KEA FELT THE BLOOD RUSH TO HER FACE. RAFE! IT WAS RAFE!

Someone had tricked her. She wanted to cry out in anger. Whenever she'd dreamed of meeting him again it had never been like this. She'd imagined she would sweep into the room where he was, quite by accident, and those dark, moody eyes would settle on her, revealing the depths of his pain at losing her. She realized now what a childish daydream it had been.

"I've been called in on your case," he said.

"Not by *me*," she retorted icily.

"Forgive me. I thought it was with your consent." His tone had become formal, a tone he would use with any patient in need of care and compassion. She hardly recognized it. "May I look at you?"

Kea hadn't the strength to refuse his request. And now that he'd spoken to her, touched her, all she could think of was her longing for him. She couldn't think of any way to drive him away. . . .

A CANDLELIGHT ECSTASY SUPREME™

TENDERNESS AT TWILIGHT

Megan Lane

A CANDLELIGHT ECSTASY SUPREME ™

Published by
Dell Publishing Co., Inc.
1 Dag Hammarskjold Plaza
New York, New York 10017

Dell ® TM 681510, Dell Publishing Co., Inc.

Candlelight Ecstasy Supreme is a trademark of Dell
Publishing Co., Inc.

Candlelight Ecstasy Romance®, 1,203,540, is a registered
trademark of Dell Publishing Co., Inc.

ISBN: 0-440-18574-2

Printed in the United States of America
First printing—October 1983

For Dr. H. Cline, who so kindly and patiently answered all my questions; for J. Teal and D. Searle who helped; and for my brother-in-law, Ray, who always has time to care

To Our Readers:

Candlelight Ecstasy is delighted to announce the start of a brand-new series—Ecstasy Supremes! Now you can enjoy a romance series unlike all the others—longer and more exciting, filled with more passion, adventure, and intrigue—the stories you've been waiting for.

In months to come we look forward to presenting books by many of your favorite authors and the very finest work from new authors of romantic fiction as well. As always, we are striving to present the unique, absorbing love stories that you enjoy most—the very best love has to offer.

Breathtaking and unforgettable, Ecstasy Supremes will follow in the great romantic tradition you've come to expect *only* from Candlelight Ecstasy.

Your suggestions and comments are always welcome. Please let us hear from you.

Sincerely,

The Editors
Candlelight Romances
1 Dag Hammarskjold Plaza
New York, New York 10017

CHAPTER ONE

As Kea lay in the frightening silence of the hospital room, her face bandaged, unable to see anything except the blackness of her own eyelids, she wondered how her life had unraveled to this point.

Had it been only eight months since she had married Roxwell? Since she had seen Rafe that final time? God, the mental anguish was almost more unbearable than the physical pain. She ached so in spirit, and she knew she was terribly broken in body.

When she heard the faint rustling sounds of a nurse's uniform and the soft squeaking of rubber-soled shoes on the floor, she whispered against the rough edges of the bandages surrounding her mouth, "My husband, Roxwell, is he all right?"

Her throat was incredibly dry, and the question came out raspy and thick. Kea licked her cracked lips, and she was relieved not to feel any injuries there.

For a moment there was no response, then the nurse came over and patted Kea's hand. "He can't see you now. He was injured, too, in the plane crash. You rest. The doctor will be in after a bit."

Ah, yes, Kea thought, the plane crash. "Nurse." Her mouth ached with the movement, but she knew her mind was more fractured than her body. The nagging questions kept bouncing around and around in her head. "How badly injured was he?"

Again the pause. "We've done what we could," the woman finally answered cautiously.

Kea felt her heart sinking. That didn't sound encouraging, and she was very much afraid that she was to blame for her husband's condition. She and Roxwell had been arguing; perhaps he hadn't done the preflight check as carefully as he should have. Perhaps his anger had impaired his judgment.

She sighed tiredly. She had found out all too soon that there was no hope for her marriage, but she knew she shouldn't have discussed it with him before he took the controls of the small plane. Even though he had badgered her, egged her on, becoming surly and obnoxious with his comments, she should have had more self-control.

She had never understood why Roxwell had married her anyway, but she had always wanted to make the marriage work. That was before he had told her about the other woman. She flinched inwardly as she thought of Roxwell's mistress. She had been shocked when he had told her that he was still seeing someone else, and that he had no intention of giving her up. After all, he'd said casually on the way to the plane, no one raised a brow in this day and age if a man had both a mistress and a wife.

Kea felt her face flame with the memory. The joke had been on her. She had thought she would find respectability with Roxwell, and she had found only more humiliation. She'd probably been the last to know that Roxwell was still having an affair.

Raising her hand, she touched her forehead and was mildly surprised when she encountered the bandage. In her anger and remorse she had again forgotten that she was here, broken, in pain, and hopelessly uncertain about everything.

"Don't touch the bandages," the nurse admonished gently.

Kea lowered her hand, and when she heard the nurse

begin to walk away, she licked her lips. "Am I blind?" she whispered almost inaudibly.

The nurse's voice was full of sympathy. "No."

"Then why are my eyes covered?"

"You were battered pretty badly inside the plane when it went down."

"Oh, God," Kea moaned. "My face—how bad is it?"

She couldn't see the nurse shake her head. "You'll take a bit of fixing up, but you'll be just fine eventually. You'll see."

A bit of fixing up, Kea thought dully, repeating in her mind the casual way the woman had said the words. "Has anyone notified the station?" she asked, the effort making her mouth ache. Her head hurt terribly, but she didn't know if that was from her injuries or her memories.

"That's right. You're the talk-show hostess from L.A., aren't you? I thought I'd heard the name. It's rather unusual."

"Where am I?" Kea asked.

The nurse mentioned a town Kea was only vaguely familiar with, but she knew that it was behind one of the mountains just outside the Los Angeles basin. "You'll be transported back to Los Angeles when we're sure your vital signs are stable. We want to make certain you don't encounter any more difficulties."

"How extensive are my injuries?"

"The doctor will talk to you about them. He'll be here in just a little while."

"I see," Kea murmured. She tried to turn over in bed and moaned in pain.

"You've suffered some bruises and lacerations and a sprained ankle, so you'll be uncomfortable for a while," the nurse said. "Would you like something to help you sleep?"

Kea had never been one to take pills, but today she needed the sweet oblivion of sleep. "Yes, please."

The woman left and then returned a few minutes later with the medication. She raised the bed so that Kea was better able to take the pill, and Kea could feel the extent of her injuries. Her body ached in general, and there was an awful pain in one of her eyes.

"Are you sure my eyes are all right?" she asked nervously.

"I think so," the nurse replied. "The doctor will discuss your injuries with you, but you're going to be fine. Really you are. Now you get some rest."

She lowered the bed again and walked away. Kea wanted to obey, and though she hadn't asked the nurse the hundred questions she had, her mind continued to pound out the painful messages as if there were an electric typewriter inside her head.

How badly injured was Roxwell? How badly injured was she? What did her face look like? The nurse had said she would take a bit of fixing up. What did that mean?

And then, suddenly, as she had thousands of times in the past, she thought of Rafe. She wondered if he were away now, on one of his jaunts into the back country of Mexico to give new faces and new hope to the disfigured—those who couldn't afford to pay him. They were in sharp contrast to his usual clientele in the Beverly Hills area and throughout the vast domain of Southern California who came to him because of his reputation, spending exorbitant sums of money, seeking all kinds of repair work to hold back the years.

Rafe lifted faces, tucked tummies, reduced bags under the eyes, all work that he enjoyed and considered important, for it aided the psyche so much, but his true love was the work he did for the poor in countries all around the world. He heard about first one case, then another, and he went to heal and give new hope or to bring patients back to the States for care.

Kea sighed raggedly, and the sound told of a world of

heartache. Her life-style had been too incompatible with Rafe's. She loved him, she knew, as she had loved no other man, no matter how much she had tried to deny it to herself, but he had been right when he said she didn't understand him or his work.

How they had quarreled over his desire to change the fate of mankind. She had told him a thousand times that he couldn't reconstruct every damaged face that nature had cruelly created, or accidents had altered—especially since he insisted on doing the work free, so that, despite his rich patrons, he was far from wealthy himself.

He was a philanthropist, a true philanthropist, if ever there was one. It had been the reason Kea had first interviewed him three years ago. Three years. Where had they gone? Three years in which she had kept hoping that Rafe would settle down to the life she knew and marry her.

In those three years she had come to know pain and love, but not marriage. Rafe had been the first man in her life that she'd wanted and hadn't been able to get. Born to money, adored by her father, Kea had always had the best: the most outrageous and expensive clothes, summers in Europe, exclusive finishing schools. But even her father hadn't been able to influence Rafe, not that she would have wanted him to.

It had been a terrible blow to her when her father had died two years ago, but it hadn't been at all unexpected; he had been in his early fifties when Kea was born, and he had had a long life. Still, she had grieved deeply, and she would give anything now to talk to him.

She sighed again. Perhaps she was glad after all that neither of her parents was here to see what a mess she had made of her life. Her father wouldn't have approved of Roxwell, and certainly not of the hasty way Kea had married him.

The cold truth was that Kea had married Roxwell in a fit of anger. And the mistake had been evident almost at once. At twenty-eight she had certainly dated enough men to know when the one she really wanted had come along. It was funny, though, that she had never given marriage much thought until Rafe came into her life. She had everything she wanted—more than she had honestly dreamed possible—and she had achieved it all on her own, refusing her father's intervention as she worked her way up from secretary to her present position at a very prestigious television station.

But there had never been any real doubt in her mind that Rafe Jordan was her one true love. Gradually she had begun to dream the silly dreams of hearts, flowers, and houses with white picket fences that she had spurned while a line of handsome men pursued her. They had offered it all, and more. Rafe had never offered her more than a few hours in his arms when he was in town.

Abruptly Kea had gone from a carefree single woman to a possessive and demanding one. She had loved Rafe too much, and she had been embarrassed time and time again because there seemed to be nothing permanent in their future, at least not as permanent as she wanted—a home, a family, Rafe's name. Rafe's name of all things! It was almost comical after so many years of scrupulously avoiding matrimony.

She had always loved her job, and she had been both awed and pleased by the accompanying benefits—the high visibility, the celebrity status, the best tables in restaurants and seats on planes, the showers of compliments about her show and herself.

At first she had been self-conscious and embarrassed by all the attention; she truly hadn't been prepared for it and she hadn't known how to handle it, but she had kept her head and quickly adjusted—and enjoyed—her position. The job wasn't all sweetness and light, for she worked hard at home studying future shows, pondering the implications of the guests and the issues when the subjects

14

were controversial, considering the best ways to present the material and the person. The job had its moments of panic when a guest clammed up and couldn't utter a single word, or when one simply didn't show up at all, but Kea loved the show with everything in her. Even the occasional severe critic couldn't shake her happiness at finding herself the hostess. Sometimes she lay back in bed and smiled to herself, unable to believe her good fortune as a new day dawned.

Meeting people, both on the set and off, had been the most thrilling part of all. Kea found them all fascinating, from the person on the street who recognized her from her show, to the rich and famous who invited her to their homes and parties all over the world. Her life was a whirl of fun and excitement, and every day she was grateful.

Only Rafe had darkened her sunshine with his elusive brooding shadow and his contrasting life. Soon it had become all too obvious that he didn't share her desire for matching wedding bands. He was too busy changing the world, helping the poor, putting young doctors in foreign countries through medical school so that they could serve the needs of their desperate communities, or even buying food for the family of a child patient so that the child could get the nourishment he needed during the critical healing time.

Kea had admired him and thought that it was all noble and wonderful, but her attitude had changed somewhat when she realized that Rafe's dedication to his cause meant that he would never be hers in the truest sense of the word.

At first she had been hurt, then humiliated. Her friends kept asking when the wedding was going to be, and she kept saying Rafe was going here or there, doing his duty to a disadvantaged world. She couldn't count the times she had made jokes about caring for a man with a fever to do good.

15

She had even replied lightly and good-naturedly when people had teased her about Rafe taking his nurse with him. Kea had been jealous of Trena, terribly jealous. Though the woman was plain and meek, there was no doubt in Kea's mind about her dedication—or love—for Rafe.

She hid her pain well, but Roxwell sensed her vulnerability. He had stayed by her side, flattering her with pretty phrases and flowers, escorting her to local parties and functions when Rafe was too busy or too far away to attend.

Roxwell Mason: Rafe's opposite, polished, refined, monied, fun-loving. He was older than Rafe's thirty-four years by fourteen, but he was silver-haired and handsome, with money to burn from a chain of prosperous supermarkets.

Kea pushed at the flood of thoughts that surged into her throbbing head, but it was no use. For the hundredth time she recalled how she and Rafe had quarreled that night she had foolishly flown to Las Vegas to marry Roxwell. She wouldn't offer excuses for herself. There were none. She had wanted to punish Rafe, and she had wound up punishing only herself.

She remembered how awful she had felt when she had first seen the big writeup in the paper as the media made a to-do about the event: *Kea Montgomery, beautiful talk-show hostess marries entrepreneur Roxwell Mason in surprise ceremony in Las Vegas.* She had known only the most fleeting feeling of satisfaction as she considered Rafe's reaction.

But she had never heard from him again. Not a note, not a telephone call, not even a message delivered by mutual friends. And she certainly hadn't been inclined to contact him after it was all said and done. What could she possibly have said?

"Mrs. Mason?"

16

She was startled when a man addressed her. She hadn't used the name Mason much; she had continued to be known by Montgomery. "Yes?"

"Good. You haven't gone to sleep yet. I wanted to speak with you before I left. I'm Dr. Graines. I'm sure you've been anxious about your condition, and I'm here to tell you what I can."

"How is my husband?" Kea asked worriedly.

The doctor patted her hand reassuringly. "Let's talk about you first," he said in a manner that precluded further questions about Roxwell. Kea complied because she was afraid of hearing something she didn't want to hear.

"All right," she whispered, wishing she could see the man.

"You've suffered some injuries to your face, a severely sprained ankle, and a few minor bruises and lacerations to other parts of your body, nothing really serious there, and nothing to the face that can't be bettered. Miracles are done with reconstructive surgery these days."

Miracles, she thought frantically. Would it take a miracle to make her whole again? "How much damage is there?"

Why did she think of Rafe, and why did the mere thought cause such a stab of pain to her heart?

"Well," the doctor replied with disconcerting vagueness, "you have a number of stitches in your face, especially around your right eye. We don't have a plastic surgeon available at this hospital, and we couldn't wait for one. You were losing a lot of blood, so we went ahead and sutured the wounds. I suspect that you might have a few scars which will need to be revised later on."

"Scars?" This time Kea couldn't keep the alarm out of her voice. She had never considered herself especially vain; her beauty had been an accepted part of her all her life. But she had always been aware of the advantages, and she knew her face and figure were part of her success in

17

an extremely competitive field where the image was all important. Her flawless skin and fiery red hair had been her trademark, and she couldn't imagine scars marring her beauty. "How bad will they be?"

"We'll have to wait and see, but don't be too upset. It will all work out. Tomorrow we'll transfer you back to Beverly Hills where you can be treated by your own doctors. Things will work out just fine. Is there someone we should call?"

Kea's mind suddenly rushed frantically over the people in her life, and she struggled with the most ridiculous urge to say Rafe Jordan. "No," she murmured at last. Her mother had been dead since Kea was seven, and her only other living relative, her mother's brother, had long ago made it clear that he wanted no further family ties with the Montgomerys. She had some very dear friends, but they could be notified when she reached Beverly Hills.

She tried to move, and she felt the pain in her eye again, as well as new pain in her arm. The pill was beginning to work, but it hadn't eased her suffering yet.

"What's wrong with my eye?" she asked. "And my arm hurts." She reached for her upper right arm and the doctor caught her hand.

"Your arm is badly bruised, but it will be fine. Your right side took an awful pounding. I believe you have an orbital fracture of the right eye. Don't let the term throw you. It sounds awful, but a good plastic surgeon can fix you right up. You were unconscious for a short time, and you'll need to see a neurosurgeon before definitive work can be done, but the first thing you know, you'll be back on that television show."

Kea tried to smile as the doctor offered a few more reassuring comments, but his comment about her television show had sent shivers up her spine. She had never had any doubts about that before; the show was hers. She and the show had grown together, and though she had a tem-

18

peramental producer, she had eventually achieved all her goals, and they had been met with public approval and critical acclaim. She had even received the coveted Emmy for her work. But she knew without hearing from anyone else that scars and pretty women on television didn't mix. Had her future, her career, been injured along with her body? And what would she do if it had? She couldn't give up her show!

Her injuries sounded very real and very frightening all of a sudden, and she was fearful for her future. Resisting an urge to give in to the rising panic inside her, she closed her eyes, and before she could stop it, Rafe's face rose to haunt her. As she drifted into the welcome blackness of sleep, she once again recalled the rapture she had so often known in her lover's arms.

She had gone out with Rafe dozens of times before she had finally given in to her desire for him. He was tall, dark, and enticing—with huge, liquid brown eyes that filled with deep sorrow when he suffered so intensely for a world too vast to help, or danced with a dark, mysterious glow when he drew Kea into his arms.

Kea often suspected that she could see some Mexican or Spanish heritage in Rafe, and she knew he spoke Spanish like a native, but he never discussed his family or his background, and somehow she had never found the right time to indulge her talk-show hostess's penchant for asking a hundred personal questions. Rafe was secretive and very private, and Kea dated him for many months without ever finding a way to learn all the things she wanted to know about him.

In fact, she had promised herself that she wouldn't become involved with him beyond the pleasure of an occasional date with a fascinating man. She loved her life—the glamour, the excitement, the jet-set crowd of movie and television moguls, corporate heads, old money reeking of class, and new money living life to its financial maximum.

She was in her element with these people, who, like her, had reached the peak in their professions and knew how to enjoy life.

Rafe, on the other hand, patiently listened to every sob story and reached deeper and deeper into his pocket to bandage humanity's wounds, or held out his own hands to heal the physical flaws of mankind. He somehow made Kea feel guilty about her life-style, even though she faithfully hosted charity benefits and donated a portion of her generous salary to needy causes. She cared deeply, and she was involved, but not to the exclusion of all else.

As she slipped farther and farther into sleep's endless depths, she dreamed of the first time she and Rafe had made love. That evening he had cooked for her in his house, and Kea had known when she accepted the invitation that she would finally succumb to his amorous advances.

After a delicious meal and two glasses of wine, she and Rafe had gone to the living room where Kea sank down on a plain brown couch. When Rafe walked over to turn on the stereo unit, she gazed after him hypnotically. He wasn't particularly tall, probably not over five feet ten inches, compared to Kea's five feet seven, but his body was beautifully proportioned and defined, from his intriguing face, broad shoulders, and lean hips down to his loafer-clad feet.

Despite the sorrow Kea detected in him, which sometimes seemed to permeate his entire being, his steps were firm and confident, his posture tall and proud, leaving no doubt that he was sure of himself in the way that some successful men have. Life's inequalities might have disappointed him, but they had not daunted him.

His body was muscled from a weekly regimen of jogging and from the arduous treks into isolated spots around the world, places hard put to find a doctor for the most necessary of treatments, let alone the so-called luxuries, such as cosmetic surgery. Kea found herself thinking that this man before her was truly gorgeous in every sense of the word.

When he unexpectedly turned around, his eyes met hers and she could tell by his gaze that he had recognized her desire for him. Being here in his home was her undoing; she was so very aware of how much his house reminded her of him and his virility. The living room, like the man, was almost Spartan; the few pieces of furniture were solid and well-chosen. There was no excess and no clutter. The one concession Rafe had made to luxury was his art objects from all over the world, many of them quite erotic, so that Kea was intensely aware of the obsession many primitive people had with fertility.

Rafe crossed the room very quickly, and Kea felt the excited beating of her heart as he stood before her, his dark gaze holding her. "I want you," he murmured huskily as he held his hands out to her. Kea was trembling when he drew her up against his hard body, embracing her to move her slowly and provocatively to the soft strains of a love song.

She could feel every line of his muscled thighs as they pressed enticingly against her long, shapely legs. The blue silk dress that clung to her curves offered no barrier to Rafe's touch.

When he held her more possessively, hugging her to his chest while his fingers played sensuously on her back, Kea felt her pulse pound at her temples. Rafe lowered his head to kiss the curve of her neck with warm, moist lips and Kea was alarmed by the shiver that raced up her spine.

Rafe's magic was powerful and enchanting, and when his lips found Kea's, she was lost to his heady appeal. He stopped guiding her around the floor and she found him even more irresistible as he pressed his hard length to her and swayed with her to the music, their feet still while their teasing bodies set their minds on fire.

21

Kea had known the excitement of Rafe's touch before, but she had been very careful not to let the embers of desire become flames. This time it was too late to caution her heart, for her body had overruled it already.

"Sweet temptation," Rafe murmured against her lips when he had freed them.

Kea was hungry for more of his touch, and when he scattered kisses down her neck, she felt her nipples tighten against Rafe's chest. His beautiful hands closed down over her breasts, and his thumbs teased the rigid peaks with the gentlest of circling caresses.

The fires of passion burned high in Kea's veins, causing a warmth somewhere down deep inside her. She ached to know Rafe intimately and there was no denying the desire he aroused in her. She could feel heat flooding through her, and she closed her eyes as a flush raced up her cheeks. When she looked at Rafe from beneath lowered lids, he was gazing at her, his own excitement burning deep in the dark depths of his eyes.

"I want you, Kea," he murmured again. "Tonight. I won't be refused." He drew her against him even more firmly, and Kea was intoxicated by his appeal and virility as she felt his full desire.

"Rafe," she murmured half protestingly, but before she could utter another word, he lifted her up in his arms and strode toward the bedroom.

The light spilling from the living room barely outlined the king-sized bed. Kea hadn't expected the richness of the room; it was extravagant in contrast to the others, and she reveled in the feel of cool silk beneath her bare shoulders when they touched the sheets.

She watched, fascinated, as Rafe removed her high heels and stockings, sliding the sheer nylons down the length of her legs with the utmost care, making the moment incredibly intimate and provocative. When his mouth trailed back up her legs, kissing them with a deliberation that was maddening, Kea raised her hips so that Rafe could ease her bikini panties down her legs.

After he had completed his leisurely undressing of her, she lay before him naked and a little shy under his penetrating perusal.

"You're the most beautiful woman I've ever seen," he told her with a solemnity that caught her unaware.

His exploring fingers strayed over her body and face, and her qualms vanished in the heat of his caresses as the flames built higher and higher inside her. She knew she wanted no less than complete possession by this man.

At last he began to undress and Kea held her breath as he stood before her in all his manly glory. He was covered with thick, curling silky black hair, and she longed to run her fingers over his chest and down his stomach and abdomen to the thickest thatches of hair.

She found Rafe immensely appealing, and she waited breathlessly as he lowered his body to hers, stretching out over her, his manhood burning against her flesh.

"Rafe," she whispered hungrily, wanting him to know how he fired her blood, but embarrassed to be so eager after all the times she had refused him.

His hips began to move against hers, driving her wild with desire as his aroused body teased hers with its promise of unknown pleasures.

When his mouth found hers again, she parted her lips, wanting to taste him, to make him as consumed by the fires of desire as she was.

He eased her thighs apart with his knees as his hands slid beneath her hips, and Kea sucked in her breath, drawing his seeking tongue deep into her mouth as Rafe moved slowly and powerfully into her velvety depths.

"Mrs. Mason. Mrs. Mason."

Kea was startled awake by the sound of her name, and when she tried to open her eyes, she was harshly reminded of where she was.

"You were having a nightmare, honey," a pleasant voice said. "You were calling out for your husband."

The dream came back to Kea all too vividly, and she blushed beneath the white bandages. She must have called Rafe's name.

"Thank you for waking me," she said thickly. But she wasn't thankful at all. The nurse touched her shoulder and then Kea heard fading footsteps. Once more she was left to the night darkness of her bandages and her troubling dreams. This time they were much more unpleasant. Roxwell's face came time and time again to torment her, and all the while, buried deep within her heart, Rafe remained to haunt her.

Two days later Kea lay in a hospital in Beverly Hills, her long-time friends, Jon and Ellen Wagner, at her bedside, each holding a hand reassuringly. The doctor had finally told her the truth—that Roxwell had not survived the accident, and the knowledge burned against her dark eyelids, bright and accusing.

The nurse had sedated her, but Kea's conscience would not let her retreat into the blackness of sleep. She had not really loved him, nor he her, but she had lived with him for eight months as his wife and she could not escape the fear that he would still be alive if it weren't for her. Her family physician stood by her bed, offering solace and encouragement, but Kea couldn't shake the guilt that weighed so heavily on her heart.

Roxwell had wanted to take care of her, as if she were a helpless woman in need of nuturing. He had initially been attracted to her because of her celebrity status, but once they were married, he had wanted her to be totally dependent on him. She'd soon realized that he saw her as a trophy, a prize that he wanted to put on display to his wealthy friends. Kea had known then that the marriage had no chance. Had that been when Roxwell had gone back to the other woman? When he had discovered that Kea would not give up her job?

She heard her family physician telling her that time would ease the pain, and she whispered tremulously, "When can I get these bandages off my eyes?"

Perhaps if she could see the world around her again, she could deal with it more rationally. Everything was so black now, inside and out. It was all too sudden, too cruel.

"I want a plastic surgeon to take a look at you right away," Dr. Draper said firmly. "Rafe Jordan is the best. Now that the neurosurgeon has checked you, we can get started on the definitive work."

Kea's heartbeats quickened. Rafe Jordan! It was unthinkable! She couldn't bear for him to see her like this. She wouldn't allow it in a million years. And anyway, she was sure he wouldn't want to be the one to help her.

"No," she said coldly. "Not Rafe Jordan."

"He's the best," Dr. Draper repeated.

Kea knew the doctor was aware of her prior relationship with Rafe, and she was distressed and embarrassed by his persistence.

"No."

"Don't let pride rule your mind, Kea," Jon said gently. "He's just returned to town. At least talk with him about it."

Kea was aware that Ellen hadn't commented, but she could envision Jon's and Ellen's concerned faces without having to see them. Jon, so good, so ordinary in all things —looks, job, social status—he really was the epitome of the boy next door. Both he and Ellen had lived in the same neighborhood with Kea when she was younger, and they had grown up together, sharing the highs and lows of adolescence. They had been friends for half their lives, and they knew each other in that intimate way that long-time friends can, the best and the worst traits, the accomplishments and failures, the strengths and insecurities, but they didn't know what they were asking of her this time.

She knew Jon's blue eyes would be troubled; he would be running his slender hands through straight brown hair that was a bit untidy. Ellen's large green eyes would dart worriedly toward her husband.

Yes, she thought and felt comforted, she knew and loved her friends, but they couldn't have any idea of the torment they were asking her to suffer by having Rafe as her doctor. She shook her head, and the motion caused a shooting pain in her right eye.

"Am I blind, Ted?" she asked Dr. Draper anxiously. "My eye hurts quite badly."

His voice was calm and confident. "No, you're not, but you'll have a little trouble with that eye for a while." He explained the problem that the first doctor had mentioned, and Kea felt herself growing fearful again. Her eyes—she had always taken them so much for granted. She had always been told how enchanting and lovely they were, their gray color mysterious and changeable with her clothing.

"God," she moaned. "Why did all this have to happen?"

Jon squeezed her hand. "You're going to be all right, honey. Things seem a lot worse than they are. Time will take care of most of it."

Kea managed a trembling smile, but she drew little comfort from his words. Time. Time hadn't been kind to her in the past. It hadn't taken care of the problem with Rafe; in fact, with the passage of time it had only hurt more.

"Let Rafe take a look at you," Jon urged softly. "He really is the best, and you know it."

"No, Jon. No." Kea didn't argue about Rafe's competency. She never had. But that was not the point. Whatever Rafe felt for her, it could not possibly be compassion;

26

it was more likely contempt. And she would not give him that kind of power over her. Yet, for one brief instant, her heart had raced at the thought of seeing him again. She was a fool, she knew, for she loved him. Still. And that was the worst pain of all.

CHAPTER TWO

Dr. Draper had set up a meeting with a plastic surgeon, and Kea lay waiting in the early-morning quiet of the hospital, wondering what the doctor would say when he had examined her, wondering how badly she was injured, wondering if she would see well again.

The seconds seemed to stretch into agonizing eternities as she waited, filled with doubts and uncertainties. She was as taut as a bowstring as she listened for the sound of a man's footsteps on the floor; she hadn't slept well last night, despite having taken a sleeping pill, and she wanted more than anything to get this over with so that she could get on with her life—whatever that was now.

When she heard the sure steps of someone coming toward her room, she lay in tense expectation, wanting to run and wanting to stay as she heard step after step. She was eager, but afraid. What if she really couldn't be put back together again? Inexplicably, the footsteps stopped. Kea strained to hear, but there were no more.

She sighed wearily and drew in a deep breath. She was imagining things. The person hadn't been coming into her room at all. She knew she had to make herself calm down, and she drew in another steadying breath.

The tall, dark man standing in the doorway stood motionless, his intense, brooding eyes focused on the woman in the hospital bed. Rafe Jordan's jaw muscles were tightly clenched and his hands were balled into fists as he stood gazing at Kea. He had never before seen her looking helpless and vulnerable, and the sight almost made his knees buckle.

He had been awed by her vibrancy and energy whenever he had been with her; she had always been more vital—and more beautiful—than any woman he had ever known. She had been like a splendid butterfly, flitting here and there as she pleased, calling the shots, plotting the course of her life as if fate itself had no hand in her future.

He had admired her passion for life, but he had also been afraid of it, for he had known that it would spell doom for their relationship. Kea couldn't live in his world with its drudgery and hardships and sacrifices, and he wouldn't live in hers with its superficial glitter and fantasy. It had almost been a relief when she married Mason, for he had known that it would happen sooner or later. With money to spend and time on his hands, Mason had been just the partner for her.

At first it had hurt like hell, and he had despised her for the way she had let him find out, but as the months passed, the pain eventually eased. He had made himself face the fact that it was all for the best.

Even Kea didn't know how he had brooded and become inflamed with jealousy when she caught the eye of every man in the room everywhere they went. It seemed almost impossible that she was so beautiful in all ways, with her fiery red hair, gorgeous face, and those incredible gray eyes. Her shapely body didn't have a flaw or a curve out of place, and those magnificent long legs were the loveliest he had ever seen.

He could still recall how silky her skin had felt to his fingertips, and how warm and pliable her full mouth had been under his. When he made love to her, he felt as if she had touched his very soul. At first he had thought he would die inside when she married Mason, but he hadn't, of course.

He had thrown himself deeper and deeper into his work to forget her—the work over which Kea and he had often been in conflict. Kea had never known how much he owed to so many, especially his adoptive father, Dr. Hadley Jordan, the man who had changed his life, and the life of his poor sister Maria.

Rafe was drawn sharply back to the present when Kea moaned softly. He stared at her again. There had been no way of explaining his life to Kea, and he hadn't tried, for there would have been no purpose. Her brilliant wings would have lost their luster and her flaming soul would have died in his world of suffering.

He had had no right to ask her to be his, and he hadn't. But now, seeing her there before him, he recalled all the times she had touched his soul and given him a reason for living.

Suddenly, he found himself bitterly resenting that she had asked for him. He knew that Roxwell was dead, and he knew that Kea's face was damaged, but he didn't know if he could repair it. Not that he wasn't physically capable. He had no doubts about that. But was he emotionally strong enough to work on her? He loved her too much—still. Had she summoned him to torment him further, or now that she needed him—however briefly—had she consented to allow him back into her life? He gazed at her for a moment longer, then turned on his heel and started to leave. He would not be a fool for her again.

Hearing the steps resume, Kea tensed in confusion. Had someone come in? She could feel a growing sense of panic rising inside her. "Hello. Is someone there?" she asked, her voice filled with apprehension. God, but it was awful to be trapped behind these bandages. As the silence continued, Kea's apprehension increased.

Then her nostrils flared in fear, for she thought she

smelled a scent once so familiar to her that it took her breath away. She sniffed the air and she imagined that she recognized the faint muskiness of Rafe's after-shave lotion.

Bracing himself against the wall with one hand, Rafe paused at the sound of Kea's rich voice. He didn't think he could bear to turn around, and yet he couldn't walk away now.

"Hello?" she murmured again with such uncertainty, such vulnerability, that Rafe closed his eyes and gritted his teeth. He had never stopped loving this woman, no matter how far away he had traveled, abroad or in his own mind, and he realized now how he had hated her when she had married Roxwell, even though he had known that she would marry eventually. He had seen all the signs of her wanting a husband, and he had known that he wasn't the man for her.

Finally he turned around and looked at her again. It was almost his undoing. She had pulled the sheet up and was clutching it over her full breasts, making it outline them in all their beauty. Rafe knew that she was frightened, and he wanted to comfort her, to hold her in his arms, to make it all right again, for him and for her.

And now there was no going back. Ted Draper had been wrong to persuade him to take the case, regardless of Kea's wishes. And yet he had known the minute Ted had mentioned Kea's name that there would be no way he could refuse. She wanted him, and he couldn't say no.

Drawing in a steadying breath, Rafe began to walk toward her. "Kea," he said in a deep voice, "it's Rafe."

Kea felt the blood rush to her face. Rafe! It was Rafe! Someone had tricked her and she wanted to cry out in anger, but she couldn't think of a thing to say.

Her breath caught in her throat at the sound of her name on his lips once more. She waited until she sensed that he was at her bedside, and still she could think of

31

nothing to say. She wanted to order him away, but she didn't know how to. Glad after all that she couldn't see him, she continued to wait for him to speak, and all the while her emotions were in turmoil.

Whenever she had dreamed of meeting him again, it had never been like this. She had imagined that she would sweep into the room where he was, quite by accident, and those dark, moody eyes would settle on her, revealing the depths of his pain at losing her. She realized now what a childish daydream it had been.

"I've been called in on your case," he said.

Kea began to read all kinds of disturbing ideas into his tone. Wasn't it cold? Remote? Harsh? Did he despise her now? Why had he come? The questions poured into her mind as silence lay like a shroud over the room, and the most bothersome question of all filled the emptiness. Did he still care, even a little?

She was aware that she was feeling for her wedding band with her thumb, as if the fact that she had married someone else could still offer her protection from Rafe. But Roxwell was dead. She toyed nervously with the ring for a moment. Finally she spoke with a coldness born out of fear and frustration. "You weren't called in by *me*."

"No?" he asked, and Kea heard both surprise and bitterness in his voice.

"No," she confirmed, and she hated the way the mere sound of his voice excited her.

There was a long pause. She wondered desperately what Rafe was thinking. Had Dr. Draper been the one so cruel to send this man on this mission, or had it been Jon and Ellen?

"Forgive me," he said at last, his voice suddenly tired and remote. "Ted Draper asked me to take the case as a personal favor. I thought it was with your consent."

"It wasn't," she said, and this time, to her sheer mortifi-

32

cation, her voice cracked, and she found herself perilously near tears. Damn Ted Draper anyway!

Involuntarily, she reached up to wipe away the threatening tears; in her distress she had forgotten about the bandages. When her fingers encountered them, they wandered tremblingly over their thickness.

Rafe stood at her side, caught in a moment of indecision. Of course she hadn't wanted him. How could he have been fool enough to think she did? She had stopped wanting him for any reason months ago. Was it his own pride that had sent him here at Ted's request? Or was it only any excuse to see Kea?

But now that he was here, he couldn't leave without seeing if he could help her. Abruptly, he lowered her hands to her sides, and she wondered if his gesture had been spontaneous and automatic, a gesture he would have made with any patient in need of consolation.

"May I look at you?" he asked in a tone so formal Kea hardly recognized it.

That was the last thing she wanted, the very last, but somehow she couldn't summon the strength to refuse his request. Rafe had obviously come here only as a surgeon doing a job. And now that he had touched her, spoken to her, she couldn't think of any way to drive him away. To her dismay, she nodded.

There was another pause and then he began to remove the bandages while Kea anxiously awaited some word, some betraying motion that indicated his shock, his revulsion, but there was none. She wondered if her injuries were less than she had imagined, or was it only that Rafe was an expert professional? Another more believable option occurred to her, but it was too painful to dwell on. Perhaps she simply didn't matter at all to him anymore.

With sure movements he snipped and peeled off the wrapping that had hidden her face from his penetrating dark eyes, eyes she remembered as well as she did her own.

Finally Kea knew a brightness she hadn't known for days as the bandages were stripped away, but to her horror she could see almost nothing. One eye was swollen completely shut, and at first she couldn't focus with the other. She struggled, squinting and blinking although the room was shuttered to allow her to adjust gradually.

Eventually she could see through the narrowed slit of her left eye. Rafe was only a hazy outline at first as Kea tried futilely to focus on him. For a few moments she was too consumed by her own panic to give him her attention. Then he became real to her. Much too real.

It was the first time she had seen him in eight months, and she was reminded of how she had hungered for him deep in her soul, how she had yearned for his intimate loving while she shared a bed with an indifferent husband.

Rafe's dark gaze met hers only briefly as his penetrating eyes studied her wounded face almost impersonally, appraising, assessing, evaluating the damage. He produced a pencil-slim flashlight to examine her eyes, and when he tilted her chin gently, Kea's gaze met his again.

Was his thinly veiled expression pained? Or was it her imagination, spurred on by the situation? It was so hard to see with her limited vision that she didn't know what to think.

"Rafe?" she whispered when he shone the light in her eye. "How bad is it?" She hadn't meant to ask that question, but she was so alarmed by the condition of her eyes. She truly hadn't wanted to sound weak and frightened with him. There were a hundred other questions quivering on her lips, but none came forth; she wouldn't allow them to.

When he didn't reply immediately, she raised shaking fingers again, and Rafe caught them and held them. Kea remembered how strong and beautiful she had always thought his hands were.

"I can make you almost as beautiful as ever," he said

with a brusqueness that pained her. "There's nothing to worry about."

His voice sounded so cold and impersonal that Kea jerked her hands away. It was all Rafe could do not to pull her against his chest and hold her until her fears and distress subsided. He knew he would have to save all the strength he had to repair her face—and to keep from falling more deeply in love with her. He hadn't forgotten that she didn't want him; she was hurt and he would help her.

He reminded himself that their past had died when she elected to marry another man. Their relationship wouldn't have worked anyway. He had always known that.

He told himself that they were no more than physician and patient, but in his heart he knew that this was the woman he loved, the only woman he would ever love. How the sight of her thrilled him! How the sound of her voice stirred old feelings and hopes. Her very nearness intoxicated him. He had thought she was gone forever from him, and finding her again here, needing him, was a heady sensation. No matter what he had told himself, he had never recovered from the shock of her marriage. She had taken his heart with her, and he had been left with nothing but dusty memories and bitter regrets. But she was back. And what now?

Nothing now, he told himself sharply, and in a remarkably controlled voice he began to outline the procedure he would follow to repair the orbital fracture. He knew that he would have to revise the scars that would result from the wounds that had been sutured around her eye and on her right cheek, but there was no point in telling her that now. There would be several operations over the next six months or so, but now the immediate worry was the surgery to repair the fracture.

"I want to see myself," Kea said with a firmness that contrasted with her earlier vulnerability, and Rafe was pleased. She would need her fiery temper and her fighting spirit to get through the months ahead.

Sooner or later she would have to look at her face, of course, and he was glad he was the one here with her to cushion the blow of the first time. He knew there was no way she could be prepared for the sight that would confront her.

He produced a hand mirror that he had brought with him and held it up before her. Grasping it with both hands, Kea gasped when she looked into it. She couldn't believe that the woman in the mirror was she!

Her right eye was swollen shut, and the left was a mere slit. All the area around both eyes was bluish-purple and hideously puffy and stretched looking, and two long, ragged gashes that bit into her cheek had been sewn up.

But worse than that, a crescent-shaped cut curved from the side of her forehead, slicing through the tip of her right brow and snaking under her eye; the wound had been sutured so that it reminded Kea of railroad tracks. The face men had once admired was now an appalling sight, and no matter how much she had imagined the extent of her injuries, she hadn't expected this much damage.

She sagged back against the pillows, ashamed that Rafe had seen her ugliness. She had *known* that she didn't want him here. His presence only made this moment more painful. What she had expected, she had no idea, but a little fixing up hadn't sounded like this. She hadn't been prepared for this broken, distorted mask where a face with clear and fine features once had been. Never again would Rafe say she was the most beautiful woman he had ever seen. No one would say it.

When she closed her eyes, she felt tears well up behind the lids. "Go away," she whispered wrenchingly.

Rafe reached up to catch the tears that escaped her tightly closed lids. "I can help you," he murmured so poignantly that Kea wanted to run and hide forever from the pity etched deeply in his thick voice.

She tried to cover her face with her hands but the tender skin ached from the slightest touch. Once again Rafe captured her hands; holding them to his lips, he whispered against them, "Kea, it's going to be all right."

Trying to escape, she turned her head to one side. She didn't want him to look at her anymore, to pity her. "Go away," she commanded bitterly. "Just go away."

"You don't mean that," he said softly. "I want to help you."

"I don't want you!" she all but screamed. "Don't you understand? I didn't ask for you. I don't want you! Don't touch me! Don't talk to me! Don't look at me!" She began to sob, tears cascading down her cheeks unabated, and Rafe backed away as if she had struck him. Keeping her eyes tightly closed, she refused to look at him.

He released her hands, quietly laying them on her chest. He had been wrong to come here, wrong for both their sakes. He had thought he could help her, but he had been wrong. He gazed at her briefly, then turned away. She didn't see the tears that sprang to his eyes or the way his jaw muscles worked convulsively.

Kea heard his retreating footsteps, and she sighed raggedly. Immobilized by the shock she had suffered, more sorry that Rafe had seen her disfigurement than she was for the actual injuries themselves, Kea lay crying all alone.

It seemed that only seconds had passed before a nurse came bustling into the room to partially rebandage Kea's face. This time the swathing wasn't as thick, but no amount of bandaging would wrap the sight from Kea's mind.

The nurse produced a needle and Kea knew that the woman had been instructed to give her something to calm her. She despised her own weakness, for she was sure the

37

nurse thought she was weeping for her lost beauty; in reality, it was so much more complicated. She was crying for what had been, what might have been, what had happened and never could happen again. She was crying for Roxwell, for herself, and for Rafe.

At last her tears ceased and she fell into a fitful sleep. But even in her dreams she wept because she knew now that Rafe Jordan would forever torment her, his memory bittersweet and unfulfilling.

She left orders with Dr. Draper that Rafe wasn't to be allowed into her room again and said she didn't wish to know if he attempted to see her. Actually, she was sure she need have no real fear of that: Rafe undoubtedly had no more desire to see her than she did him.

A nurse's aid awakened her much later, insisting that she eat something. Kea wanted to refuse but she knew she needed nourishment. As the woman started out of the room, she hesitated and then flipped on the television set. "It'll give you something to distract you," she commented.

The news was on, and as Kea sampled the food on her tray, she tried to focus on the picture with her limited vision. To her surprise she saw her own likeness—or what it used to be—on the evening news. She listened, her heart pounding, as the report was given on her and Roxwell's accident. Then the picture changed, and she was surprised to see Roxwell's son, Shane, standing in front of the house. He looked so much like Roxwell that Kea's heart began to break just watching him. She felt along the edge of the bed until she found the remote-control unit for the set, then she quickly switched it off. She didn't want any more reminders of her life right now.

Another twenty-four hours passed before Dr. Draper again approached her on the subject of plastic surgery. "Kea," he told her, concern in his voice, "you must get that eye repaired. The sooner you have something done, the better. Those sutures will come out in a few days, and there'll be no reason to keep you here longer than a week or so. You were fortunate that you didn't suffer more serious injuries. Your face is all you'll have to deal with."

"Yes," Kea said bitterly. "Only my face, of all places."

"It could have been worse," Dr. Draper reminded her firmly, and Kea nodded.

"I know, Ted, and I'm not trying to be difficult. I'm just so troubled. I feel so guilty about Roxwell, and I almost wonder if I'm not being punished. You know that we never should have married, and the way he died—"

Ted took her by the shoulders and made her look into his eyes. "Kea, don't do this to yourself. You know as well as I that Roxwell wasn't the first pilot to crash in that area. You can't change what happened, and you mustn't dwell on it. I hate to use that old cliché, but life is for the living. Things will be confusing enough settling Roxwell's vast estate. Let's take one day at a time. You need to get yourself back in shape first of all. You have your future, your work to think about."

"There is no work for me, no future in television now. You know that, Ted." She gazed vacantly toward the tall window. "I think I'll move away."

"Now isn't the time to move," he insisted. "You need to be among friends. And what do you mean—no future?" He pointed to the beautiful flowers and the many lovely cards that had started pouring in after the piece on Kea on television. "Does that look like no future?" he asked. "The viewers love you."

Although Kea had been moved and touched by the outpouring of love, she knew that the viewers were thinking of the old Kea. "But they haven't seen me like this," she murmured thickly. "This is not the same person they're sending cards and flowers to."

She couldn't stop the memory of the way her producer had looked at her when he had come to visit yesterday. He had managed to say a few bright, clever things, but Kea could read the terrible disappointment in his eyes. And she feared for her future. She could find small comfort in the fact that her contract hadn't yet expired; it was only a matter of months.

"You will work again, Kea," Ted said. "Proceed with that goal in mind. Save your other decisions until you're better able to cope." He gazed at her thoughtfully for a moment. "Why don't you stay with friends for a while?"

She laughed lightly. "I don't want to be a burden to anyone."

Ted made a wry face. "Nonsense. You won't be. How about staying with Jon and Ellen for a while?"

Kea shrugged offhandedly. She could do that, of course; she had always known that she could turn to them at any time, but she felt that she needed to be left to herself for a while. Besides, it wasn't as if she were an invalid. "I'll just go home. I'll be fine, better there, in fact, than anywhere."

Ted pursed his lips thoughtfully, and Kea could tell that he had something on his mind. "Kea, you're going to need some assistance for a while. Even though the bed rest has helped your ankle heal, it will still be tender for a while. And there are your other injuries to consider—your eye in particular. You've suffered a very serious injury to it. These things take time to heal. After any surgery, you need bed rest for a time. Who will be at the house to help you? I understand that Shane's living in the house, but—" He looked away briefly, then back, and Kea was puzzled. "But I don't think he'll be much help."

"Shane's staying at the house?" Kea asked, her voice full of surprise. He had never stayed with her and Roxwell, not even overnight. He had never approved of her, no matter how she went out of her way to be nice to him.

"Yes, I spoke to him this morning."

40

Kea didn't know what to think. "The housekeeper will be there."

Ted shook his head. "I believe Shane let most of the household help go, including the housekeeper."

"But why?" Kea whispered.

Looking at her gravely, Ted murmured, "Kea, he's gone public to accuse you of marrying Roxwell for his money. He's just trying to be difficult. You mustn't let it get to you." Again he lowered his eyes, briefly studying the bed sheet.

Kea closed her eyes in disbelief. Shane's behavior was humiliating to say the least. There was sure to be a scandal —and on her very own medium. And Shane couldn't honestly believe his accusations. The money had never been a consideration.

Ted's words broke into her painful thoughts. "Shane has planned the memorial service for tomorrow."

Clenching her hands into fists at her sides, Kea exclaimed, "Not tomorrow! He'll have to wait until I get out of the hospital."

"Kea," he said soothingly, "let him have it tomorrow. He has already arranged everything. Besides, you won't be out of here for many days, and even then you won't be ready for something like this. No one is going to condemn you for missing the service."

Kea pressed her fingertips to her lips as if the motion could still her misery. Suddenly she felt as if she were drowning in her unhappiness. She couldn't take any more punishment right now; she was raw and aching, and feeling very despondent. "I don't know why Shane is being so awful," she whispered to no one in particular. Then she raised her gray eyes to meet Ted's. "Yes, I do. He's been that way from the beginning. He resented me terribly, and I'm sure that resentment is worse now. He's always been afraid that I would get a nickel of Roxwell's money, and I tried to tell him that it was never a factor. Oh, Ted," she

41

murmured in a tear-choked voice, "I just want to be left alone. I can't go through any more."

"Forget about Shane. Roxwell left a will. Wait and see what happens with it. Time will work it all out, but I really wish you would stay where someone can help you the first couple of weeks after you leave here. You aren't going to feel as well as you think after the surgery."

"I'll manage," she said stubbornly. "If it comes to it, I'll hire a nurse."

Now it was Ted's turn to sigh tiredly. "Kea, I want you to remember that you're still beautiful and desirable. Plastic surgery is a modern miracle, and no one will know the difference when your treatment is completed."

"But they'll all be looking to see, won't they?" she asked resentfully. "I know that everything has been revealed about me except my slip size, and maybe even that. Did you see that bit on the news about me last night, Ted?"

He nodded, and his eyes widened a little. "Did you watch it?"

"Only a little. Shane was on briefly before I turned the TV off." Something in his tone alarmed her. "Why? Is that where Shane made his announcement?"

Ted nodded, and when Kea looked stricken, he shrugged lightly. His brown eyes were sympathetic even if his voice wasn't. "What can I say? People love a scandal, and especially here in this town. When you became a public figure, you became a prime target for gossip. But take heart, next month it will be somebody else."

He managed a smile. "That's the good part. Your turn will last only until something more interesting comes along and there are a lot of things more interesting than a contested will."

Hard put to find any humor in the situation, Kea nervously played with the sheet. She wished she'd never heard of Roxwell Mason, but no one had made her marry him. She'd done that all by herself.

"Ted, will you send flowers for me, please, and ask Shane to come talk with me, won't you? I don't want this to get any worse between us."

Ted glanced at her sadly for only a moment before he nodded. There was an awkward pause, then he asked, "What about Rafe?"

Kea stared at him. She hadn't expected the question, for she had been so clear about her feelings on the subject. "What about him?" she asked with a carelessness she was far from experiencing.

"I want him to do your surgery."

"No."

"Kea."

"No. We've already gone over this. I don't want to see Rafe again. Ever. Anyway"—she heard the tremor in her voice—"he only came as a courtesy to you."

Ted shook his head disgustedly. "That man doesn't go anywhere as a courtesy to anyone. He doesn't have to. He's agreed to do it, and I think you should put personal consideration aside and let him."

Personal consideration! she wanted to shout. My heart? My life? My face? Mere personal consideration! "There are other doctors just as good," she insisted. "I don't want Rafe. Personal consideration has nothing to do with it."

"Liar," he accused softly. "Foolish little liar. Rafe wants to do it, and I think you're showing extremely poor judgment not to allow it."

He was goading her and she knew it. What she didn't know was that he was setting her up for Rafe. When she didn't reply, he said, "I'll be back later."

She watched as he left, then her gaze returned to the window. Why was everyone so determined to force Rafe back into her life? Didn't they know that she was barely holding together now? She stared at the place where the summer sunshine played across the windowsill, dancing into the room on a stream of gold. It seemed to mock her and her misery.

When the door opened again, she glanced around to find Rafe walking into the room. Her breath caught in her throat as he quietly closed the door behind him.

Kea lay before him, speechless for a moment, staring at him as he strode over to her in that easy manner that spoke of such latent power and confidence.

"Ready to talk about the particulars now?" he asked as casually as if she had agreed beforehand.

"I told you I don't want you to do the surgery," she stated. She wished she could hide from him, snap her fingers and vanish. Ellen had brought some beautiful gowns to the hospital for her, and though she was wearing one today, it didn't help her self-image.

"Why not? Don't you think I'm capable?"

In spite of herself Kea met his eyes. Then she laughed a little, and the sound hung between them, mirthless and strained. "No, Rafe, you and I both know you're very competent, but you're simply not the doctor for me."

"Don't worry," he said with abrupt harshness, his dark eyes flashing. "I won't intrude on your personal life. I'll restore your beauty for some other man, and you can go on with your life as though you'd never seen me again. Pretend that I'm any surgeon doing a job."

Kea was taken aback for a moment. Biting down on her lower lip, she gazed at him in surprise. The cruelty in his voice was a shock to her. Was he angry because he thought *she* expected *him* to become involved with her again? Obviously it was an idea he found distasteful.

Or was he angry for other reasons? Had he cared at all when she married Roxwell, or had he been relieved? Maybe she had only been fooling herself when she thought she had hurt him. And if he hadn't been interested then, he sure as hell wasn't interested now, she told herself bitterly.

44

"You *can* view me as just another physician, can't you, Kea?" he needled, his words stinging her to the quick.

Kea felt her temper rise; she *couldn't*, of course, but she would never let him know it. Now pride alone demanded that she let Rafe do the surgery.

"Of course I can, *Dr. Jordan*," she flung at him. "With the greatest of ease," she added, her gray eyes cold and steely. "I think the past has proven that."

"Good." The word was like a jab to her soul. "The first surgery will be tomorrow morning." He moved closer to her, and it was all she could do not to slap his face. He gave her another thorough examination, his fingers moving lightly over her face, and she set her jaw in grim determination and endured his touch.

He quickly partially replaced the bandages, then he was gone, leaving Kea to her inner turmoil.

CHAPTER THREE

Lying back against the pillows, Kea trembled with fury and disappointment. She had never expected such callousness of him—Rafe who had treated the least and the best of his brethren with concern and compassion. She wondered if she had imagined that he had cared for her, loved her, all those times they had shared.

Well, at least he wasn't pitying her now. She could cope with his arrogance much more easily than she could his pity, but it didn't ease the pain, or the shame she was feeling. She would show Rafe that he had meant no more to her than she apparently had meant to him.

Sighing, she closed her eyes and recalled every single word of her exchange with Rafe. And she vowed that she would see him no more than absolutely necessary. He *would* be "just another physician" to her, no matter what it took. And it would take a lot, she knew, to hide the love she felt for him, the love she was afraid she would always feel for him.

Struggling to her feet, she worked her way stiffly to the bath in her private room, and she made herself stare at the reflection in the mirror. Most of her face was uncovered now, and it was a fresh shock to see the aftermath of her injuries, but as she studied the face she knew so well, she thanked God that her eyes would be normal again, with the help of Rafe, and she was grateful that her lips hadn't even been scraped, the lips that had once clung so longingly to his.

She straightened her spine, causing her battered body to cry out in protest, and she made herself a promise that she wouldn't let her situation conquer her. At least she was alive, and that was more than poor Roxwell was. She shivered, and she would not permit herself to think of him. Ted had been right; Kea had to carry on. She would do so with Rafe's help, whether she wanted to accept his aid or not.

For a time she stayed there before the mirror, supporting her weight on one foot while the other throbbed with pain, taking stock of herself and her future. She was frightened, yes, but she would survive. Maybe she would even come out of this disaster stronger than she had been before, but at the moment she had serious doubts. Life as she had known it was irrevocably gone, and she didn't know what the future would hold for her.

When she had been back in bed for only a few minutes, the door opened and she was pleased to see Jon come into the room. "Hello," she said with much more cheer than she was feeling. "Where's Ellen?"

"She's running the shop today." He walked over to stand beside the bed. "You're looking better every day. How are you?" He had a big bunch of red roses in his hand, and Kea was delighted that he had been so thoughtful.

"I'm going to be all right," she said, and for the first time she actually thought the words might be true.

"Sure you are," Jon agreed. "I'm happy your attitude has improved. What's brought about this miracle?" His blue eyes twinkled and he smiled broadly.

She found herself returning his smile, but she couldn't quite answer his question. Had Rafe goaded her out of her self-pity? Or had Rafe's mere appearance been enough to affect her attitude? She wouldn't permit herself to explore the question.

"Time, I guess. Ted told me that life was for the living, and I think I've finally realized that I'm still among them."

Jon set the vase on the table and eased down on the side of her bed. "You are that, Kea, and I can't tell you how pleased I am to see you doing better. I was really worried."

"You're a treasure," she murmured gently, grateful for his friendship. "I truly don't know what I'd do without you and Ellen."

He reached out to take her hand in his. "I don't know what I'd do without you. I realized that when I heard about the accident. You're such a part of my life, a beautiful part, and have been for so long."

"A beautiful part?" Kea asked, laughing at herself for the first time. "You must care for me if you can refer to anything about me as beautiful with this face."

Jon patted her hand. "Your face will soon be good as new." His smile was so warm and compassionate that Kea wanted to hug him.

Instead, she squeezed his hand, then freed hers. "You know how much you and Ellen mean to me." She laughed, feeling completely relaxed with him. "I'm convinced we're related in spirit."

"Listen," Jon said solemnly, "Ellen and I have talked it over, and we want you to stay a few days at our place when you're released. The doctor tells me that you'll need someone to care for you for a while, and we want to be the ones to do it."

Kea wanted to say no; she wanted nothing more than to be by herself for at least a short time so that she could pull herself together again, but how could she refuse? She had realized when she hobbled to the mirror in the bathroom that she couldn't get around without great difficulty with her sprained ankle, and she knew that once she had

48

the surgery on her eye, she would be bedridden, at least temporarily. If Shane had fired most of the household help, she couldn't count on them, and she definitely couldn't count on Shane. She glanced at Jon again. She would be comfortable with her friends, and when the bleak times came, she would find solace with them.

"We insist," Jon said, taking her hand again.

Kea's gaze searched his face. Yes, it would be good to spend some time with her friends. They all had been far too busy in the past few years, he and Ellen with the florist shop they owned, and Kea with her talk show. Their warm and spacious home was a good place to hide from the memories that often became too painful and the heart-aches that called too frequently.

"Thank you, Jon," she decided abruptly. "I just might take you up on the offer."

"That's wonderful." He patted her hand again, and Kea found herself thinking that the accident had made them all look at life differently. She had never thought about just how much Jon and Ellen really meant to her, or how much they cared for her. They had always been there for each other, but now it was different. She sensed it.

She smiled at Jon again. His timing couldn't have been better. His reassurance and concern were just what she needed after Rafe's insensitivity.

A week later Rafe stood at Kea's bedside examining her for the last time before her release from the hospital. He hated to let her go, but he knew she would be all right with her friends. The operation had been a success and the fracture was healing nicely. The eye patch had been removed, and the sutures would come out in a couple of days. The sutures from the other wounds had already been taken out. As he traced her face with his fingertips, he knew he had touched her more often than necessary, lin-

49

gered over his daily visits to her, savoring the bittersweet time with her, agonizing over the future.

Kea had been aloof and impersonal, but stoic and uncomplaining throughout. Rafe had admired her courage, for he knew how deeply troubled she was. He had heard about Mason's son's hostility, and he knew the papers were having a field day with the boy and his comments about Kea. He had accused Kea of marrying his father solely for his money, and he had hinted that she was glad Roxwell Mason was dead. Rafe knew Kea was in for trouble with the boy, and he would have gladly borne her pains, both physical and mental, if he could have.

She had such fierce pride. And until now she hadn't known about the harsh realities of life—how the spirit and body could suffer and starve from verbal wounding as well as physical. She hadn't lived life as he had known it, as it had been in his most formative years, so that he could empathize with those hurt and broken.

His dark eyes raked over her face, taking in the features that had lived on in his mind, making him toss and turn in the night. He was glad that he was the one to restore her beauty, even though he knew that once she was out from under his care, he would be sending her from him forever.

She wouldn't need him then. Once again she would be beautiful—beautiful to other men, as she was beautiful to him now. He drew strange comfort from the knowledge that he would have a few more months with her, though it would ultimately add to the pain that still burned inside him, filling him with fresh need and raw regret each time he saw her.

"How do you feel?" he asked curtly, hiding his feelings behind a stern face and dark eyes.

"All right," she replied, evading his gaze by looking off at the far corner of the room.

"You're doing very well," he said. "I think you can

safely go home now, but it's important for you to take it easy for a few weeks. No lifting or bending. You need bed rest for a few days, and then you need to resume your regular routine very gradually. You're still a little swollen and bruised, but that will soon disappear." He trailed his fingertips around the area he was examining, then traced the scars on her cheek.

"We'll see how these mature. Later we can revise them if that's what you want."

Kea nodded, and she trembled inside when he bent down to check her bruised upper arm. "Sore?" he asked, looking up at her. Their eyes locked, then Kea quickly glanced away.

Didn't he realize how he made her heart beat faster when he pinned her with his dark gaze? She didn't know what was worse—the fear that she might see pity in his eyes, or hatred.

"A little," she admitted.

"That's to be expected, but nothing's broken." He straightened. "The soreness will probably remain for a week or so."

"I see."

When he moved to the foot of her bed and lifted the bedcovers to examine her ankle, Kea tensed. There was something so intimate about him gently exploring her ankle that she felt a shiver race up her spine. She had been an utter fool to agree to having him as her doctor, for every time he had touched her it was sheer agony. She hated him seeing her so ugly and vulnerable, and her shame was almost intolerable. At least it was nearly over.

"Are you getting around any better on this ankle?"

"Yes."

"Does it hurt much?"

"No."

"Stay off it as much as possible. It still hasn't healed completely. Walk on it a little more each day."

51

"All right."

Rafe stood staring at her a moment longer, and Kea sensed that he had something more to say. She waited, tense and anxious, wondering if this entire week had been as heartrending and humiliating for him as it had been for her. Of course it hadn't, she told herself. He wasn't the one who had been injured, who was suffering mentally and physically, fighting with confusing feelings and desperate longings, dealing with guilt and self-doubt and embarrassment.

"I'll see you in the office on Friday."

"Fine."

"Kea . . ."

She glanced up at him when he called her name ever so softly and their gazes held for a moment.

"Take care of yourself. If you need me, call me at the office or at home, day or night."

She saw it clearly this time—the pity—and she was appalled by it! "I won't need you," she said firmly.

Rafe's voice was sharp-edged once again. "No, I don't suppose you will. Good day."

"Good-bye."

At last he was gone and Kea could breathe more easily. She stared down at her hands. The ring Roxwell had given her had been removed when she had surgery, and she hadn't put it back on. What was the point? It had no significance now. A memory from long ago burned brightly in her mind as she recalled how desperately she had wanted Rafe's ring. She had never gotten it. She would never get it.

She drew in a steadying breath; there was no point in regretting that either. She had to think about the future now. She was beginning to feel better, at least physically. She had been so worried about her eyes, and now she could see out of both of them again. She knew that her face was still a little swollen, but except in the most recent area of repair, the ugly purples and blues had faded to pale yellow.

"Hello! Hello!"

Kea smiled when Ellen walked into the room, distracting her from her thoughts.

"I just saw your doctor and he tells me you're all ready to go home with me."

"More than ready," Kea agreed.

"Well, let's find somebody to wheel you out of here and we'll get under way."

"I'm all for that," Kea said with a small laugh.

She didn't relax until she was in the car and headed for the Wagners' comfortable home on a quiet tree-lined street. Kea knew it well; it was the home Jon had been raised in, and it had been left to him by his parents when they died. She adored the house, and she even had a guest room she considered her own.

"Is Jon still at the shop?" she asked as Ellen drove past familiar landmarks.

Her friend laughed. "No. Actually he's cleaning the house, if you can believe that. He's so excited about you staying with us, and so worried that you won't be happy. He's planned Scrabble games and invited friends over— the whole bit. He wants you to get back into the normal swing of life."

Looking away, Kea hesitated to comment. She wasn't ready to get back in the swing, but she knew she couldn't hide out forever. The sooner she could begin to forget the accident, Roxwell, and especially Rafe, the better it would be.

"Don't throw a party too soon," she said at last. "We don't want to scare anybody." She laughed lightly, but Ellen responded to the tension in her voice.

"You really don't look bad, Kea. Just a bit bruised and swollen. That accident didn't destroy your beauty— there's more to you than a face. Anyway, those scars are so mysterious and fascinating," she teased. "They make you seem like a figure in a novel." The teasing tone left her voice, and her green eyes became unusually bright when she gazed at Kea.

"Why did you decide to let Rafe be the surgeon? You seemed so adamant about not having him beforehand that I was surprised when you chose him after all."

"I didn't choose him," Kea said sharply. "Ted sent him in without my permission."

"But you allowed him to operate," Ellen persisted.

Kea shrugged with a nonchalance she was far from feeling. "What does it matter? He's the best around, and it's done now."

Ellen looked back at the road. "I was just surprised that you changed your mind. Has—is there anything—oh, you know what I'm trying to ask," she finished in exasperation.

"Yes, I do believe I know what you mean," Kea answered. "And, no, of course there's nothing between Rafe and me. There hasn't been for some time as you well know." Her laughter was brief and bitter. "If I had been suffering under some kind of delusion that Rafe still cared for me, he quickly set me straight."

"Then why did you agree? I don't understand."

"He asked me if I couldn't view him as just another physician, meaning, obviously, that was all he was and would ever be to me now." She glanced out the window. "What could I do but accept the challenge?"

"You could have requested another doctor," Ellen said bluntly.

"I tried, but Rafe was determined so I decided to use him."

"To *use* him?" Ellen asked, her voice playing with the words.

"Even *you* thought he should be the one to work on

me," Kea retorted defensively, ignoring the implications of the question.

"I had my reservations," Ellen murmured. "Not about his competency, of course, but because of your past relationship. I think he still cares for you, Kea, and I'd hate to see you try to dredge up the past right now just because you're feeling low and not your most attractive. Things didn't work out between you two. Don't make him pay again. The last thing you need in your life right now is a man."

Kea was so surprised that she could think of nothing to say; before she could respond, Ellen changed the subject. "I hope Jon's finished with your room by now. He was so frantic about getting it just so. He's quite worried that you won't be comfortable."

"I've always been comfortable in your home, Ellen. You know that and so does Jon." She switched topics as easily as Ellen had, but the other woman's comments had upset her terribly.

Use Rafe? Had it been a subconscious word choice because she so deeply resented Rafe's attitude toward her? But why should she? No matter how he felt about her, he was justified in light of the way she'd treated him.

But Ellen's comment about him still caring for her was the most surprising of all. Not that she believed it for a moment, and neither would Ellen if she had seen the way Rafe treated her in the hospital. He pitied her, perhaps, but pity and caring weren't quite the same thing.

Kea hadn't even told Ellen how much she still loved Rafe, or how unhappy her marriage to Roxwell had been. Ellen had guessed that it wasn't all a bed of roses, of course, but Kea had been too ashamed to confide in even her closest friends after what she had done. Everyone had been shocked when she married Roxwell so unexpectedly, but her friends accepted it without condemning her.

She wanted to assure Ellen that her fears were unfound-

55

ed where Rafe was concerned, but before she could voice her thoughts, Ellen spoke again.

"We just want to make this difficult time as easy as possible for you," she said warmly.

Kea was so absorbed in thoughts of Rafe it took her a moment to realize that they were talking about her stay in the Wagner home.

"Your accident was one of those things we always think won't happen to those we know and love," Ellen continued. "It only happens to someone else, doesn't it? The reality of this has brought it home to us. We love you and this was such a dreadful shock."

When Kea felt the tears rise at the back of her eyes, she swallowed hard. She didn't want to get maudlin now; she had made herself a promise that she would leave the past behind and look to the future. But she was moved by Ellen's concern and love. "Thank you," she whispered, feeling the terrible inadequacy of those two words.

Ellen smoothly guided the car into the driveway. Then she opened the garage with an electronic device and carefully parked inside. "Jon will go over to your place later this afternoon and pick up a few items. We'll make a list. We'll even bring Mickey if you want."

Kea laughed softly. Mickey was a stuffed toy she had gotten from Disneyland when she was a teen-ager, and she had kept it throughout the years. She knew it was ridiculous, but she was genuinely fond of the toy.

"I think Mickey can take care of himself just a little longer," she said. "He's a big boy now, all grown-up like the rest of us."

Jon came bounding out to the garage before Ellen and Kea could get out of the car. They had only a few things to carry—gowns, robes, and minor personal items—but Jon was there, eager to help, and Ellen gave him the overnight bag.

"How are you?" he asked Kea.

She smiled at him indulgently. "You saw me yesterday, Jon," she teased. "I haven't changed a whole lot. Bruised face, limited vision, but not too bad all in all."

His grin was boyish. "That's good to hear. Just as long as you're still in a decent frame of mind."

"What mind I have left," she joked, a hint of the Kea of old surfacing.

"I've prepared lunch," Jon said enthusiastically.

Again Kea smiled. "Let me guess. Quiche Lorraine." She was amused at Jon's surprise. "How did you know?"

Both Kea and Ellen laughed. "Jon, it's Kea's favorite and your best dish," Ellen replied. "After fifteen years she can make a pretty good guess about what you'll do."

When they were settled at the table, they engaged in light banter, and Kea began to relax for the first time in many days. It had been the right decision, coming here to stay with her friends.

She glanced at Jon as he served her a second portion of quiche, noticing the way his hair fell so carelessly over his forehead. He was slender and fair; his features could be described as less than sensational, but his friendship meant the world to Kea.

Her gaze shifted to Ellen with her pixie looks, her blond hair and flashing green eyes. She could have had her pick of the guys, but she had been in love with Jon since they were both fifteen.

"Let's fatten you up," Jon said teasingly as he placed a large portion of the egg dish on Kea's plate.

"You want the rest of me to look as bad as my face?" she asked. She bit down on her lower lip as the words filled the air, bringing with them an unexpected tension. She had been teasing, but she saw the glances her friends exchanged.

Her fingers strayed to her cheek, and she traced the

57

wounds with her fingertips. It was no longer painful to the touch, but it caused her pain, nevertheless.

"I don't think you have to worry about putting on any extra pounds," Ellen said as casually as if their happy time hadn't been shattered. "Your figure has never been anything short of gorgeous, and I doubt that it ever will be. The rest of us began to add poundage years ago, but not you."

Kea managed a brief laugh. "It's known as sheer vanity. I worked my rear off—literally—to stay in shape."

The former mood was lost, but at least the tension eased somewhat and they finished lunch in a reasonably pleasant atmosphere.

While Ellen did the dishes, Jon and Kea made a list of the things she would need from the house. Mostly she wanted comfortable dresses and pants outfits; she had no intention of sitting around in gowns and robes like an invalid. His list in hand, Jon kissed Ellen on the cheek and left.

When Ellen had finished the dishes, she and Kea talked for a while as they awaited Jon's return. They were surprised when he came back empty-handed after a short time.

"What happened?" Kea asked, and frowned worriedly, causing her injuries to be more noticeable.

"It's that damn son of Mason's," Jon exploded, running his hands angrily through his brown hair. "He refused to let me in. He said you couldn't touch a thing in that house until the estate was settled."

Kea gaped at him in disbelief. "I don't believe it! He can't be serious!"

At just that moment the doorbell rang. "That will be Shane now with an explanation and an apology," Kea said confidently.

Jon strode over to the door and dragged it open. To his surprise he found Rafe Jordan standing before him.

"Is something wrong?" he asked, seeing Jon's distress.

"Come on in." Jon indicated a chair, then slumped down on the sofa.

Looking at Kea, Rafe asked, "Are you all right? I had intended to give you a prescription for pain before you left the hospital, but I forgot to see if you needed something." He wondered if his reason for stopping by sounded as phony to them as it did to him; in truth, he had wanted to make sure she was settled in comfortably.

Kea shook her head. "I don't need anything, thanks." She was as startled as Jon was to see Rafe, and she didn't want to prolong his visit.

"She does need something," Jon interjected. "Mason's son won't let me take any of Kea's personal belongings from the house—not even her clothes. He wouldn't even let me in!" His blue eyes sparked with anger.

"I'm sure there's some explanation," Kea murmured. "Surely Shane didn't mean that. He doesn't know you that well, Jon. Perhaps if I phoned—"

"He knows me all right," Jon countered. "He's just behaving like a jackal. He's afraid you've instructed me to take something more valuable than your clothes."

Kea stood up abruptly, forgetting about her injuries, and she winced as she put her weight on the sprained ankle. "I'll go myself. He won't refuse me."

Rafe stood up. "Sit down. You're in no condition to go. I'll do it. I know how to deal with this kind of thing."

He said it with such fierceness that none of them dared attempt to dissuade him. But it was the last thing Kea wanted. She didn't want him involved in her affairs, especially this messy confrontation with Roxwell's son; however, she was so weakened by all the turmoil that she knew she didn't have the strength to face Shane herself. Her head was aching terribly now, and she felt faint.

Seeing her paleness, Rafe insisted that she go back to bed. "You're supposed to be resting," he said curtly.

"I can't sleep," she protested.

"I'll give you something to help. Go lie down."

To her consternation Kea saw a flash of sympathy in his dark eyes, and that, more than anything, convinced her to leave the room. She couldn't cope with any more humiliation. Her head was pounding as she made her way clumsily back to her room and gratefully sank down on the bed.

Hovering around her, Ellen smoothed down the light spread and plumped Kea's pillows. "You try to rest. I'll go get the prescription filled."

"Thank you." Kea sighed wearily as Ellen left. Through the partially open door she could hear Rafe giving instructions about the prescription to Ellen. Kea closed her eyes, seeking some relief from all the unhappiness she was feeling.

She had hoped that Shane wouldn't make this any harder on her than it already was. She knew he had resented her marriage to Roxwell, but she hadn't realized how much he disliked her. For the most part he had ignored her, and he hadn't had much to do with his father unless he wanted money or was in some kind of trouble. Now even Rafe knew how Shane felt about her. Why had he come back into her life just to see her in this awful state?

She heard Rafe and Ellen leave, and when she heard Jon's steps in the hall, she kept her eyes tightly closed. At this particular time she didn't want to talk to anyone, not even him.

He nudged the door open farther, and Kea could feel his gaze on her for a moment. Then she heard him walk away. Exhausted, she rolled over on her side and tried to get to sleep, but it was impossible. Her mind was spinning with anger and frustration. If she weren't here, injured, she would march to Roxwell's—her—house and tell Shane just what she thought of him. But she *was* injured—broken in mind and spirit—and so very, very weary.

It seemed like forever that she lay there, tossing and

restless, before she heard a light tap on the door. She wanted to ignore it, but she knew Jon was aware that she wasn't asleep. The tapping sounded again, and she opened her eyes.

"Come in, Jon."

He slipped into the room and closed the door. "Can't you sleep?" he asked softly, concern etched deeply on his features.

"No." She admitted the obvious. "My mind is running in circles and I can't seem to make it stop."

Walking over to her bed, he sat down on the edge. "Ellen has gone to get the prescription filled. She won't be gone too long." He patted her hand reassuringly.

Kea gave him a faint smile, grateful for his concern. He was so uncomplicated and easy to be with.

Jon's fingers tightened over hers, and Kea felt his warm breath on her cheek as he bent down over her. "Kea, I promise you it's going to be all right," he whispered.

Knowing how much he wanted to comfort her, she agreed. "I hope so."

"It will," he said. "You're still beautiful to me," he suddenly murmured fiercely.

As Kea looked at him, she was suddenly aware of a tenseness in him. Slipping her hand from his, she sat up in bed, a little uneasy, but not quite sure why. He was looking at her so intensely that his eyes glittered with unusual brightness.

"Thank you, Jon," she murmured uncertainly.

He reached out to brush her hair away from her right cheek, and unexpectedly he bent forward and kissed her scars, then embraced her.

Kea had been hugged by him as many times as she had by Ellen, but there was something upsetting about his embrace now, and she had an awful feeling growing inside her.

"Kea," he whispered against her hair, "I'll take care of

you. I realized when you were injured how dear you are to me."

Drawing back, she tried to free herself from his possessive grasp. "I'm grateful," she replied stiffly, but she could not disguise the unease she was beginning to feel.

"So beautiful," he murmured as he held her close. "I've always thought you were the most beautiful creature I've ever seen. You're a very desirable woman."

Kea tried again to pull away. "Jon, you don't know what you're saying. Ellen—" Before she could finish, his mouth came down on hers.

Kea made a muffled protest and tried to free herself, but found that she was too weak. Still, she pushed frantically against his chest as he pressed her back against the pillows.

At that precise moment Kea heard the door to the bedroom open. "Kea, I'm back."

Ellen's words froze in her throat, and her face turned ashen. Both Kea and Jon turned toward the familiar face with the same horror in their eyes. "What are you doing?" Ellen rasped. "Jon? Kea?"

If Kea lived to be a thousand, she would never, never forget the shocked, haunted look in her friend's wide green eyes. Kea had known pain in her time, but almost nothing compared to the way she was feeling now.

CHAPTER FOUR

While Jon awkwardly moved off the bed, Kea licked her lips and tried to think of the right explanation to give Ellen, but she was still too stunned herself to know what to say to her childhood friend.

She was aware that Ellen closed the door with incredible softness, and she listened to her friend's retreating footsteps, but still she couldn't move. When they heard the car start in the garage, Jon rushed down the hall. Seconds later Kea heard his car start, but she was still too devastated even to think. My God, how had this happened?

Her life was crumbling all around her; everything that she had known and loved, had thought was forever, was shattering and breaking up day after day like the ice on a lake being pounded by a relentless warm sun. The terror that rose in her heart made it pound ominously, and she wished that she had died in the accident along with Roxwell.

In the midst of her distress she sensed that she was still being watched, and her misery increased tenfold when she looked up to find Rafe standing in the doorway. His eyes were dark, with an unreadable expression, and his arms were filled with Kea's clothes and other personal items, including the stuffed toy, Mickey. Her heart contracted and she tried to speak, but no words came.

Rafe closed his eyes for an instant at the plea he read

in Kea's. He had arrived at the house in time to see Ellen race away. No one had answered the door, which Ellen had left ajar, so he had come in, fearing that something had happened to Kea. He had gone down the hall to find Jon grasping her hand, his face guilt-stricken. Kea had been on the bed, struggling to sit up. Their demeanor had painted an ugly picture, and Rafe didn't like the conclusion he had drawn—but what else could he think?

Kea couldn't hold his gaze when she saw the questioning look in his eyes. She was too distraught to know what to tell him. She didn't know how much he had seen or heard, but it was all too clear that it had been too much. She didn't want to incriminate Jon, but she couldn't abide the idea of Rafe thinking she was to blame for what had happened here. A deep scarlet tainted her face, and she lowered her lids to hide her eyes from him.

Rafe still didn't comment. Struggling with old and fierce inner demons, he was waiting for the woman in front of him to make some kind of appropriate explanation. And while he waited, his mind raced ahead. Had Kea made love with Jon? He knew it was a critical time for a woman in a situation like this, especially a woman who had been so beautiful. She would be seeking reassurance, wanting to know that she was still attractive, still appealing. But to Jon? Ellen's husband? Her longest and dearest friends? And was this the first time?

Although Rafe didn't want to think the worst, the situation more or less spoke for itself, and Kea was doing nothing to defend her actions—or lack of them. At first Rafe had been angry with the Mason boy, and now that anger was intensified and directed at Kea; he felt oddly betrayed, as though she had cheated *him,* as well as Ellen. In his case it wouldn't be the first time, of course.

He walked into the room and set down her belongings, and still he waited for her to say something. Let her tell

64

him he was wrong, that it was all a mistake, he thought silently. Let her somehow explain the inexplicable.

Again she raised her eyes to meet his, and when she saw that accusing look, she pressed her lips tightly together. Rafe had already judged her! She didn't owe him any explanation. She hadn't asked for his involvement, and she couldn't begin to explain what had happened here, or to convey the anguish she was feeling for herself, Ellen, and Jon.

It took her an eternity to regain her composure, to force her mind to function rationally. She had suffered blow after blow in the past few weeks, and Jon and Ellen had stood by her through it all. They had been her friends, the only ones who understood—or so she had thought. And now this. Without Jon and Ellen she had no one. No one. Certainly not this cold, condemning man standing before her.

Never in her wildest dreams had she imagined that Jon would approach her as he had, and, in truth, she really didn't believe he had meant to do it. He must have thought he was helping her by the declarations he had made. He was foolish and his timing had been incredibly bad, but deep in her heart she didn't believe that he had intended to get involved with her. He loved Ellen; Kea was sure of it. She had seen how deep that love was in his eyes when he had seen Ellen's pain.

He had wrongly thought that Kea felt she was no longer lovable, and he had wanted in some way to prove to her that she was. The way he had chosen had been the wrong one, but she could almost understand the desperation, the confusion, that had distorted his perception of her.

Kea couldn't erase Ellen's tortured face from her mind. Her friend had been crushed, cruelly and uselessly crushed, for had the scene happened a few minutes earlier, Kea was sure she could have straightened it all out before Ellen ever came home.

It hurt terribly to think that Ellen had thought Kea a willing participant. The mere idea was abhorrent to her, but she could imagine how it had looked to Ellen. It was an old story, Kea knew, of the unhappy friend finding solace in the husband's arms, but it hadn't been *her* story. God knows she hadn't wanted Jon to touch her like that. She had loved him as a brother—deeply and sincerely, without stipulations—just as she loved Ellen.

Now she feared she had lost their friendship. She had other friends, yes, but Jon's and Ellen's friendship had been rare and precious, and such a big part of her life. She would be lost without them, for she had always envisioned the three of them going into old age together, sharing the highs and lows of life.

Abruptly, without any comment, she stood up, the effort in itself something of a feat. With incredible determination she made her way over to Rafe and began to gather up her belongings. She paused only briefly when she saw that he had brought her flute along. She admired his sensitivity in bringing the toy and the flute, for he knew how much she treasured both; however, she didn't have time to ponder his consideration. She had to leave here, of course, before Jon and Ellen returned.

"What are you doing?" he demanded.

"I'm going to stay at a hotel," she announced as if she had already worked it all out in her mind. The idea had come to her when he had asked, and it sounded as reasonable as any.

"You can't stay in a hotel in your condition," he told her firmly.

Her laughter was brief and bitter. "Well, I certainly can't stay here."

He stared at her without comment, still waiting for an explanation that she was never going to give. He knew that she had to be in pain, and even if he thought she deserved some punishment for her conduct with Jon, pain of this kind wasn't it.

"You can't stay alone. You need someone to wait on you."

"I'll manage if I hire a nurse," she retorted.

Rafe saw her strength and her bitterness, and despite his doubts he had to admire her fortitude. "Come home with me," he said on impulse. But the moment the words were out of his mouth he regretted them. He was letting his compassion overrule his common sense. Still, he waited expectantly for her answer.

Kea glanced at him in surprise. How could he even suggest such a thing? "No, thanks," she said with an edge of sharpness in her voice. "I've had enough kind offers for one day."

"It's not a *kind* offer," he retorted. "You don't have to worry about *anyone* making advances to you at my house."

Her head snapped back, and she quickly disguised the hurt that she knew must be visible in her gray eyes. No doubt he thought he was reassuring her, when he was really reminding her again that she had lost him, that he no longer desired her.

"You'll have all the privacy in the world," Rafe continued, too busy hiding his own pain to recognize hers. "I'm not home much, but my housekeeper will be there to help you."

"Do you make this offer to all your patients?" she asked bitterly.

"Not all," he returned. "But some."

Sighing tiredly, Kea didn't argue the point, for she remembered that it was true that he sometimes let patients stay in his house. Of course he would—the magnanimous Rafe Jordan. She knew that he would bring patients in from countries that didn't have the facilities to treat them,

67

and yes, they often lived with him until they could return to their homeland.

She smiled bleakly to herself. She should have remembered it with no trouble. During those times she and Rafe had spent their private moments at her place instead of his. The memory caused a fresh surge of pain to her heart.

"Save your rooms for your more seriously injured patients," she said quietly. She could not put herself in his power again, no matter what her circumstances.

She turned toward the hall, seeking the phone, but when she put her weight on her ankle, a shaft of pain shot up her leg, causing her such discomfort that she gasped softly.

Rafe knew she was in pain, for he had seen her careless and angry stride, and abruptly he took her things back from her. All his hostility left him as he watched her struggle to compose her expression. A wave of sympathy washed over him as he saw her helplessness and her confusion.

Cupping her chin so that she had to raise her sad gray eyes to meet his dark, penetrating ones, he said softly, "As your doctor, I'm concerned for you. I don't want you to undo my work with your rashness. You're not up to the struggle of finding a room, getting settled in, and hiring a nurse. Please, let me take care of you until you can manage better."

His words touched her more deeply than Jon's plea, for she thought she heard real tenderness in his voice. Suddenly she felt utterly defeated. That flicker of feeling she sensed in Rafe crumbled her last defense. She was so weary, so tired of the battles of her life. She wanted nothing more than to sink into the oblivion of Rafe's arms and let the world disappear. It was an impossible desire, of course, for all that he had offered her was the solace of his home. And she was going to take it. He had defeated her with his gentleness.

She tried to force a smile, but she couldn't. "All right. You win," she said thickly. "I don't want you to have wasted your time and your talents on a patient who behaves recklessly." She had wanted to be flippant, light, but her weary voice reflected her state of mind.

He laid her things on the bed. "Let's get you settled in the car, then I'll bring these," he said.

Kea obeyed, walking slowly toward the front door. When Rafe had opened it, she made her way down the walk to his car, a car she had been in many times. Very gently, as if she were made of fine, fragile china, Rafe supported her with his arm as he helped her into the car.

Her heart beating madly, Kea glanced at him, seeing his strong jaw and dark eyes, free for the moment of their bitter mask. Their eyes locked briefly, and his look seemed to reach inside her to strip her of her fears. Finding herself here in his car, again gazing into his eyes, experiencing his tenderness, Kea couldn't keep back a flood of memories of other times with Rafe. Times when there was sharing and caring. Times when they were happy in each other's arms. Times when passion had soared to unimagined heights.

"I'll be right back."

Rafe's words shattered the moment, and Kea watched as he went back up the walkway, his stride confident and masculine. A short time later he returned with her possessions and put them in the backseat of the car.

Sitting stiffly at Rafe's side, Kea was all too aware of him as they drove toward his house. She hated being here with him, helpless; she hated giving him the power to direct her life at the moment, but she knew, too, that she wanted to draw whatever strength she could from him for a short time. She needed him—as never before.

As they made their way past lavish homes, Kea remained silent. She couldn't seem to get a bearing on her life right now. She was acutely aware of Rafe sitting so close beside her, and she had to resist the urge to caress his muscled thigh as she had done so often so many months ago. She coldly reminded herself of who she was now, what she looked like, and why she was here. That was all it took to put things back in perspective, despite that moment when his eyes had drawn her back in time and his hands had touched her with a brief, blazing memory of lost desire. But the silence in the car and Rafe's black expression told her that moment had been no more than an illusion.

When they finally arrived at his house, Rafe helped her from the car, and to her chagrin, he whisked her up in his arms. "You've been on that ankle too much today," he said. "I know it must be painful."

It had been, but now she had forgotten all about the pain. She could feel her heart hammering wildly inside her chest, and she wondered if he felt the frantic beating. Did he have any idea what torment it was for her to be held in his arms like this after all the many months of longing? He couldn't know, of course, and Kea fought with herself to keep from locking her arms around his neck.

She wondered what he really thought as he looked at her face, the face he was making whole again, and she wondered if he, too, remembered the other times they had shared. Times when neither of them could have imagined this nightmare. Then she remembered the dark accusation in his eyes after Jon had rushed from her room, and she wondered exactly what Rafe thought of her now. The question sobered her, bringing her ruthlessly back to the present.

"You don't need to carry me. I can manage on my own."

He didn't reply, and Kea pressed her lips into a thin line. When they reached the front door, he stood her on her feet. Finding herself back here once again filled her with a sense of unreality. She had never thought she would be welcome. She stood nervously by his side as Rafe opened the door.

When they had entered, she awkwardly waited for him to direct her wherever it was he wanted her to go. Her eyes swept over the familiar rooms, which brought back the thousand memories they held for her. In the past, that time so long ago, she would have walked confidently into his house and made herself at home, settling down on the couch, or mixing a drink for each of them. That was what she would have done then. Now was a different matter altogether.

"Would you like something cold to drink?" he asked her as he led the way down the hall to a bedroom. Kea glanced into his plush room as they made their way past it, and the pain she felt as she recalled the times in his arms there was almost physical. She found herself wondering if his nurse, Trena, had slept there in that bed with him, too, and suddenly she wanted to run away. She wondered what on earth she was doing here. She had been a fool to come, for it was sure to add to her already considerable misery, but she couldn't seem to get time or space enough to know what to do with her life right now.

"Kea?" He opened the door to the blue bedroom for her, then repeated the question. "Would you like something to drink?"

She nodded. "That would be nice."

"Orange juice? Apple juice?"

"Orange juice will be fine." She waited until he had gone, then sat down in the nearest chair. Assessing the room, she told herself that it was appropriately done in blue; it suited her mood perfectly.

In a few moments Rafe returned with her clothes and personal items. "I'll bring the juice," he said, laying the flute and a few pieces of clothing on a chair. He had a small overnight case with him, and Kea found herself thinking sarcastically that it had been generous of Shane to let him take it. "The housekeeper will put these things away for you tomorrow," Rafe told her.

Kea nodded, but she had every intention of hanging up her own clothes. She didn't want to inconvenience anyone. When she glanced at the closet, however, she was a little shocked to see a woman's nightgown barely visible at the end. She was convinced that the garment must belong to Trena, and she ached at the thought. Abandoning her good intentions, she hobbled over to the bed and climbed wearily beneath the blue spread. She tried to go to sleep, but the nightgown mocked her, the painful sight unexpectedly dragging her back into her own past with Rafe—to a time when she had been the object of his affection.

In spite of his brooding nature he had been both a tender and generous lover. A smile played on Kea's lips as she recalled the first gift Rafe had ever given her; she had been so thrilled with it, and so very surprised to discover that it was a sheer lavender nightie and a tiny vial of lilac perfume. The recollection came unbidden to her mind, filling her with warmth as she recalled the special night that had followed. He had had her model the nightie, then he had chased her madly around the bedroom until he caught her and they both fell laughing into bed. When the laughter had stopped, they had made love so tenderly that Kea didn't think such a time could ever come again. But it had. And each time with Rafe seemed more special than the last.

She closed her eyes again, wanting to be asleep before Rafe returned, afraid the rosy glow on her cheeks would betray her precious memory of that special night with him. When she opened them again, afraid that she would dream of him, Rafe was standing by the bedside.

"Here."

Rafe brusquely handed her the tiny white pill he held in one hand, then the glass of orange juice.

With trembling hands, Kea somehow managed to take

them. Then she gave the glass back to him and again closed her eyes. She never knew that Rafe stood by her bed staring down at her for a long time, his soul twisted in torment.

He had told her that they would be patient and doctor, but seeing her here made his resolutions so difficult. He wanted nothing more than to smooth back the red hair that had fallen across her brow and stroke the pale skin there. Finally he turned on his heel and quietly walked out of the room.

The next morning Kea was awakened by a loud rap on her door. She awoke to the smell of coffee brewing and bacon cooking. "Breakfast!" a cheery voice called out.

"Come in," Kea responded, stretching and trying to recall where she was. As she awakened fully, it came back to her vividly—yesterday's humiliation and disappointments. Despite the previous day's events she had slept well and dreamlessly, and she found that she was in a better humor than she had been in some time.

The door opened and a jolly white-haired woman entered with a broad smile on her plump face. "Good morning. I'm Mrs. Fortune. Dr. Jordan sent me over for the day. I'm his housekeeper, and his patient-in-residence caretaker."

"I'm pleased to meet you," Kea said, pushing herself up against the pillows.

"What would you like for breakfast?" the woman asked. "I'll bring you a tray."

Kea shook her head. "There's no need for that. I'll come out to the kitchen."

"I think it best if you stay in the bed," Mrs. Fortune said firmly. "Dr. Jordan's orders. Now we don't want to make our ankle worse, do we?"

Gazing at the woman, Kea couldn't resist the urge to tease her a little.

"Is your ankle sprained, too?" she asked in mock innocence.

Mrs. Fortune stepped a little closer to her. "Well, no. I was talking about *you.*"

Kea smiled. "But you said *we,* did you not?"

Mrs. Fortune laughed. "Having a little fun with me, are you? Now you know that's just a manner of speaking. I picked it up from the doctors I've known."

"Not from Ra—Dr. Jordan," Kea said knowingly.

Mrs. Fortune gave a hearty laugh. "No, not from him. He doesn't even think in the term we."

I could testify to that, Kea thought ruefully.

"I'll be back with your breakfast in a jiffy," Mrs. Fortune said.

Kea nodded, but as soon as the woman was gone, she struggled from her bed, put on her robe, and painfully made her way to the bathroom. In a short time she had bathed and slipped into a jade-colored dress and house shoes and was gingerly making her way to the kitchen.

Mrs. Fortune was bustling about, cleaning up the remains of Rafe's breakfast. The woman turned around to watch Kea work her way over to the kitchen table, but her gaze wasn't altogether disapproving. "Hard-headed, are you?" she asked.

Kea couldn't resist laughing. "I guess I am at that, but I didn't want to lie in bed all day." She drew in a deep breath. "It looks like a good day," she commented, glancing out the window.

"Well, I'm glad to see your attitude's good," Mrs. Fortune said, studying the redheaded woman thoughtfully. "I never know what kind of reaction I'll get from the patients when I get here. Some of them are so bitter."

"Some have reason to be," Kea couldn't help but say.

Mrs. Fortune's shrewd brown eyes made a swift appraisal of Kea. "I don't see that you're in such bad shape."

She shrugged offhandedly. "Looks like you got off lucky to me."

"But you don't know what I look like under these clothes," Kea teased a little.

"Oh, yes, I do," Mrs. Fortune said. "Dr. Jordan tells me what to expect injury-wise before I come—and sometimes otherwise."

And what did he tell you about me, Kea desperately wanted to ask, but she didn't dare. Laughing lightly, she agreed, "Yes, I'm fine from here down." She indicated her neck with her hand. "Only my head is a mess."

She liked the housekeeper already. It was good to have someone to talk with, and Mrs. Fortune had a no-nonsense way about her that Kea admired. She had a notion that no one, no matter how badly they were injured, indulged in self-pity with the formidable Mrs. Fortune around.

Holding out her hand, Kea said, "I'm Kea Montgomery. It's nice to meet you."

Mrs. Fortune shook her hand warmly. "Yes, I know who you are. The doctor told me, of course, but I have seen you on television."

"I'm flattered," Kea said. "Bet you didn't know I looked like this without all that makeup, did you?"

The older woman laughed, and it was a warm, hearty laugh, coming up from the belly and booming good-naturedly so that it brought a smile to Kea's lips. "You and I are going to get along just fine," Mrs. Fortune said. "You're going to be okay."

Mrs. Fortune poured herself a cup of coffee. "I'll join you for coffee," she said. "I haven't had mine yet this morning. I think I like the smell of coffee brewing better than I like the taste of it. I always feel cozy and secure when I smell that rich aroma. Creates atmosphere, don't you think?"

Actually Kea had never thought of it quite like that, but yes, it did. "Exactly," she agreed.

Mrs. Fortune had drawn the draperies back, and as Kea gazed out over the swimming pool, she recalled the dozens of times she and Rafe swam in the pool in the dark of night, naked, and she felt the color rise to her cheeks. She was soon lost to a million thoughts of times long gone.

When Mrs. Fortune set a plate of scrambled eggs and bacon before her, she looked up sharply. "Toast?" the woman asked.

"Yes, please."

Mrs. Fortune went back to the counter and picked up a plate with two pieces of whole-wheat bread and returned to hand it to Kea. Then she sat down across from her. "So, what are you going to do with yourself?" she asked bluntly. "You need to keep busy, you know."

Kea smiled again. Here was this stranger, coming into her life with advice and less than gentle nudging, and Kea had to admit that the woman was right. She did need to keep busy, but she didn't know at what. She wondered where Rafe had found Mrs. Fortune, and if he knew what a treasure he had here.

Shrugging, Kea said, "I'm not sure yet. Once these eyes look better, I'll consider my options."

Mrs. Fortune shook her head. "Have you ever worked anywhere besides television? I haven't seen many television personalities who look less than absolutely perfect."

Kea gazed thoughtfully at the woman. How much did she know? Again she had to fight the urge to ask how much Rafe had told her. He had told her about Kea's wounds and her career, but had he told her how he had once held her long into the dark nights, stirring her soul and body with his hungry loving?

Brushing away the images the thought conjured up, Kea met Mrs. Fortune's brown eyes with an even gaze. "I trained to be a secretary, but I *will* go back into television." She hadn't realized it herself until the woman had made her put it into words.

"Doing what?"

"What I do best. Working as a talk-show hostess."

Mrs. Fortune arched her heavy brows and for once she didn't have a ready comment.

"I can, you know," Kea said with conviction. "Why should my scars alter my career?"

"Let's look at this realistically," Mrs. Fortune said solemnly. "They shouldn't, but you and I both know they will. You tell me how many successful people you know in television who've suffered injuries like yours."

Averting her gaze, Kea studied the tabletop. "Maybe none ever tried. I'm already established."

Mrs. Fortune reached across the table to take Kea's hand in hers. "Don't make it too hard on yourself. Your injuries are still new, and you haven't made up your mind what to do. You're obviously bright and talented. You do have other options. Consider them. There comes a time in all our lives when we have to make changes."

Kea met the woman's eyes with a steady gray gaze. Suddenly resolute, she shook her head. "I *have* made up my mind what to do. I love my job, and I won't give it up. I have a contract, and I'll see that it's honored."

"Who's doing your job now? Hasn't the contract been broken by your inability to perform?"

Kea had never given much attention to the contract, honestly. Her father's lawyer had gone over it when she had first gotten the job, and it had been renewed periodically. She hadn't had to worry about terms. "I'm not sure," she admitted. "But I do know this. I *will* work in television again."

Mrs. Fortune nodded, but they both knew she didn't believe Kea could, and it made Kea all the more determined. If she were willing to go back to work, why shouldn't she be permitted? After all, she was the same person with the same capabilities, the same potential.

She knew the answer to her question: It just wasn't done. All the women in television were, if not beautiful, attractive. Kea knew all too well that in the television game packaging was all important. But her stubborn streak surfaced. Now that she had made up her mind, she would not be swayed.

When Rafe had revised the scars—something that wouldn't happen for months—she knew she would still be scarred. But she would live with that, and she had no intention of giving up the life she knew because of it. She was still able to do her job, and if anything, the accident had matured her, broadened her horizons.

Kea stared across the table at Mrs. Fortune; the woman had made her look at her life as no one else had. Rafe had been clever in getting this woman, and she marveled at his perception.

"I'll clean up this mess, straighten the house, and be on my way," Mrs. Fortune announced, picking up some of the dishes.

Kea stood up when the other woman did, offering her help, but Mrs. Fortune refused it, instead ordering her back to bed.

Distracted by her thoughts, Kea told Mrs. Fortune how pleased she was to have met her and excused herself. She returned to her room and stood before the long mirrors on the closet doors. She *did* want to go back into television.

She stayed before the mirror a long time, trying to decide what she should do about it all, but really it wasn't a decision she could make right now. When her eyes had healed completely, she would contact her producer. What would happen then was anybody's guess. After his one visit, he had phoned often while she was in the hospital, and although he had assured her that her job would be there when she was ready, they both knew that her contract was almost up. All he had to do was let it run out while she was on sick leave, and then not renew it. Kea knew as well as Mrs. Fortune that the odds weren't on her side, but she wasn't going to give up without a fight—and she had the ratings and her past performance on her side.

"Kea."

Hearing Mrs. Fortune call her name, Kea looked at the door, surprised to see the woman. How long had she stood there before the mirror?

"I'll be going now. Is there anything more I can do for you before I leave?"

Kea shook her head. "No, you've done quite enough, thank you. I really enjoyed our conversation."

Mrs. Fortune beamed. "I've left lunch in the refrigerator, and there's a roast with all the trimmings in the oven. I'll see you tomorrow."

The woman was soon gone as quickly as she had come, leaving Kea to ponder the future with new eyes. Feeling suddenly drained again, she hobbled over to the bed and lay down. She had a great desire to call Ellen and tell her what she had decided, and when she remembered that she couldn't do that, she was overcome with sadness.

She wondered if she should call and try to explain, but she didn't know what Jon had said, and she didn't want to make things any worse than they were.

Finally, she determined to leave the situation alone until things calmed down. Perhaps one of them would try to contact her through Rafe, but she doubted it. Forcing herself not to think about how badly she missed them or how bitterly she resented what had happened, she closed her eyes and tried to nap. Someday, she knew, she would attempt to explain to Ellen what had happened, but not right now. She was terrified of making the situation worse.

Sleep proved elusive, but a brief rest refreshed Kea somewhat, and she soon got up and went into the living room to turn on the television set. Subconsciously she had turned the dial to her station, and she sagged down in the nearest chair as she stared at the people filling the screen. Her afternoon show was on and Janice Royal had taken her place as easily and as naturally as if Kea had never been there. Chic and blonde, in her early twenties, she positively oozed charm and flirtatious beauty as she talked with a young male movie idol.

Kea sighed wearily. And McDonald Hollister had vowed that he would never give Janice her own show. So she saw all too soon that the producer's words of comfort were hollow. Ambitious to the point of being obnoxious, Janice had been nipping at Kea's heels for months, trying to work her way into top spot on one of the two shows Kea hosted, but she hadn't been at all worried. Her place was assured; her ratings were high. Or had been.

Now she wasn't so sure what would happen. The thought alarmed her terribly. What would she have in her life without her career? She would never have Rafe, and he and her career were all that she longed for.

CHAPTER FIVE

Kea watched the show until the end, then wondered what to do with herself. She hadn't eaten lunch, but she wasn't very hungry. She found herself wondering if Rafe would be home for dinner. Though the smell of the roast was permeating the house, it didn't tempt her with its delicious aroma. She was at loose ends, and she began to ask herself how people occupied the long hours in the day when they didn't have a job to go to.

Her hobbies, reading and playing the flute, held no interest for her at the moment. She gazed around the familiar room, seeing too much of Rafe everywhere she looked. It was almost as if she had been transported back in time, for she could recall her times in this house as vividly as if they had happened yesterday—the night she and Rafe had come back to the house after being drenched in a rainstorm and had made love in front of the fireplace, the year he hid her Christmas present in a bar of soap and made her wait for the water to wear the soap down while they showered.

Turning away from the memories, Kea left the chair to pace the house; walking very carefully on her injured ankle, she disobeyed orders to rest in bed and aimlessly wandered in and out of the rooms. She had left the roast in the oven, warming, thinking—no hoping—that Rafe would come home for dinner, but as the hours dragged by on leaden feet, she realized that it was not to be.

Kea caught herself in time to stop her foolish thoughts: she had no right to wonder where Rafe was, much less to be angry because he had left her alone. After all, he had offered her privacy, not his company. Her face flamed as she recalled his blunt words. He had left no doubt about his intentions.

Angry with herself for caring, she turned the oven off, took the roast out, and served herself. When she sat down at the table, all alone, she discovered that she could only pick at her food, despite her lack of lunch. After she had nibbled at the vegetables for a few minutes, she dumped the contents of her plate in the garbage disposal, washed the plate, and shoved it back in the cupboard.

She had to think of some way to occupy her time, but how? She had never been a person given to boredom; she had a host of interests outside her friends and her career, but at the present she couldn't think of a single thing. How she longed to talk with Ellen and Jon, or Mrs. Fortune. She found the idea of calling old friends abhorrent, for she had no wish to hear their murmurings of sympathy, no matter how well intentioned. She had appreciated the many cards she had received, and she would acknowledge them, but not right now.

More than anything in the world, she wanted to talk to Ellen, to get the ugly business out of the way and to go on with their friendship. Finally, she could resist no longer. She had to see how Ellen was, how she felt about the friendship now. She had to know if Jon had made her understand that neither of them had meant to hurt her.

Picking up the phone, she began to dial the number she knew as well as her own. Before she was halfway through, she replaced the receiver. What would she say? How could she begin?

"Oh, God," she murmured aloud. Then she picked up the phone again and quickly dialed the number with trembling fingers. How she hated being in this position. How she wished she could wipe out the whole ugly scene and pretend that it had never happened, but wishing wouldn't make it so. The phone rang twice and then Ellen answered. Kea could hear her heart pounding savagely.

"Ellen?"

There was a pause, and Kea, unable to stand it, quickly filled it. "Ellen, I want to try to explain what happened—I feel so bad about it, and really it was all a misunderstanding . . ."

Ellen let her struggle wildly, and Kea resented her insensitivity in not responding.

"Ellen," she said urgently, "you know I would never do anything to hurt our friendship."

Ellen's voice came over the wire, tired and hurt. "But you did, didn't you, Kea? You did the one thing I never expected of you. And you can't expect me to forgive you for that. Not for Jon."

"Ellen, it wasn't that way—"

Abruptly Kea heard the click on the other end, then the dial tone. For a few seconds she stood with the receiver to her ear, speechless. Somehow she felt worse than if she hadn't made the effort to explain at all. Why did she feel so damned guilty when she had done nothing?

For only a moment she was tempted to call back and try again, but she didn't have the heart. She couldn't stand to be hurt anymore. She had tried to right a wrong situation, but she would wait a while longer. Ellen clearly wasn't receptive now.

The phone rang, scattering her thoughts, and Kea was caught in a moment of indecision. This wasn't her home, and she didn't know if she should answer or not. At last she picked up the receiver on the fourth ring. Perhaps it was Ellen.

"Hello?"

She could hear someone breathing, but no one spoke. "Hello?"

Abruptly the party on the other end quietly replaced the receiver. For the second time Kea stood with the phone held to her ear, listening to the dial tone. Had the caller been Ellen? No, she was sure it hadn't been. Then *who?* One of Rafe's girl friends? If it had been, the woman had gotten an unpleasant surprise by hearing a woman answer. The thought unaccountably made Kea smile faintly, and then she hung up. The poor woman—if it had been a woman—should have had the courage to have spoken up.

Kea was certainly not a threat to any other woman desiring Rafe. Holding on to the thought that both annoyed her and, oddly, gave her new resolve, Kea went back to her bedroom.

After selecting her prettiest gown, she went to the central bathroom and filled the tub with warm water. When she had undressed, she struggled to get into the tub, stepping in with her good foot and awkwardly lowering herself without putting weight on her injured ankle. She was determined to go on with her life somehow. She found that the water was immensely soothing to her body, but it did very little to revive her spirit.

The way before her would be rough, and she would have to travel it all alone. With this face. With this past. Without Rafe. How had she clung to the idea that he would regret not making her his? It had been so foolish. Or had it only been the notion of a woman hopelessly and futilely in love?

She found herself listening for his key in the door, his footsteps in the hall, and she submerged herself a little deeper to escape. She had real problems to consider. In a few days she must deal with Roxwell's son. She would not allow Shane to keep her possessions from her. She would find an apartment and begin to live her life again. Away from Rafe. Away from the memories of Roxwell. Away from Jon and Ellen. She would work again, make new friends, develop new interests.

The painful thought tore at her; she would be giving up everything she held dear, those things treasured and familiar. Refusing to give in to the feelings of self-pity stirring inside her, she told herself that she was lucky to be alive, lucky to be getting the chance to start all over.

Feeling the need to escape her troubling thoughts, she stood up and carefully stepped out of the tub onto a plush smoke-colored rug. As she leaned over to dry her legs, she caught sight of herself in the tall mirror over the sink. Her long red hair had fallen forward, hiding her face. The body reflected in the mirror was quite lovely, Kea knew, and she paused to draw sustenance from that thought.

Her legs were long and shapely, her hips well-rounded without being too broad. Her breasts were as perfect as anyone could hope for—full and high, with rosy nipples that thrust up enticingly just the slightest bit. Her back was smooth and well-shaped, her waist a trim twenty-three inches. Her face might have changed, but her body was still her own; she had not, after all, lost *everything*.

Turning away from her image, she pulled on the beautiful sheer white gown, and it settled softly around her, the gauzy material barely shadowing her lovely body, making her beauty seem both virginal and voluptuous. She avoided looking at her face. When she had brushed her long hair, she returned to her bed and lay down with a half-read novel. She found that it caused her eyes to ache when she attempted to read, and she placed the book on a night table and closed her eyes.

Rafe. Rafe. Why was it always Rafe? Rafe as she had known him all those months ago, as she had known him last night, as she would never know him again.

She was almost asleep when the phone rang again, dragging her back to painful reality. Wearily, she reached over to the phone on her bedside table.

"Hello?"

Nothing again. This time she was angry, for in her

85

semiconscious state she had imagined that it would be Rafe calling with some explanation. He had worked late. He was staying elsewhere tonight. Something. Something she had no right to hope for.

Now it was she who silently replaced the phone in the cradle. It obviously hadn't been Rafe, and Kea was left feeling uneasy. Who was calling and why did they keep hanging up?

She was wide awake again, and she couldn't force herself to remain in bed. Putting her weight very gently on her injured ankle, Kea was inexorably drawn to Rafe's room. She glanced inside to see his bed still made up. He hadn't come home yet, and she couldn't help but wonder where he was.

As she lingered by the door in her sheer gown, her eyes roved over the bed where she had once spent so many hours wrapped in Rafe's arms, thrilling to his touch. She could still feel his warmth, his hard, long body, the way he smelled faintly of soap and cologne, his skin clean and tantalizing. He had taken her places in her mind no other man could; she knew that all too well, for her husband had failed miserably to replace Rafe.

Her eyes were attracted to a picture on his bureau, and she couldn't resist walking over to it. Holding it in both hands, she was amazed to see that it was a picture of the two of them. She was laughing up into his face, her own face radiant and lovely. She stared at the photograph for a long time, recalling the good times they had shared, then she caught sight of herself in the floor-to-ceiling closet-door mirrors beside the bureau.

She hadn't heard Rafe's footsteps on the carpet, and she didn't know that he stood in the doorway, watching her as she studied her reflection in the mirror. He had stayed away from home as long as he could. But ultimately, he had been unable to run from Kea and his memories of her. He was aware every moment that she was here in his house, all alone. He asked himself why he had invited her here.

Just looking at her, her red hair tumbled about her shoulders, her tall shapely body outlined so gloriously and provocatively in that tantalizing white gown, he wanted her. He was only tormenting himself by having her here again. She had dropped him for another man as easily as if he had meant nothing at all to her. She was only here now because she needed him; she had nowhere else to go and really no one to help her, so she had accepted his invitation. And now how would he keep her out of his heart?

When she had healed and was stable again, she would find some other man, and he would be left to his recent wounds, reminded of how much he had lost. He never should have taken her case, but how could he have refused? He couldn't bear the thought of someone else working on that beautiful face, restoring her beauty, her beauty as only he knew it, having touched each fine feature with his fingertips and his lips.

He was about to enter the room when Kea suddenly reached out to the image in the mirror. Rafe watched, transfixed, as she began to trace the face before her. Rafe couldn't know what she was thinking, but he could see the depth of her torment.

As Kea traced the broken face in the mirror, she thought of the mess she had made of it and her life. Never again would she see that carefree woman in the picture. She was overcome with guilt and unhappiness; she had ruined all the major relationships in her life—what she had shared with Rafe, the treasured friendship she had had so long with Ellen and Jon, even her marriage to Roxwell. She didn't know this tortured stranger standing before her. A single tear trickled down her right cheek, and slowly others followed as her eyes overflowed with her grief.

As he watched, Rafe was overwhelmed by the torment he read in her bowed head and tear-stained cheeks. Her suffering was almost more than he could bear. He wanted to take her in his arms and make her forget—to wipe out her troubled past, her painful present, and her uncertain future with his love and his touch. But once he closed the space between them, he knew there would be no turning back. If he let her into his heart a second time, she would only shatter it again.

Still, how could he keep away when she so obviously needed him? She was broken and bleeding inside and his heart cried out to her that he was here! He would keep her safe.

When he could no longer hold back the tide of compassion and caring that swept over him, Rafe silently crossed the room and took Kea in his arms. Drawing her against his body, he whispered words of consolation, words he was powerless to contain.

Kea tensed, momentarily startled by his sudden appearance, but as his hands caressed her tenderly and his deep, soothing voice filled her ears, she knew that she had no will to push him away. She needed him now—needed to know that he had not turned from her, disgusted by her weakness. His warmth, his presence, his understanding were like a salve that touched her wounded spirit and slowly began to heal it. She would let him hold her, if only for the moment.

Lifting her up in his arms as if she were a fragile and wondrous treasure, Rafe carried her to the bed and gently laid her down. He lowered his body beside hers, holding her against him, resting her head on his chest. With a fingertip, he erased the tracks of her tears, and then his fingers found their way to her long hair to stroke it ever so gently while he murmured encouragement to her.

Kea held on to him, wrapping her arms around his waist, bonding to him, feeling his strength flow into her.

She knew she shared a communion with him she had never before known, something splendid and ethereal. The moment was far more precious to her than any other, and she knew intuitively that her healing had begun and that she was going to be all right.

Slowly Rafe's hands left her hair to wander down the slim column of her throat, caressing and touching with a tenderness that moved her. And just as slowly the tenderness gave way to desire as his warm hands began to travel over her breasts, gradually giving wing to her hunger for him, creating delicious shivers inside her.

He groaned deeply against her breasts as he cupped them, scattering hot kisses over the full curves exposed in the diaphanous white gown. Kea found his thick dark hair with her fingers and drew him more possessively to her, reveling in the feel of him so near once again.

She hardly dared to breathe, so afraid was she that Rafe would leave her. Here in his arms, glorying in his loving was where she belonged, where she wanted to be. She had been too long on an emotional desert, thirsty for what she could not have, and now she was drinking her fill.

His hands sought out each curve of her body to caress it, to explore it with hard and eager fingers, and Kea held Rafe to her as if there were no tomorrow. When his mouth found hers to claim the sweet treasure there, Kea met the fire in his kiss. The kiss deepened and Kea parted her lips wider so that she could savor the thrill of Rafe's searching tongue.

When he drew back from her, he whispered, "Kea, Kea," so hauntingly that she raised her gray eyes to look up into his face. He cupped her face with both hands and his thumbs began a sensual tracing of her ears. Suddenly the movement ceased as Rafe's dark eyes roved over Kea's face.

He realized that he had let things go too far. He had only meant to hold her, but the awareness of her body so close to his had awakened old hungers that had never been fully appeased. And he had wanted to make love to her. But he knew he would have been taking advantage of her weakness. He had promised her that no one would make advances to her here, yet already he had brought her to his bed.

Kea had not seemed to mind, it was true, but perhaps she did not realize how much he wanted her. Or did she? For a brief time he was caught between his raging desire for her and the urgent need to consider her emotional state. He didn't want to take her now, like this, when she was vulnerable and shattered. Drawing her head forward, he rested it on his shoulder, and for a short time he held her in his arms, then he let her go. There was nothing else he could do.

"I'll get something to help you sleep," he said hoarsely. And then he slid out of bed and left the room.

Kea listened to his heavy footsteps as they disappeared down the hall, and she had to clasp her hands together to keep them from shaking. He had left her so easily, without a backward glance. And though he had said nothing, she knew why he had gone.

Lying there all alone, still burning from his touch, she bit down on her lower lip and forced back forming tears. She would not cry for herself again. Rafe had looked into her face—and he had not wanted her.

She brushed at her tumbled red hair and drew a shuddering breath. It was better this way; she didn't want his pity, and she was glad he hadn't made love to her for old time's sake.

For whatever reasons—his disinterest, her unattractiveness—she was glad he hadn't taken her. She had gone into his arms, hungering for his touch, so eager to begin again what had long been gone.

What he must think of her! Roxwell had been dead less than two weeks, and she had rushed into Rafe's arms as if Roxwell had never lived, as if she had never married him, as if eight months and a thousand bitter memories hadn't come between them. As if she were whole and desirable.

But she wasn't sorry, she realized, that she had let him hold her. In that one tender moment when they had transcended past and present, he had made a future for her. She had known that she was going to be all right, really all right. For that moment she would endure the humiliation of Rafe's rejection. He had given her that new hope, and it couldn't be taken from her. Clinging to the thought to save her sanity, she awkwardly hurried down the hall to her own room.

Rafe followed only seconds later, and though she had closed her eyes and was pretending to be asleep, he said huskily, "Take this."

As he had last night, he handed her a glass of orange juice and a little white pill. Kea took them, and when she had drained the glass, she gave it back to Rafe without a word. Then she rolled over on her side, praying that he would go away.

For a moment he stood there silently gazing at her. He had made a promise to her, and he would keep it. He didn't want her to turn to him out of loneliness and pain. When she came to him again, he wanted to know that she cared. If she still did. If she ever had.

The sun blazed into Kea's room like a vicious thing, stealing over her with cruel brightness, forcing her to greet the new day. Her mind muddled from the sleeping pill, she pulled herself from the kaleidoscope of her confused dreams. Could it be day already? She hardly felt rested at all.

Then she heard the loud tapping on her door that must have awakened her. Why did her foolish heart begin its silly rapid song?

"Kea?"

The breath escaped from her lips in a tired sigh. "Yes, Mrs. Fortune. I'm awake."

"May I come in?"

"Yes, of course." Kea struggled up in bed and brushed at her tumbled red locks. She was sure she was a frightful sight with her hair in wild disarray, testimony to her troubled night, her eyes still heavy from the drug-induced sleep.

"My, my don't you look lovely in that gown," Mrs. Fortune exclaimed, bursting into the room, full of vim and vigor, making Kea want to hide from all that energy when she felt so washed out and faded from her restless sleep.

Glancing down at the beautiful white gown, she smiled bleakly. Now she remembered. She had put the gown on to prove to herself that she was still attractive, and Rafe had come home and caught her in it in his room. And he had made it all too clear that she *wasn't* attractive—at least not to him—anymore.

She laughed bitterly to herself, and Mrs. Fortune said brightly, "I'm so glad to see you in a good mood. Slept well, did you?"

Kea's smile was more natural this time. She was far from in a good mood, but Mrs. Fortune was determined to see only the good side, so why fight it? She was delighted to see the woman again, and she did take comfort in her happy disposition.

"I slept tolerably," she said, stretching the truth considerably. "How are you today?"

"Same as always. Just fine. Life's what you make it, you know, and it's all in your attitude."

Kea nodded. "So I've been told, but don't you think once in a while life hands you just what it wants to?"

Shaking her head, Mrs. Fortune denied the statement vigorously. "No, indeed! We are the captains of our souls."

Kea smiled at the woman. She didn't think her soul realized that it had a captain. "If you say so. What's the status on breakfast? Has Dr. Jordan eaten?"

She bit down on her lower lip. Now why had she asked that? What she really wanted to know was if he was still home. She couldn't bear to face him this morning, and she was going to plead illness if he hadn't gone to work yet.

Mrs. Fortune answered quickly enough. "He wasn't in when I arrived. He must have left early today."

"I see," Kea murmured. And she *did* see. Apparently Rafe could not face her this morning. Perhaps he could not bear to look at her and remember how close he had come to the past that was no more. She knew she should not be surprised, but Rafe's rejection hurt her more deeply than she could have imagined. Clearly he wanted only the paitent-doctor relationship he had insisted upon from the first; most of all, he didn't want to make love to her. Then why had he taken her in his arms last night? Why couldn't he have left her to her own private pain?

"I'll be driving you to your appointment later today," Mrs. Fortune said, interrupting Kea's painful speculations. "Dr. Jordan has already made the arrangements."

"Thank you," Kea said, but she moaned inwardly. She had forgotten that she would have to see him in a professional capacity today; she was tempted to change doctors right now, but she had too much pride. She would show Rafe that she cared no more than he. Her car was still at the house, and she bitterly wondered if Roxwell's son intended to refuse her permission to take her own car from the premises. She felt well enough to drive her car the short distance home, and, anyway, today or tomorrow she would have to go and face Shane. She wasn't going to let him treat her this way.

She tensed at the thought of the confrontation. She didn't want any more ugly scenes in her life. The reading of the will was going to take place the day after tomorrow.

She would need to see Shane today. She thought of all her good intentions where he had been concerned; she had never wanted Roxwell's money and had meant to tell Shane so, but he had not given her the chance. Besides, she didn't expect her husband to leave her anything anyway. She didn't know what all the fuss was about. They had not made a prenuptial agreement as was often done in this town, and Kea doubted that Roxwell's will had been altered from whatever it had been before their marriage. She sighed tiredly. She would have to face Shane sometime, and she might as well get it over with.

"Breakfast in a few minutes," Mrs. Fortune said, and Kea nodded.

Today she was ravenous; she had eaten very little yesterday, and though it wouldn't hurt her to lose a pound or two, she certainly didn't need to. Her usual daily routine included a regimen of exercises. She shook her head tiredly. Would she ever return to what had been so normal in the past, so taken for granted?

When she had dressed in comfortable clothes and put on some soft slippers, Kea slowly made her way to the kitchen. She had discovered yesterday that her ankle was much improved, and she decided to try to walk on it even more than she had in the hope of strengthening it. When she reached the kitchen, she found that Mrs. Fortune already had everything well under way; all Kea had to do was make herself comfortable at the round kitchen table. Although Rafe had a formal dining room, it was rarely used. Mrs. Fortune had opened the draperies and Kea gazed out at the glorious California morning, watching the sun spill gold across the pool and the courtyard shaded by fruit trees.

She had always enjoyed Rafe's yard. It was landscaped Mexican style, with a large patio and two fountains that attracted the most fascinating birds. Kea had loved to unwind there on long weekends with Rafe, both of them

94

in casual attire, coffee cups in hand as they idled away the hours, talking, swimming, or making love behind the high stone walls that surrounded the back yard.

Mrs. Fortune set a tempting plate of food in front of her, and she was soon eating with enthusiasm, enjoying the morning and the company of the outgoing woman across from her.

Both of them looked up in surprise when Rafe unexpectedly entered the room. Kea felt the blood pound at her temples as she stared at him. Dressed in navy shorts, a navy T-shirt, and white tennis shoes, he had obviously been out jogging this morning. Kea couldn't keep her gaze from skimming down his well-defined body, from his broad shoulders, trim waist, and lean hips, down to his hairy, muscled legs. A faint red tainted her cheeks as she recalled how close she had come to making love with this man hours before.

When her gaze reached his face once more, she saw that he was looking levelly at her. Was it her imagination, or was the expression in his eyes sad? She noticed that he looked weary, in contrast to the exhilaration he had shown in the past after an invigorating run.

"Good morning, Kea," he said solemnly. Before she could speak, he turned to Mrs. Fortune. "Will you bring a cup of coffee to the bedroom for me, please. I'm running behind today. I'll drink it while I dress."

"Don't you want some breakfast?" she asked, frowning at him.

He shook his head. "No, thank you." And then, as suddenly as he had appeared, he was gone.

Mrs. Fortune immediately got up and put a couple of pieces of bread in the toaster, then poured a cup of coffee. "He should eat something," she grumbled to no one in particular.

Kea watched the woman distractedly, no longer taking pleasure in her own breakfast. She hadn't been prepared to see Rafe this morning, and now that she had, she didn't feel any better about last night. Clearly something had changed for the worse between them, and the thought made her terribly unhappy. Kea sat quietly at the table, lost in thought, as Mrs. Fortune buttered the toast, then hurried from the room with the toast and coffee on a tray.

Rafe had spoken to her only to be polite, she was sure. Did he truly despise her now? She drew in a weary breath; there was nothing to be done about it. She would stay on here only until after the reading of the will, then she would make her own life.

Mrs. Fortune returned to the kitchen with the toast. "He didn't want it," she announced, setting the plate down on the table. "You eat it, Kea."

Kea shook her head. "Not me. I'm full."

"Oh, you two," the woman said in exasperation. "Neither of you ate well."

Kea smiled. She had been eating well—before Rafe came into the room. "You eat the toast," she urged.

"I might as well. There's no point in letting it go to waste."

Watching as Mrs. Fortune ate the crisp pieces of bread, Kea tried to think of something to say, but she knew she was straining to hear Rafe's footsteps when he left, wondering if he would come back by the kitchen. Her answer wasn't long in coming. As she sat there, trying futilely to concentrate on Mrs. Fortune's chatter, Rafe returned his coffee cup to the kitchen and nodded to the two women. "Good day," he murmured, and he was gone again.

Kea gazed after his retreating figure, thinking unhappily about her afternoon appointment with him. "Will you be staying long today?" she asked Mrs. Fortune.

"I'll be here all day today. It's my main cleaning day, and, of course, I'll be taking you to your appointment, but this is the day I don't prepare dinner."

"No?" Kea questioned, wanting to ask what Rafe

would do for dinner, but knowing it was none of her business. The refrigerator was full, so she knew she need not be concerned about her own dinner; she wouldn't starve.

The morning again became pleasant as the two women settled back into easy conversation. Mrs. Fortune laughed heartily when Kea began to ask all kinds of questions. Kea had become so accustomed to it on her job, making light chitchat, trying to get a prospective guest to open up before a show or to relax when he was on the air. It had become second nature to her to ask questions.

Purposely putting the disturbing picture of Rafe in the back of her mind, she talked easily with the amicable Mrs. Fortune. The time passed rapidly, and Kea discovered that Rafe would soon be having another guest in the house: a twelve-year-old girl, Carmen, who was suddenly left deaf by a tragic accident that had destroyed one of her ears. Rafe had already reconstructed the ear for esthetic purposes, even though the girl would never hear again. In a few days he would be taking Carmen back to her home deep in Mexico.

Mrs. Fortune casually pulled a paperback book from her mammoth handbag. "Do you know sign language?" she asked.

Kea shook her head.

"I'll just leave this here for you, then," Mrs. Fortune said ever so casually. "You speak some Spanish, don't you?"

Kea laughed. "A bare minimum." She picked up the book. "In other words, you're leaving this with me because you think it will give me something to do, as well as enable me to communicate with Carmen. Well, I really do appreciate the thought, but I won't be staying here that long, for one thing. For another, I couldn't learn sign language quickly enough to use it with anyone."

Mrs. Fortune shrugged as if it were of no consequence,

but she left the book on the table. "Some of the signs are so universal and easy that you can memorize them in no time. Anyway, I don't need the book myself. I made it a point to learn years ago, so I'll just leave it—in case you might want to look through it."

Kea laughed again. The woman was a jewel, and as transparent as cellophane. "Thanks," she said.

Despite Kea's statements, she found herself thumbing through the book when Mrs. Fortune finally left the table to do her housework. Kea was still sitting at the table when Mrs. Fortune returned to prepare soup and tuna sandwiches for their lunch. When they had eaten, Kea was amazed to see that it was time for her to get ready for her appointment with Rafe. To her consternation after she had taken a leisurely bath, she selected one of her loveliest dresses—a chic navy blue trimmed in white, which flattered her fair complexion and red hair. She pulled the three-inch heels she usually wore from the closet, knowing it was absolutely ridiculous even to consider them with her injured ankle. It was healing nicely, but it was far from ready for high heels.

Eventually she settled for a one and a half inch heel, knowing that even that was silly when she had plenty of flat shoes, but she wanted so much to look good today, and she found herself trying to offset her injuries with her clothing. She sharply reminded herself that she was going to a doctor. Nothing more, nothing less. But her heart told her she was going to see Rafe, and she wanted more than ever to look as good as she could. She was wearing her hair down because he had once loved it that way; she was wearing some kind of heel because he had always admired her legs; and she was wearing blue because it was his favorite color on her. The scene from last night was indelibly imprinted on her brain, and she could not—would not—forget what had happened.

"Well, don't you look lovely?" Mrs. Fortune said when

Kea went to the living room where the woman was waiting. She commented on the dress, saying all the right things to make Kea feel good about herself. And she did. She knew that her red hair was glowing with golden highlights from a fresh washing. She had put on a bright lipstick and had even tried to hide her scars with powder, but she felt it had been to little avail.

The ride to Rafe's office was brief, but Kea's hands were perspiring by the time Mrs. Fortune dropped her off. She wasn't sure what kind of reception Rafe would give her, and the fact that this was her first real trip out into the world didn't help any. Although it was a cowardly thing to do, she had asked Mrs. Fortune to stop at a local drugstore and buy her a pair of dark sunglasses. They would at least obscure her eyes, and she thought she would be more comfortable hiding behind them this first time.

There were several people waiting when she went into Rafe's office, and she had the odd sensation that each and every one of them had turned to stare at her, even though some were in much worse shape than she. Kea wondered if Rafe hadn't insisted that she see him here in the office to make her view her own situation in perspective. Surely he could have examined her at home and removed the stitches there.

Holding her head high, she walked past the others to the front window. She had perched the sunglasses on her head, and she knew that she hadn't imagined someone whispering her name. When she glanced around, everyone suddenly seemed engrossed in magazines or each other. Damn, she told herself, she was becoming absolutely paranoid! She knew Rafe's office girls, and she smiled when they both came to the window to greet her.

"Hello, Miss Montgomery!" Mary said cheerfully.

"How are you, Mary? Sue? I have a four-o'clock appointment."

"Yes, Dr. Jordan told us," Sue said, handing Kea a chart to fill out. "Please be seated. You shouldn't have to wait very long."

More than glad to oblige, Kea stiffly made her way past the others to a chair by the door.

The small group around her began to hum with news and speculation about her and her injuries. Kea couldn't keep from listening to the murmurs of sympathy, and today she regretted being well-known. She was sure someone said it was too bad about her career, and when another commented on Shane, Kea felt a fresh surge of color to her cheeks.

Fighting for self-control, Kea picked up a magazine and pretended to be lost in its contents, but her mind was racing furiously. If she couldn't handle this little group, how would she handle the public? Would she ever be ready to face the kind of critical scrutiny that would surely come? Did she really want to go back on television with her "new" face? First Rafe, and now these people . . .

After what seemed an eternity, the room emptied and her turn came. Painfully, she hobbled in the direction of the office Mary had indicated. When she had sat down on the examining table, she fought the urge to slip off her shoes. She looked up in surprise when Trena, Rafe's nurse, came into the room. She didn't know why she was so surprised; she hadn't thought the woman had magically disappeared from Rafe's life.

"Good afternoon, Miss Montgomery. How are you feeling?"

"All right. How are you, Trena?"

The preliminaries over, both women looked away. The air was filled with tension, and the awkward moment stretched to the breaking point. Although Trena had never said a sharp or unkind word to Kea, or vice versa, they were acutely uncomfortable with each other.

All too well Kea remembered the jokes her friends had made about Rafe and Trena in the back country. She knew that this woman was part of the reason she had married Roxwell, part of the reason she had given up Rafe, and regardless of the fact that Trena wasn't really to blame, she couldn't help but see her as a rival she resented.

With stiff movements Trena examined Kea's face, then washed the area around the eye. "The doctor will be in soon."

Kea nodded, and she couldn't resist the urge to watch Trena walk away. A small, dark woman with long black hair and warm brown eyes, Trena was hardly exceptionally good-looking, but there was something about her that was appealing. Perhaps it was the serenity one sensed in the woman, or the genuine interest Trena seemed to take in each patient. Kea didn't know what it was, but she imagined that Trena was fine and noble and dedicated to her profession—as well as to Rafe.

When the door opened again, Rafe entered the office. "Good afternoon," he said impersonally, and though Kea had a sinking sensation inside, she matched his aloof tone. She was so intensely aware of Rafe that the room seemed to have grown smaller since he entered it.

Was it her imagination that he was even colder now than he had been this morning? Well, he didn't have to worry; he was in no danger of having her fall into his arms again. She had learned her lesson, and it had been too bitter to forget so soon.

"Good afternoon."

At least he didn't make any pretenses of indulging in polite conversation. He examined her, then removed the stitches from the right eye. "You're doing very well. I'm pleased with your progress."

Their eyes met only briefly, and she wondered at the dark, forbidding message she saw so fleetingly in his. What could it mean? "Thank you."

101

For the first time Rafe let his eyes skim down her pretty blue dress and on down her legs. His brows lifted almost imperceptibly when he noticed her shoes. He reached for her leg and lifted it slightly to examine her ankle, feeling it gently with his fingertips.

Kea held her breath and hoped he couldn't hear the erratic beating of her foolish heart. She was trying so hard not to tremble that she didn't hear him when he spoke.

"I beg your pardon," she murmured.

"I asked if you're going out." He released her leg and let his eyes roam over her appraisingly again, much to her consternation. "You look lovely."

She scoffed at his words, and she wondered if he was mocking her. Did he know that she had dressed especially for him? But, of course, she didn't want him to know that. She felt at the moment that she never wanted to go out in public again, but she told him, "I'm going by the house. I want to pick up my car."

She made herself meet his penetrating eyes, but she couldn't read the expression in them when they darkened mysteriously. "I'll drive you."

"No, thanks. I'll take a cab. It isn't that far."

"It's no trouble at all. I insist," he said resolutely.

Kea didn't feel like arguing, but she was afraid that Shane would make another scene. She didn't want Rafe to witness any more of her embarrassment. He had seen enough.

"Really, I prefer to go alone."

"Don't be so damned difficult," he snapped. "You don't even know if anyone's home. Let me drive you."

Kea was beginning to feel the start of a headache; she really didn't want to fight with this man. His work was finished with her for the time being; she wanted to get on with her life and let him get on with his, and yet, when she met his eyes, she knew she would agree to let him drive her. She wanted him to, in truth. And it wasn't as if Rafe didn't already know the boy.

"Fine, if that's what you want." But even as she agreed, she knew she would be sorry.

CHAPTER SIX

Both Kea and Rafe were silent as they left the office and made their way to Roxwell's elaborate home on Hillcrest Road. Kea felt her throat constricting as Rafe drove up the long, winding driveway to the house. It was hard to know that never again would Roxwell come home to this place. Kea resisted the urge to cry; she couldn't change what had happened, and brooding about it wouldn't make it any better. Still, she couldn't shake the sadness she experienced at seeing Roxwell's home again.

"Looks like someone's here," Rafe noted, pointing to the open draperies at the windows.

"Probably some of the household help," Kea said. Then she remembered that Ted Draper had said Shane had dismissed the housekeeper and most of the staff. She wondered who, if anyone, was left.

"Ah, yes," Rafe murmured, "the household help." He asked himself how he could have forgotten the luxury Kea was used to, had been reared with. It was a sharp reminder of their ever-present differences. Maids and chauffeurs had never been a part of Rafe's life, not even when he could afford them.

He felt guilty about having Mrs. Fortune, but she was such a help in so many ways that housekeeping had long since become a secondary chore for her. Rafe had never been able to give her orders anyway. A tiny smile curved his lips as he recalled the day the cleaning service had sent her over. When she had asked him what she was to do, he had told her clean the house as she saw fit. It had been the last time they had discussed it.

When he had parked the car, he walked around to Kea's side and opened the door. Her ankle was giving her a bit of trouble now, but Rafe didn't comment about her hesitant walk. He knew Kea's temper and her pride, so he remained silent on the subject. They walked to the front door and Kea knocked loudly before producing a key.

She tried twice to fit it into the keyhole—and then she knew: someone had changed the lock! Her key wouldn't fit. Anger and humiliation caused her to grit her teeth. He couldn't do this to her! This was her house—at least until the will was read, and even then there was the matter of community property! Shane couldn't just lock her out of the place where she had been living.

She put her finger to the bell and pressed. How, oh how she wished Rafe weren't here by her side; again her instincts had been correct. Him coming with her could only add to her embarrassment.

Finally, Neal, the houseman, answered, opening the door only a tiny bit. For a moment he simply stared at Kea, then he recovered with remarkable swiftness. "Good evening, Mrs. Mason. How are you? I was sorry to learn of your injuries."

"I'm all right. Thank you for your concern, Neal," she responded through stiff lips. She started to move past him and a most grievous look crossed his face.

"I'm sorry, Mrs. Mason, but Shane has forbidden me to allow you to enter." His face was suffused with color and his eyes were wild with distress.

Kea drew in a steadying breath, despite the fact that she was ready to explode with rage. "Is he here?" she demanded.

Reluctantly, Neal nodded.

"Send him to the door!" she commanded, her lips quivering with fury.

The delay was interminable and Kea and Rafe stood like strangers on the familiar porch while Shane kept them waiting. At last he strolled to the door, and in spite of his careless manner Kea knew that he was nervous. She was both sad and sorry that he had decided to treat her this way; she had hoped that they might help each other through this distressing time.

"Kea!" he cried upon seeing her. "What are you doing here? I thought you'd still be bedridden. You look—I—" he stammered into the awkward silence.

Kea clenched her hands into fists, but she felt the tears spring to her eyes, hot and wet. "What on earth is wrong with you, Shane? Why are you doing this? Why have you barred me from my own home?"

Shane straightened rigidly. "The Mason family owns this house. It's been in our family for years. It does not belong to you."

Kea could hear Rafe's sharp intake of breath beside her, and she knew he was furious. "Day after tomorrow the will announces who owns the house," she said sharply. "In the meantime, I want to take some of my personal belongings."

Shane shook his head. "I'm sorry, Kea. You'll have to wait until the will reading."

"Where is my car?" she demanded. "I *will* take that with me."

"Dad paid for it," Shane said belligerently.

It was as if Rafe had finally exploded; he shoved into the hall and grabbed Shane by the shirt collar. "Unless you want to see a doctor yourself, boy, tell her where her car is. I don't like physical violence, but my patience with this game has ended."

"Hey, man, take it easy," Shane whined; his earlier

bravado had completely vanished. "A friend of mine borrowed it."

Rafe tightened his hold on Shane's shirt, and Kea touched his arm. She didn't want any more ugly scenes. "Let him go, Rafe. It will all be resolved in two days. I can wait until then." The effort to speak calmly cost her a great deal; she wanted to scream with frustration and anger. But she knew that she must stop Rafe before he did something he would regret later. The threat of violence was not likely to change Shane's mind. Now that she had seen him, she doubted that *anything* would. He had his own personal vendetta going, and he wasn't going to stop it.

Rafe recognized the truth in what Kea had said, but still he was reluctant to let Shane go. He wanted to teach the boy a thing or two, but he knew this wasn't the time.

Giving Shane a final threatening shake, Rafe said, "Don't think this is over, Mason. I won't stand by and let you humiliate Kea this way again. Next time *think* before you act." With that he released the boy, who retreated into the house without a word.

When Rafe had walked outside, Shane slammed the door, and Kea heard the dead bolts move into place. She also heard him raging at Neal.

She wanted to turn away from this house of her unhappiness and never once look back, not for love or money, but Shane's behavior stirred a primitive fighting spirit. She had never been less than warm and kind to him; she had done nothing to incur his wrath; and she vowed now that she would not stand by idly and let him heap insult upon insult on her.

And it infuriated her that she had to watch helplessly while Rafe fought her battle for her. She already owed him too much.

Rafe took her arm and started back toward the car. She wanted to pull away, but she could not bring herself to do it. He seemed to sense her need for silence and that only hurt her more. Was this sensitive man, who had fought so gallantly for her a moment before, the same one who had rejected her last night? He seemed to change every instant, and she never knew what to expect.

When the silence between them was its heaviest with unspoken pain, Rafe finally shattered it with his deep voice. "What are you going to do about Shane?"

With difficulty Kea brought her thoughts back to her recent confrontation. "I'll have to wait and see. Of course no matter what Roxwell left me, I won't stand by and let Shane keep my personal belongings. I'll go to my own lawyer, if need be." She glanced at him, and seeing the darkness of his eyes, she quickly looked away. "I had so hoped to avoid all this. I don't know why people feel the need to hurt each other so deeply. I've never done anything to Shane." She stared at her hands. "I guess he thinks I stole his father from him, but that isn't true, of course. He and Roxwell never did get along exceptionally well. They were too different."

Rafe's voice was fierce. "I can assure you that Shane won't keep your things."

Kea looked over at him in surprise, seeing the glitter of his dark eyes and the determined set of his jaw. Why was he so angry anyway? Was it just his urge to help the unfortunate, or was it something more?

No, she reminded herself with a vengeance, he had made it clear last night that he had nothing more than sympathy to give her. She averted her eyes, staring out at the passing scenery.

"How about dinner?" Rafe asked unexpectedly.

"Where?" Kea flung at him, the memory of his rejection burning her throat. "At a table in the kitchen somewhere? Hidden away? I don't want to frighten anyone else. Neal and Shane were obviously shocked by my appearance."

Rafe's jaw muscles began to work convulsively, and

when he spoke, his voice was stern, belying his anguish for her. "It's not like you to indulge in self-pity, Kea. Of course when someone sees you for the first time, he's surprised. It's only natural. You're going to have to live with that. The scars are going to fade, but they aren't going away. Even when we revise, there will still be scars, a lot less visible, but scars. You can't hide, and you can't change them."

"I'm not trying to!" she retorted, clenching her hands into fists at her sides. But that was exactly what she wanted to do at the moment. All afternoon people had been staring at her, and she had had enough. Yet she knew that it had only begun—the looks of stunned surprise, the expressions of sympathy, and, worst of all, the pity. She might as well learn to accept these things now. It would not get any easier with time.

"Let's go to the Brown Derby," she suggested contrarily, resolving not to hide.

Rafe glanced at her obliquely, but he didn't comment on her choice. He knew she knew she was likely to run into almost anyone there, and, consequently, suffer more stares and comments. When he had suggested a restaurant, he hadn't quite had that in mind.

In fact, the choice momentarily made him angry. The Brown Derby had been their restaurant—his and hers. They had gone there frequently when they dated, and he wondered if she had consciously chosen the restaurant to torment him. Or worse yet, had she and Roxwell gone there? He had continued to eat there without Kea, perhaps searching for some sign of her, but he had seen none.

He brushed away his ridiculous thoughts. The Brown Derby was probably the first restaurant that had come to her mind. Kea was headstrong and rebellious, used to the world being her oyster, and now that it wasn't, she was striking out at it. She would learn everything the hard way; it was in her nature. This evening would be no different. The Brown Derby was just the place for renewing her pain. All the beautiful people went there, and she was sure to see someone she knew. She had made the choice, and although he thought her unwise, he had to admire her strength. He knew what kind of courage it took to face the stares of a hostile world.

After they had reached the restaurant, Rafe took Kea's arm, as if to give her a little of his own strength, and despite the memory of last night she was grateful. As she looked around the crowded room, she realized this would be more difficult than she had imagined. But she forced a smile to her lips and followed the maitre d' to a table.

Getting a table for two was no problem because Rafe often dined here. Kea was pleased to be in the restaurant once more. She liked the atmosphere and she never ceased to enjoy looking at the pictures of movie stars on the walls, many of them old-timers. The food was excellent, especially the famous Cobb salad. She had not come here in a long time—not since the last time with Rafe.

Once they were seated, Kea began to relax a little. Rafe smiled at her. "Let's really unwind tonight. How about a drink?"

"That sounds wonderful," she quickly agreed. In fact, it was just what she needed—both the drink and the unwinding.

When they had ordered drinks and been served, they took only a couple of minutes to select their food. Then they settled in against the booth back and sipped their beverages.

"Do you remember the time that woman from Kentucky came up to you and asked if you were a movie star?" Rafe asked. "We were sitting in this same booth."

Kea had to smile. "Yes. How could I forget?"

Rafe laughed. "She was convinced that you were the star on some series that was popular at the time."

Kea laughed. "Well, she thought you were Omar Sha-

110

rif. She was really disappointed when you said you were a doctor. I recall her comment. She said, 'Heck, we've got doctors in Kentucky. You're nothing.' "

Rafe laughed good-naturedly. "I told her it was lucky for her they had doctors. Remember? She wasn't at all impressed with that comment either."

Kea laughed again with genuine amusement. The woman had been incredibly rude, but they had laughed all evening over the incident, making a game out of her remarks, exaggerating them more with each time.

The old story set the mood for the entire meal. Rafe and Kea grew more comfortable with each other as they topped one story with another; then the conversation gradually turned to work—his practice and her talk show. They sat close together, talking as they had done so many months ago, discussing funny experiences and serious ones, and though Kea wondered why Rafe was being so charming, she began to enjoy herself for the first time in a long time, despite her doubts. She had needed this time with him for so long, and though they both carefully and delicately steered clear of painful topics, there was the beginning of the breaking down of barriers between them. A new intimacy was growing.

Kea could feel stirrings of the old magic in the air as she tilted her glass, then looked over the rim at Rafe. She could see his eyes sparkle as they appraised her, and she was sure she wasn't imagining the fire in them. She had seen it too many times before. Forgetting the events that had led up to this moment, she let her gaze stray to Rafe's handsome features, his dark eyes, his strong, straight nose, the determined jawline she found so appealing, his lips, so full and inviting. She was being lured back into the wonder of him. As she set her glass down, she could feel her fingers trembling, so aware was she of Rafe at this moment.

He reached out and caught her fingers in his and her

111

eyes were drawn to his again. "Kea," he murmured softly, "I've missed you."

God, how she had yearned to hear him say those words. Her heart soared at the sound of them, and she could feel the excitement coursing through her veins. She didn't know what to say, how much she *should* say. Their eyes locked, and Kea moistened her mouth with her tongue.

The moment was irrevocably shattered when someone stepped up to the table. Kea glanced at the intruder with glazed eyes, but it didn't take her long to regain her composure. It was Danette Thomson, the gossip bitch of all of Southern California.

"Kea, darling, it's so good—" Danette seemed stunned into silence as she peered at Kea over her bifocals, her face revealing her disbelief. "Darling, I had *no* idea," she exclaimed in exaggerated tones, drawing the attention of people at nearby tables. "Your *poor* face. *Whatever* are you going to *do*?"

When Kea saw that several people were staring openly at her, she clenched her hands into fists beneath the table. She did not want to make a scene, but she was very much afraid she could not contain her distress. Everywhere she went it was the same story, and she was afraid it would be so for the rest of her life. *Kea, your poor face! Whatever are you going to do?*

Closing her eyes, she forced herself to breathe evenly. Well, she knew what she was *not* going to do. She was not going to give Danette the satisfaction of seeing her cry. "Excuse me," she said shakily, "I was just on my way to the powder room."

Danette stepped back a little too quickly, and Kea heard Rafe draw a deep, ragged breath.

"The powder room?" Danette asked, the question clearly implying that makeup would be a futile effort in Kea's particular case.

Kea did not respond. Before she broke down completely, she turned her back and walked quickly away, aware again of her injured ankle. Once inside the powder room she leaned against the door and drew in several steadying breaths. She had too much pride to be brought to her knees by someone like Danette, but today had been full of comments like hers, and it was hard to take. She couldn't make herself walk back to her table.

Instead, she left the rest room and made her way through the crowded restaurant to the car. She knew some people were staring at her, and she held her head high and her pain inside, where they could not see it, until she reached the safety of the car.

Only when the door was closed and locked did she give in to the torrent of tears that had been building in her since last night. She heard the opposite door open and knew Rafe had slid in beside her, but she did not look at him. Why must it always be Rafe who witnessed her humiliation? Rafe who saw the pain that others did not see.

As he put his arm comfortingly around her shoulder, she shivered, but her tears did not cease. It was one of life's cruelest jokes that Rafe should be here beside her, close enough to touch her, but so far away that she could not begin to reach him. Damn him anyway!

When her tears had subsided a little, Rafe moved his arm and started the car. He quickly moved into the traffic, working his way past the lavish Rodeo Drive shops.

"It had to happen sometime," he said at last, "but I think you forced it a little too soon."

Kea wiped her eyes and did not respond. He was right, and she knew it, but just now she could not bring herself to agree with him.

"You'll find it gets easier as the time passes."

There was real compassion in Rafe's voice, and Kea had to fight back a new wave of tears. Didn't he realize that his pity was worse than his hatred?

113

"I know how you feel," he continued when she still did not answer.

"You *don't* know," she cried. "Don't patronize me! I don't want your pity!"

"And you won't get it!" he growled, sobering her at once. "You have a few scars on your beautiful face. Other people are a lot worse off. Stop feeling sorry for yourself!"

A sob hung in her throat and Kea blinked her gray eyes as she looked at him. The tears began to fall again and Rafe looked back at the road, unable to bear her misery. In the restaurant, he had felt like slapping that bitch's face for her insensitivity, but Kea hadn't given him time to do more than give the woman a few well-chosen words about her behavior. And now he wanted nothing more than to hold Kea in his arms and make the world go away, but he knew that she *didn't* want his pity—*or* his love. He was only fooling himself to think that he could somehow lure her back into his life with his presence and some stories from better times they had shared. He stepped harder on the gas pedal and the car shot down the crowded street much too fast.

When they reached the house, Kea got out of the car without waiting for Rafe's assistance. After he had unlocked the door, she made her way down the hall to her room and closed the door behind her. Damn Rafe! How she hated him!

She dropped down on the bed and slipped off her shoes. Running trembling hands through her long hair, she sighed tiredly. It wasn't Rafe's fault at all, and she knew it. She also knew all too well that she didn't hate him; she would be a lot better off if she could. It wasn't like her to place the blame for her mistakes on someone else. Rafe hadn't chosen the Brown Derby. She had done so herself, perversely, and she had gotten what she deserved.

Rafe was right; of course people were shocked the first time they saw her. She would be shocked to find someone's

114

face injured when she hadn't been anticipating it. And though there were those, like Danette, who were deliberately cruel, those like poor Neal hadn't meant to hurt her. He had reacted from surprise and concern. Oh, God, she wondered, when was it all going to stop? When would her life return to normal? She stretched out on the bed, feeling another bad headache coming on.

In the kitchen Rafe was rummaging about in the refrigerator, slamming dishes and bottles around, directing his hostility at inaminate objects, wishing all the while that he could strangle someone. It was almost a physical pain for him to see Kea hurt and miserable, and again he wondered why some people were so petty and malicious that they enjoyed hurting others. Didn't they know that no one ever knew when he would be in the same or worse shape? Why didn't they care? What had happened to man's compassion for his fellow creatures? He shook his head. He didn't want to start asking all those questions again.

Taking yesterday's dessert out of the refrigerator, Rafe served up two portions of the creamy custard. The phone rang shrilly, and he lifted the receiver of the kitchen wall phone. "Hello."

"Rafe?"

"Yes," he answered irritably, reacting harshly to the hesitating voice on the other end.

"Rafe, it's Jon. I—I wanted to know how Kea is. Is she all right?"

"Yes," Rafe replied brusquely. He wondered how often Jon had called in the past two days. Had he talked to Kea? Maybe even come to see her? Rafe forced his suspicious thoughts aside. He had no right to feel this way; he knew he was acting out of jealousy and old hurts. Why shouldn't Jon call here? Perhaps he *was* having an affair with Kea. Perhaps he had more right to her than did Rafe. Anyway, it really wasn't his business.

115

"She's resting, but I don't think she's asleep. Do you want to speak with her?" he asked as calmly as he could.

Jon hesitated, then murmured, "No, I won't bother her, but will you tell her I called?"

"Yes." Rafe hung up the phone as if it had scorched him. Well, there was one person who didn't find Kea unattractive now, he told himself resentfully. His mind strayed to Ellen, and he wondered what had happened between the couple. More than that, he wondered how serious this thing between Kea and Jon was. Had she turned to him because he, like Rafe, could help her through this difficult time? Had she become that uncaring of Ellen's feelings?

By the time he walked down the hall to Kea's room he had no wish to share the dessert with her. Angry at her, angry at himself for caring, he rapped sharply on the door. Why couldn't he get her out of his heart and mind? What they had shared had been over for so long now. He had dealt with it all before.

Brushing her tears aside, Kea went to open the door. Rafe handed her the dish. "Jon just called," he said without preliminaries.

He watched the confusion that altered her features, and he didn't know what to make of it. He had hoped to see something that would ease his suspicions one way or another, but he was disappointed.

Kea frowned worriedly, sorry that Jon had phoned when Rafe was here. "What did he say?" she murmured.

"Just to tell you that he called," Rafe said as impersonally as he could. "He wanted to know how you were, and I told him that you were resting, but not asleep. He didn't want to bother you."

He said the last words more sharply than he had intended, but Kea didn't seem to notice. Caught in her own indecision, she didn't know whether to call Jon back or not. Had Ellen told him she had called? Had he really

116

wanted to talk to her, or had he been grateful that Rafe had answered? She didn't think she could cope with more rejection right at the moment, but she was grateful that Jon had cared enough to ask about her. For a time she stood before Rafe, lost in thought.

Abruptly, he turned on his heel and left without further comment. Kea stared after him, wondering how much he dispised her to treat her so coolly when she was at her lowest. Finally, she closed the door and took the dish to the bedside table. For some time she gazed at it, too upset and too drained to be interested in something so frivolous as sweets. It was small comfort, under the circumstances, to know that Rafe had thought of her with the custard.

Kea heard the doorbell ring, and she listened tensely, hoping that Rafe wasn't entertaining tonight. She couldn't bear to see anyone else today. Minutes later she heard Rafe knock on her door again. When she answered, he had already gone, but she saw that he had deposited a bunch of beautiful red roses in a magnificent vase on the floor.

A tiny thrill raced over her; she was moved that some-one had cared enough to send her flowers. She recalled the many cards and gifts she had received at the hospital, but this was totally unexpected here at Rafe's house—unless . . . Turning the small card over, she read it, and her brief elation turned to dismay.

"I'm sorry. I didn't mean to hurt you. Jon."

Kea set the roses on her bedside table, shut the bedroom door, and lay down on the bed. She still didn't know what to think. She knew she needed to talk to Jon, but she couldn't right now. Weary, she closed her eyes, and miraculously, she drifted into the sweeping blackness of sleep.

When she awakened some time later, she looked at the mantel clock and saw that it was ten P.M. She sighed unhappily. What was there to do now? She had slept all she felt like sleeping; she was like a prisoner trapped in her room, but she didn't want to leave its security and privacy. She had to decide where she was going to live and what to do with herself, but there was no point in doing so before the reading of the will. At least her life would begin to take some kind of direction then.

Restless, she picked up the book on sign language Mrs. Fortune had left, and began to thumb through it again. For some time she made herself pass the time with it, and eventually she became fascinated by how logical some of the signs were for such parts of the body as heart and mind. Despite her interest in the book, the hours struggled on in seconds and minutes, and Kea desperately needed some outlet for her frustration.

In a blue mood she walked over to the window and gazed out at the pool. The night was very dark, and the pool lights made the water look inviting. For a while Kea stayed by the window, lost in thought, and finally she could resist no longer. She knew that she shouldn't be swimming so soon after her accident, but pent-up energy made her nerves crawl. The night was cloaked in blackness, and it seemed to beckon to her. She had no doubts that Rafe was sleeping soundly in his bed, oblivious to her torment and haunted mind. She would swim with no interruption, and even if he did hear her, she had no fear that he would come to her. He had made that absolutely clear already.

She walked over to the mirror and slowly took off the lovely dress, letting it fall around her ankles, then she stepped away from it. The bra and panties she wore were hastily flung aside, and she pulled on a robe from her closet. Then she slipped down the hall and out through the sliding glass door of the kitchen.

The night was very still and quiet; even in summer, in Beverly Hills, the nights often grew cool. For a few seconds Kea stood by the pool, gazing at the placid water. High in the starless night the moon hid behind brooding

118

clouds. Kea was glad for the darkness for it matched her own black, stormy mood precisely.

Abruptly shedding the robe, she silently slipped over the side of the pool and let the soothing water envelop her. Then she began to stroke the length of the pool, slowly, ritually, dragging her palms through the water as if she had the power to wipe away all that had happened to her recently: the accident, Roxwell's death, Jon, the ugly words Rafe had said to her, the sympathetic stares she had received today—but most of all her face.

God, she felt lonely and adrift. She knew that she never wanted another soul to look at her as she had been looked at today. She didn't want or need pity, and somehow she had to triumph over this time in her life. Somehow she had to get back her sanity and her stability. But how? When?

As she pondered the heavy thoughts weighing on her soul, a feeling came over her as primitive as time itself. She had an awareness that she was not alone and she tensed. Slowly she turned around in the water and scanned the surrounding grounds. But there was no one. Her imagination again. Good heavens! Now she was imagining that people were staring when there was no one around. She would have laughed at herself it it hadn't been so pathetic.

Across the patio from her Rafe stood at his window, watching Kea's determined swimming. He had been drawn by the sound of the water lapping against the sides of the pool, and now that he had seen her, he couldn't get to sleep. Hidden in the darkness of his room, he peered at her from behind the edge of the draperies, and he couldn't take his eyes off her. How he wanted her! The pool lights and the ripples in the water distorted her beautiful body, but nothing could detract from Rafe's desire for her.

He was reminded that he had wanted her so badly last night that he had gone to bed aching for her. Other women —too many of them—had come into his life since Kea, but it had never been the same. He was chained to her by

119

bonds too invisible and too strong ever to be broken. He had always scoffed at the notion of undying love, but he was a victim all the same.

Kea could capture the hearts of a hundred men, and Rafe could hate her for doing so, but he couldn't stop loving her. He could feel bitter and used and hurt. He could put her out of his life, but he couldn't put her out of his heart. He could meet a hundred women in a hundred foreign countries, and any one of them could trigger a memory of Kea—a lock of red hair, wide gray eyes, long, shapely legs. And all over again he hungered for her, was tormented by what could never have been. For Kea, Rafe had known he would never be enough. There would have always been Jons and Roxwells waiting in the wings.

Kea turned in the water and looked at Rafe's window. He imagined that she had thought of him, had longed for him as he did her. It was a foolish thought, of course, for she had probably already claimed another heart. He cursed Jon softly, but the vile words didn't make him feel any better.

He was tortured by the woman swimming in the darkness. No matter what he'd told himself last night, he couldn't stay away from her. Suddenly he shoved the drapery back into place and began to strip off his clothes. When he had found a robe in his closet, he pulled it on and strode to the sliding glass door before he could change his mind. His room opened right onto the patio, and he stepped outside, crossed the Mexican stones, stripped off his robe, and plunged into the water.

This time Kea turned and saw him and her heart began to pound wildly. "Rafe!" she cried out as he surfaced beside her. "What are you doing?" She began to stroke furiously, racing toward the shallow end of the pool until her feet reached the bottom, but Rafe caught up with her before she could escape.

Turning her around, he cupped her chin with his hand

120

and forced her lips to meet his. Kea turned her head and his lips played at the edge of her mouth, tasting, teasing, stirring her blood with desire and need. She wanted desperately to resist him, but when his mouth found the curve of her neck to spill hot kisses along it, she found her resolve eroding.

"No, Rafe," she murmured thickly. "Don't."

"Kea, Kea," he whispered hoarsely, "I want you so that I can't sleep, I can't think. I hurt inside for you. I want to feel you become part of me again."

Kea tensed; it was easy for him to say he wanted her here in the darkness with her face hidden from him, but she couldn't forget how he had rebuffed her last night. She would never be able to forget. The fresh reminder made her more determined to escape, but Rafe's hands moved down her back, drawing her against his hard body.

"No, Rafe," she whispered bitterly, the words trembling on her lips. She could feel her nipples tauten as they pressed against his hair-rough chest, and she tried to ignore the waves of warmth washing through her. She wouldn't give in to him now.

Rafe's lips sought hers, found them, and conquered them. Kea tried desperately to remain impassive under the onslaught, but God knows she wanted him. With her very soul, she wanted him.

His hands moved provocatively over her body, caressing her curves, and she felt herself weakening. She couldn't turn away, body or soul. And finally, she couldn't deny herself the pleasure of him. Not tonight when she needed so very much to feel loved and desirable.

Rafe's mouth was firm and tempting against Kea's, but at the same time it was so gentle and coaxing. He kissed her long and hungrily as though his very survival depended on the honey from her lips, and Kea was powerless to draw away. Giving in to the tender pressure of his mouth, she moaned in helpless surrender, and her lips parted, welcoming the firm thrusts of his tongue.

Rafe's arms slid around Kea and suddenly he lifted her up, wrapping her legs around his hips, supporting her with his hands. She gasped with pleasure as he became one with her, moving sensually against her while the water hugged them both, swaying gently with them to a rhythm that fired Kea's blood.

She was consumed by the flames inside her and she arched her back, pressing her body more tightly to Rafe's. She did not imagine that he trembled against her as his mouth found the sensitive skin of her throat, and his tongue played hotly on it as his muscled body moved with Kea's, slowly, slowly, driving her mad with need for him. She was aware of herself as a woman as never before, for never had she needed to be desired more than at this terrible time in her life.

"Rafe," she whispered feverishly as the fires that had been banked too long roared to life hotter and still hotter. There wasn't enough water in the pool to cool the flames that raged inside her, burning higher and higher with every powerful thrusting movement of Rafe's body. How she had longed for this time again, dreamed of it. The water acted as an additional stimulant as it caressed and lapped at her body, teasing and stroking, adding to the intimate sensations Kea was glorying in.

She forgot all about yesterday and today. She forgot that she had promised herself that never again would she let this man touch her, hurt her, take her to that special place. Her ecstasy obliterated every pain and regret she had known in the past. There was only now. There was only Rafe for her, forever, no matter what happened in the future. Now was all she had, and she would not refuse it.

Locked in a timeless passionate embrace, she reveled in Rafe's strength, so vital and thrilling. At last Kea's fingers bit into his shoulders, and she sucked in her breath and closed her eyes as the night opened with a blaze of unparalleled brightness.

Rafe still held her to him, after the fires inside them had burned down to glowing embers, and Kea wrapped her arms around his neck and rested her face against his. Rafe slowly let her body slide down his, a provocative movement that fanned a small flame inside her. Kea was ashamed of her hunger for him, but tonight she was powerless against it. Tomorrow, she knew, she would hate herself.

Rafe's mouth claimed hers once more, then he lifted her up in his arms. Kea hid her face in the curve of his shoulder. She couldn't forget how he had turned from her last night, and she couldn't bear it again. Perhaps if she stayed in his shadow, in the darkness, he would forget, just for tonight, that she had changed forever.

When he carried her into his bedroom, water still dripping from them both, he reached for the light switch. Kea caught his hand. "No," she whispered urgently.

If Rafe thought the request strange, he didn't show it. Feeling his way in the darkness, he led Kea to the shower, and when they both had stepped in, he turned on the water and adjusted the spray.

Kea shivered as Rafe gathered her to him, his hands running hungrily over her body under the streams of warm water. In the darkness Rafe found a bar of soap, and Kea could feel the fires begin to burn again as Rafe's soapy hands slid down over her breasts, causing them to respond with embarrassing speed. His hands lingered, stroking, teasing, caressing as though he couldn't get enough of her. When he embraced her to soap her back and shoulders, Kea wrapped her arms around his neck, wanting to hold on to him forever.

His hands moving under the mass of wet red hair, Rafe tipped Kea's head back. Then he found her mouth and gently, tenderly caressed it with his. Kea moaned with her need for him.

Disentangling herself, she turned to leave the shower, but Rafe drew her back against him, his body warm behind hers as he held her close, his hands finding her breasts to caress them with a provocative movement that sent a flood of desire through her. As Rafe molded the hard lines of his chest and hips to her rounded softness and back, Kea could feel his excitement.

Abruptly, he stepped around her and switched off the shower water. Taking two towels from a wall shelf, Rafe found Kea in the darkness and began to dry her. She sucked in her breath when he parted her legs with his hand, then moved nearer to kiss the inside of her thigh, high up on her leg. His tongue and lips instruments of delicious torment, Rafe worked his way higher and higher.

Hungrily, Kea's fingers found their way into his dark hair, and she gripped tightly as Rafe led her down the pathways of renewed pleasure. His lips seared her flesh, causing her to cry out in passion. His mouth on her skin sent tremors of exquisite delight shooting through her.

Rafe raised himself ever so slowly, letting his tongue trail a fiery path up Kea's body until it found her breasts, then her mouth. He traced the outline of her lips, the taste of her still on his.

Kea's mouth parted, but this time Rafe didn't explore the softness inside. He let his tongue dip in and out, tracing the outline of her teeth and the gentle underside of her lips, but when her tongue touched his, he retreated. Kea was burning with desire for him, and she was surprised when Rafe handed her a towel. Trembling visibly, she began to dry him in the darkness, moving the towel over his hard muscles.

Suddenly Rafe lifted her up in his arms and strode toward the bed with her. When he had laid her down, he lowered his body to hers, his skin burning against hers. Kea drew in her breath when he entered her deeply, and a river of heat coursed throughout her body. Once again she was lost in his intimate possession of her, her passion flaming out of control.

It was almost daybreak when Kea was awakened by the first slanting rays of the sun creeping in through the sliding glass door. She opened her eyes and gazed around. Then she remembered her passionate night in Rafe's embrace. Hidden by the darkness, she had given in to her love for him when she had faithfully promised herself that she wouldn't.

This morning she was terribly ashamed of her weakness, and she glanced at Rafe quickly to assure herself that he was still sleeping. For a moment her gaze lingered on his face, savoring his handsome features. His dark hair was carelessly lying across his forehead, and she longed to brush it gently aside, but of course she did not. His jaw was darkened by the beginning stubble of his beard, and Kea resisted the urge to touch the strong angular, curve.

She hadn't been able to resist him last night, but the morning was filled with regrets, and she made herself another promise that she wouldn't be such a fool again. She wouldn't again allow Rafe to possess in the darkness the body he found so unattractive in the light. Giving him one final, painful look, Kea eased out of his bed and made her way silently down the hall to her room.

She strengthened her resolve to get her life back on solid ground. She would manage with what she had. She would create a new image for herself, a Kea that the people hadn't already seen, and she would harden her heart to further stares and questions. She would wipe out the bad in her life, and be grateful that she was alive to carry on. She could do all these things, she knew. But how would she ever forget Rafe?

CHAPTER SEVEN

Somehow Kea went back to sleep, and when she awakened again, morning was in full bloom. Sunshine spilled into the room, brightening the blue decor. For a long time she lay very still, hating to get up, for she didn't want to face Rafe this morning. Last night had been sheer ecstasy; this morning her face flamed at the mere thought of her weakness.

The time dragged on, and still she lay. Finally, she recalled that the reading of the will would take place tomorrow and she had errands to run. At some point she had made up her mind that she would look her very best tomorrow. She intended to go to her beautician's salon and get something done to her hair, and she wanted to get a new dress, always a boost for whatever occasion. When she went to the lawyer's office, she wanted to have an entirely different image, not just a different face.

When she had showered and dressed in a simple green dress with classic lines, and plain sensible sandals, she squared her shoulders and went down the hall to the dining room, hoping that Rafe had already gone. After all, it was almost nine. She breathed a sigh of relief when she saw Mrs. Fortune stirring around in the kitchen and Rafe nowhere in sight.

A small, dark girl sat huddled forlornly at the dining room table and Kea smiled at her. The girl seemed to slink down into the chair even farther, and Kea knew that this was the patient Rafe had operated on. A helmet covered her head, protecting her ear, and Kea's heart went out to her.

"Good morning, Kea," Mrs. Fortune said, smiling brightly as she entered the dining room. "The doctor told me to let you sleep as long as you wished this morning."

Kea winced. She knew why she couldn't face him, but why did he want to avoid her? Was he afraid to see her in the light of day? The thought hurt deeply, but she did not let her distress show. She was learning, slowly, how to hide her pain.

"Good morning."

Mrs. Fortune gestured to the young girl. "This is Carmen. She's going to be staying here with you for several days until Rafe takes her back to Mexico."

Why did Kea's heart plunge so at the thought of Rafe going away? It was just what she needed, some time away from him so that she could rebuild her own life without him. "Oh," she murmured. "When will he be going?"

"This weekend, I suspect."

"I see." She gave Mrs. Fortune a faint smile, then directed her attention to Carmen.

"In the hospital, Carmen was taught the very basics of sign language and she's being taught to read lips," Mrs. Fortune said. Then to Kea's amazement, the incredible Mrs. Fortune began to speak slowly to Carmen in Spanish, using her hands to make gestures.

"She is your friend," she told the girl, pointing to Kea, then interlocking her index fingers. "Her name is Kea," she said, using her first two index fingers to sign.

Although Carmen had paid painfully close attention to the woman's lips and movements, she didn't respond, other than to lower her gaze.

"It's so nice to meet you, Carmen," Kea said warmly. Then she glanced anxiously at Mrs. Fortune. "Did she understand?"

Mrs. Fortune nodded. "I believe so." She looked directly at Kea. "Carmen can talk, of course. She was injured less than two years ago, but the trauma and the resulting ridicule she suffered for her injury have resulted in what is known as elective mutism, an emotional disturbance. She hasn't spoken since the accident."

"Oh, the poor child," Kea murmured, deeply moved by the girl's plight. She wanted to wrap her arms around this small girl with the huge, mournful eyes and tell her that everything was going to be all right, but she was afraid of frightening her further. "Do you think she'll talk now that her ear has been reconstructed?"

Mrs. Fortune shrugged. "It's difficult to tell with these cases, but that's Dr. Jordan's hope, of course. Once she is no longer an object of the other kids' teasing, perhaps she will come out of her shell. Now, how about some breakfast?"

"That sounds fine. Then I'm going to run some errands."

"Oh, dear, and I hadn't been told," Mrs. Fortune said unhappily. "Well, it doesn't matter. I suppose Carmen and I could go with you, but she's afraid of the least little outing."

"Please don't bother. I'll take a cab. I'd prefer that," Kea said honestly. "You're very sweet, but an outing alone will be good for me."

Mrs. Fortune's smile returned. "If you say so." Her dark eyes began to sparkle. "I had thought that I'd let Carmen wade in the shallow end of the pool. I'm sure the doctor won't mind as long as her head doesn't get wet." She looked at the girl with genuine fondness, and Kea marveled at her big heart and deep concern for a stranger.

"You're really something," she murmured, then she sat down next to the girl, again smiling at her, but Carmen didn't return her smile.

When Mrs. Fortune had served them, Carmen barely

touched her food. Kea was troubled by the girl's unhappiness, and she wished there were something she could do for her. Perhaps while she was out, she could buy a little gift for her. She ate her breakfast hastily, then excused herself to go phone for a cab. In minutes she was en route to one of Beverly Hills' most fashionable salons.

The owner, Charles, eyed her shrewdly when she walked into the room. "Kea," he called out, "sweetheart, how are you?"

She made a gesture with her hands, indicating her face. "Like this," she said without rancor. "What you see is how I am."

Charles's features twisted into a frown and Kea could see his mind turning. She swore she would scream at him if he made a comment about her "poor face," but, of course, Charles was more tactful than that. He worked with ladies who had had all kinds of recent cosmetic surgery and Kea suspected that nothing really surprised him anymore.

At last he exclaimed, "*Voilà!* I've got it. I'll do you myself. Come along."

Without waiting for comment from her, he ushered her toward a sink and had one of the girls wash her hair. Then her shoulders were covered in a ridiculously frilly cape, and she was sent to Charles's station. She tried not to look at herself in the mirror as he lifted the masses of her long hair and let it fall down around her shoulders.

"It all has to go," he said with a finality that unnerved Kea.

"But I like it long," she protested halfheartedly. She knew his reputation and the miracles he created, and though he wasn't her regular beautician, she knew if anyone could give her a flattering hairdo, he could.

"It has to go," he repeated firmly.

Kea shook her head and smiled at his determination. Hadn't she come for a new image? "It's your hair," she said teasingly, and without further ado Charles set about his work. Kea couldn't bear to watch. She loved her hair long; to avoid the pain of losing it, she picked up a magazine and began to thumb through it while Charles worked, snipping and shaping and clucking eccentrically to himself.

At last he had created the effect he wanted, and he commanded Kea to look into the mirror. She did so almost reluctantly, but she was anything but disappointed. "Oh, Charles," she exclaimed, "you've wrought a miracle!"

He shook his head, modestly refusing such credit. "I worked with what I had," he said, "and you can see the results. This style is really much more flattering for your face than the long style. Besides," he whispered near her ear as if he had a shameful secret to tell, "it makes you look younger, and it detracts from your—injuries."

It did indeed, Kea had to agree. Charles had cut the long red hair up to chin level, parted it on the left, and let it sweep down across her right eyebrow and down her cheek with a seductive fullness that partially obscured her scars. The effect really was stunning, and when Kea turned her head, the shining hair moved, caressing her cheek. The sleek hairdo drew attention away from the scars and diminished their visibility. And it did make her look younger, more sophisticated than ever, and without the temptress look the long hair had given her.

"I love it!" she murmured. "Thank you, Charles." She was very appreciative of his effort. Suddenly she saw the hairdo as a symbolic cutting away of the past, the pain she had known. She was beginning anew, and the short style was most appropriate.

"Don't thank me," he said jokingly. "Get your money out."

Kea laughed in spite of the knowledge that his prices were only half a joke. But it had been worth every penny and more. Smiling again, she bid him good day, and set out in a considerably better frame of mind. She wondered fleetingly what Rafe would think of the haircut, then brushed the thought from her mind. It didn't matter.

She had just stepped out the door when Ellen turned the corner, coming toward the salon. Their eyes met, and Kea saw Ellen blanch. She swallowed hard and tried desperately to think of something to say.

"Ellen," she murmured at last, "I'd really like to talk to you." She wasn't at all sure what she would say, but she had to try to explain in some way.

Ellen closed her eyes for a moment and pressed her lips together as though she just wished Kea would vanish.

"Could we go somewhere?" Kea asked.

Ellen shook her head. "Really, Kea, I don't want to go into it right now. I—I'm in a hurry. Good-bye."

"Ellen, wait," Kea murmured. "You know I would never have done anything to hurt you, and neither would Jon. It wasn't what it must have looked like to you."

"Kea, please," Ellen whispered, tears welling up in her big green eyes, "I've said I don't want to talk about it." She averted her gaze and her words were almost inaudible. "I have never in my entire life felt so hurt and betrayed. I still haven't gotten over it. I just want to forget it."

Then she brushed past Kea and disappeared into the shop. Standing in stunned silence, Kea fought with her own tears, trying to make herself be reasonable. Ellen was feeling threatened; she was afraid of losing Jon. She had felt betrayed. Perhaps when a little more time passed, Kea could try again to make her understand, but that didn't ease her own pain. She needed her friends now as never before; she missed them terribly. And she was truly crushed to think that Ellen wouldn't hear her out.

Could Ellen honestly believe that she was romantically interested in Jon, of all people? Was this the same woman who had shared the last fifteen years of her life? She sighed raggedly.

The joy of her fabulous haircut had paled in the face of Ellen's pain. Forlornly, Kea trailed to the nearest restaurant and used a pay phone to call a cab; she had lost her enthusiasm for shopping for a new dress and a gift for Carmen. She wanted to run back to Rafe's and try to sort out her own unhappiness.

She returned to find Mrs. Fortune wading in the pool with Carmen, and though the girl didn't say a word, Kea could see the delight in her dark eyes. Kea stood in the kitchen gazing out at the couple for a few minutes, then she walked out to try to talk with them, glad they were here to prove a distraction from her most recent upset.

Seeing her, Mrs. Fortune waved her over to the edge of the pool. "My, my don't you look lovely with that new hairdo?" she said. "It's really becoming."

"Thank you," Kea replied, feeling her spirits lift in the face of Mrs. Fortune's enthusiasm.

"Why don't you join us?" Mrs. Fortune asked.

Kea shook her head. "I think I'll rest my ankle. Besides, I don't have a suit."

She glanced at Carmen. The girl looked more like ten years old than twelve, and Kea smiled gently at her. *"Bonita,"* she told her, speaking slowly in Spanish and pointing to the flaming red suit that set off Carmen's delicate, dark looks.

Shyly averting her gaze, Carmen didn't acknowledge the compliment.

"Dr. Jordan bought it for her," the jolly Mrs. Fortune replied; she herself was dressed in an antique black suit that more than amply covered her large frame.

But of course, Kea thought. Rafe would have bought a suit for this child. His compassion truly amazed her, and as she looked at Carmen, she began to understand why Rafe's heart went out to these unfortunate people. Carmen's whole life had been distorted because of the accident, and though Kea was sure Rafe went to great trouble and expense to repair the damage, a life was surely worth it.

"Can't you find some shorts and a top so that you can join us?" Mrs. Fortune persisted.

Memories of last night washed over Kea, and she couldn't bear to get into the water again. "I think I'll go rest a bit, then I'll come back and spend some time with you," Kea said.

"That's a marvelous idea," the other woman agreed. "Let's have lunch here on the patio—something simple. What do you say?"

"Sounds grand to me. See you in a bit." Kea watched the woman and the girl for a few more minutes, noting that both were being careful not to get Carmen's upper body or head wet. Despite the restrictions the girl was clearly happy.

After Kea had gone to her bedroom and rested for a short time, she dressed in slacks and a casual blouse and returned to the back yard. The three of them shared a lunch of cheese, bread, fruit, and sodas at a cozy little wrought-iron table while Mrs. Fortune and Carmen dried in the warm sun.

Kea was so caught up in Carmen's plight that she spent long periods of time studying the girl, trying to think of some way to help her. Although Carmen had shown no indication of wanting to communicate with her, Kea searched her mind for some of the signs in the book, then she valiantly tried to use some of them with the girl.

She thought she was telling Carmen that she wanted to be her friend, when suddenly she saw a hint of a smile on the girl's lips. Kea glanced at Mrs. Fortune, uncertain if she should be proud of herself or not. Mrs. Fortune's smile was even broader.

"You're saying something to her about your heart hurting," Mrs. Fortune said. "I think she knows what you're trying to say, but finds it a little amusing. You should actually talk to her when you sign so that she can read your lips."

Kea laughed at herself, and she saw Carmen's smile become a little stronger. She didn't care what worked with the girl; she was just happy to get a response, and, anyway, her heart did hurt, so she had been right about that. She followed Mrs. Fortune's directions and finally managed to get the signing right, and even though Carmen didn't sign in return, she gave Kea another faint smile.

Suddenly Kea excused herself and returned to her bedroom to get her flute. She felt a little silly because Carmen couldn't hear the notes, but she had never known a child not to be fascinated with a musical instrument. She settled back down in her chair with the flute in hand, and she saw that although Carmen was still reserved, she was looking at Kea and the instrument curiously.

When Kea began to play a happy tune, Carmen reached over and put her hand on the flute. Kea didn't know what she wanted, but she was smiling broadly, so Kea kept playing.

She hadn't seen Rafe come out on the patio, and she didn't know that he was standing just outside the sliding glass door watching her. She was surprised when he walked over. "She feels the vibrations," he explained when Kea abruptly stopped playing.

Kea looked up at him, her eyes locking with his. The memory of last night burned between them, bright and alive. Both looked away, and Kea realized that they would not speak of the night again. It was only a moment she must try to forget, like all the others lost in their bitter past.

Rafe gazed out at the pool for just a moment, and Kea wondered what he was thinking. Soon he returned his gaze to her, and she could read nothing at all in his dark eyes.

Taking the flute from her hand, he let Carmen examine it, explaining something to her in Spanish that Kea could not follow. All the same, she felt good about having brought the flute out. Carmen smiled shyly at Rafe before looking away, and when Rafe looked at Kea again, their gazes held ever so briefly.

Rafe pulled up a chair, and Mrs. Fortune quickly stood up. "Have you had your lunch?" she asked.

"No. I thought I'd come by and see how Carmen was doing."

"She's just fine as you can see," the older woman replied, her eyes glowing. "We had bread, fruit, and cheese for lunch. Would you like some?"

"Yes, thank you. That sounds fine."

Mrs. Fortune hurried away, and for a brief time an awkward silence descended upon the three people left at the table. Then Kea and Rafe both spoke to Carmen at the same time. They laughed and offered each other the chance to speak first, and Rafe was the one who began to talk to the girl softly and unhurriedly in Spanish, giving her time to read his lips. When Rafe chucked her under the chin, Carmen looked away in embarrassment, but Kea could see that she was pleased, and she marveled at Rafe's sensitivity. When his eyes met Kea's, she found herself following Carmen's example. She could not hold his gaze, not after last night.

Mrs. Fortune soon returned, bustling about, serving Rafe at the intimate little table. When he moved his chair nearer, his knees brushed Kea's and she felt the color rise to her cheeks.

"Sorry," he murmured deeply, and when Kea looked at him, he smiled at her. As he ate, Mrs. Fortune chatted easily about her and Carmen's morning, and Rafe nodded and commented. Kea envied the easy rapport the two of them shared, but she reminded herself that her own circumstances with Rafe were so very different from those of

135

the older woman. Still, she very much regretted that she couldn't at least say she was his friend, as she knew Mrs. Fortune could.

All too soon Rafe had to go back to work. He patted Carmen's shoulder as he stood up, then said good-bye to the three of them in general. His eyes lingered briefly on Kea, and to her consternation she found herself gazing at him breathlessly, hoping for a special word, a special look, but he turned away and left. It wasn't until the sliding glass door had been closed and she knew that Rafe was gone that she could breathe normally.

"Time for your nap, honey," Mrs. Fortune told Carmen, and the girl obediently went inside.

Kea stayed with Mrs. Fortune and helped her clean up the table and the remains of lunch. "Carmen is such a sweet child," she said. "I sure wish I could do something to help her."

"But you did," Mrs. Fortune insisted. "She was delighted with your flute playing, and so was Dr. Jordan. I could tell that he was pleased you were making an effort with the girl."

"Do you think so?" Kea asked. She hated herself for sounding so hopeful, so eager, but suddenly she wanted very much to please Rafe.

"I know so," Mrs. Fortune said, and again Kea wondered if the woman knew about her past with Rafe. She suspected not, for she doubted that Rafe was the kind of man to share something as personal as his past love life. Her suspicions were confirmed when the older woman winked at her. "I think the doctor could be sweet on you if you gave him half a chance."

Kea shook her head, suddenly terribly embarrassed. "No, I don't think so."

"Open your eyes," Mrs. Fortune said warmly. "Look at the way he watches you. I really think he thinks you're something special."

"I'm sure you're wrong," Kea murmured, but how she wished it could be true that Rafe did still care for her.

The afternoon passed in pleasant idleness. Kea and Mrs. Fortune watched television while Carmen slept, and Kea resisted the urge to watch Janice Royal do her talk show. She did decide to call the producer, McDonald Hollister, and talk to him about her position with the station. The thought caused a tremor of unease to move through her, but she knew that it had to be done.

She waited until she was thoroughly relaxed to excuse herself and make the call in the privacy of her bedroom. As she walked down the hall, she peeped into Carmen's room, and it stirred something deep within her to see the small girl huddled up in a ball in the middle of the bed, hugging her body, the helmet a cumbersome bonnet covering her dark hair. Unexpectedly, a rush of tears filled her eyes, and she asked herself how Rafe could work with someone like Carmen without getting his heart broken. The answer came to her as quickly as the question: Rafe could do it because he was making the situation better. Without him Kea knew that this girl would have had no chance for a normal life, and she felt a surge of pride.

Moments later she returned to the living room, feeling that the call to McDonald had been much less than satisfactory. He had hemmed and hawed, and clearly he didn't think Kea was able to return to work now. She wasn't disputing that; her concern was if he would ever let her go back on the show. She reminded him that she did have a contract, but they both knew that it would lapse in a matter of weeks, and she was terribly concerned that he was attempting to let it do just that before she could get back to work. She sighed wearily. She would have to cross the bridge when she came to it; the truth was that she wasn't ready to go back yet, but McDonald was in for a surprise if he thought he could pretend that she had never existed. Her job was her life, and she meant to reclaim it—one way or another.

The living room was empty and Kea trailed back to the kitchen to find Mrs. Fortune cooking enchiladas and refried beans. "For Carmen," she said conspiratorially when Kea sniffed the air. "I'd like to see that little girl put on some weight. She's so frail. Maybe if I serve her food that she's more likely to be used to, she'll eat more."

Kea laughed softly. "Maybe you're right. Can I help with anything?"

Shaking her head, Mrs. Fortune declared, "You're still a patient, too, in case you've forgotten. You've been running here and there, but you're still supposed to be taking it easy."

Kea settled down in a chair. "I've got to get on with my life. I've taken off more than two weeks to heal and think, and now it's time for action."

The other woman made a tsking sound with her tongue. "You'd better quit rushing your healing. You're lucky even to be alive, and if you keep on pushing, you'll find yourself right back in bed, flat on your back."

The mere idea was enough to frighten Kea, for never in her life had she hated anything as much as the helpless feeling she had known lying in that hospital bed, wondering what was to become of her. She realized that she had come a long way; she was at least in control of her physical self again. "You're right," she agreed. "I don't want that to happen again."

"Then you'd best be resting more," Mrs. Fortune warned.

"Really, I have been resting," Kea said. "I'm feeling quite well. My eye doesn't hurt, and my ankle doesn't give me much of a problem anymore."

"I guess you know best about your body," the other woman agreed, "but I still think you should rest more."

138

They both looked up when Carmen hovered by the door, uncertain if she should come in.

"Well, hello there," Mrs. Fortune said, motioning to her. "Come on in and see what's cooking for dinner."

Almost hesitantly, the girl entered the room, walking in the direction of the stove. Both women smiled when they saw Carmen's eyes light up at the sight of food. "I do believe your theory was right," Kea told the other woman, and Mrs. Fortune beamed at her.

"I sure hope so."

It wasn't long before Rafe came home. He greeted the three of them briefly, then went to the master bath to take a shower and change clothes. Kea couldn't still the foolish beating of her heart when he returned to the kitchen a few minutes later, his dark hair wet and glistening from the shower, his face freshly shaved. This time he was dressed in jeans and a simple blue shirt, and Kea's gaze wandered over him admiringly. She tingled as she recalled the rapture she had known in his arms only last night, and she was unable to meet his eyes when he chose the chair beside hers.

"Let me set the table," she told Mrs. Fortune, getting up.

The woman waved her back to her chair. "No, no, you just relax. I've got everything under control." She began to place the plates and silverware around the table, and Kea suddenly wished that someone had suggested eating in the dining room tonight. The table was much larger, and she knew that there she wouldn't be so painfully aware of Rafe.

The tempting aroma of Mexican food filled the room when Mrs. Fortune set the dishes on the table, and Kea welcomed the opportunity to focus on Carmen instead of Rafe. The girl didn't say anything, but her large eyes were bright as she watched the older woman burden the table with an assortment of spicy dishes.

"Well," Mrs. Fortune said, surveying her handiwork proudly, "I'll be running along unless I'm needed for something else."

"No, thank you, Mrs. Fortune," Rafe said, smiling at her. "This looks just fine, and I'm sure the ladies are as eager to sample it as I am." He poured a little sugar into his iced tea, and Kea watched as Carmen mimicked his actions.

Immediately upon Mrs. Fortune's departure, a tenseness settled over the table as the three occupants sat in stiff silence, sampling the delicious food.

Kea longed to ease the tension in the room, and she found herself making idle chitchat about the food and Carmen's improved appetite. It seemed that she and Rafe had nothing to say to each other after their passion of the previous night, and the meal time wore on in almost painful slowness. Kea tried not to look at Rafe any more than she had to, but a thousand thoughts passed through her mind, and they all seemed to concern him. She wondered if he had even noticed her hair, and she was ashamed to be bothered by such a small thing.

Across the table from her Rafe tried his best not to stare at Kea. She was more enticing than ever with her short hair, and though he had loved to run his fingers through her thick, long tresses, the new style gave her a softer, younger look, and Rafe mentally complimented the hairdresser on his choice of styles. This one came very close to hiding Kea's scars.

A heat raced through him as he sat across from her, recalling how she had made him forget about everything but her with her loving the previous night. It was obvious to him now that she regretted giving in to his pressure. He had suspected as much when she had slipped from his bed before daybreak. He was ashamed that he had had no more willpower than to force himself on her as he had. All his good intentions had evaporated when he had seen her

140

naked in the pool. His desire had burned up his common sense.

He directed his attention to Carmen, explaining in Spanish that they would be going to her home in a few days. Kea understood some of his words, and she couldn't keep from glancing at him apprehensively.

"I was telling her that I'll be taking her home in a few days," Rafe said, his dark gaze focusing on Kea. "She misses her family, and she's eager to show off her new appearance, I'm sure."

Kea cleared her throat. This didn't involve her at all, but she had a feeling of unreasonable panic growing inside her. "Will you be flying?" She knew that he usually piloted a plane himself when he went to foreign countries, or hired a pilot.

He shook his head. "The girl is too afraid. She was hysterical all the way when she was brought in. Besides, it will give me a chance to visit with my own family and some of my previous patients if I drive."

Kea held his gaze a moment and she knew her eyes had brightened at his words. How she used to wish Rafe would introduce her to his family; she had always thought it would show some kind of permanent interest in her if he would, but he had hardly mentioned them, much less taken her to meet them.

"How long will you be gone?" she asked, her voice oddly thick with emotion.

He shrugged. "Four or five weeks, depending on what surgeries I need to perform. When I go to Mexico, I travel to a given area, doing whatever needs to be done."

Kea felt stricken at the information, even though she had often known him to be gone for weeks in the past.

Rafe studied her face thoughtfully, and Kea imagined he had something he wished to say to her. Holding her breath, she watched him, but abruptly he resumed eating, and she knew that the moment had passed.

141

Then he looked at her again and she saw the hesitation in his eyes. "Would you like to go with me this time, Kea? I'm going to use the trip as a vacation as well as for work."

The question was as unexpected for him as it was for her. He had had no intention of asking her. He had never asked her in all the months they had been lovers. But somehow he sensed that she could handle it now, and he hated leaving her again so soon after he had found her. He knew that although she obviously didn't want his physical love, she needed him for a while longer.

But there was more to her going than that, he realized. He had seen how she related to Carmen this afternoon, how close she had come to reaching the girl. Perhaps Carmen realized that, because Kea had been injured too, she was more likely to understand the pain and the embarrassment. It seemed that Kea's presence might help the girl. It grieved Rafe to think of Carmen spending the rest of her life locked up inside herself, unwilling to communicate with others again because she had been so deeply hurt. He knew she would be all right if only someone could get her to take that first step and speak even a single word again.

And, in truth, he knew that he was concerned for Kea's mental health also. He knew it would help her to heal if she could keep busy. Here she had nothing but memories and problems; for the hundredth time he wondered how much she had loved Roxwell, and how broken up inside she had been over his death, but he would not ask her the question. She had left him for Roxwell, so he knew that Roxwell at least rated higher than he had. The thought sent a shaft of pain to his heart, and he didn't want to think about it again.

In Mexico Kea would find a new world, a simpler world with none of the pressures she was experiencing here. As he looked at her, he knew that he never would have asked this of the old Kea, but she had changed somehow.

Still, he knew he was taking a risk. How could he bear to be in her company day after day, watching her laugh and learn and explore? He knew what a fine and inquisitive mind she had, and he had no doubts that she would make the most of her time with the Mexican people if she chose to go. Could he stand by and watch her heal and help Carmen heal while his own wounds only grew deeper? He should not have asked. He had been a fool—again.

Kea paused, so surprised by Rafe's offer that she dropped her fork. Why had he suddenly asked her this now? What exactly was he after? Was he only acting out of pity? Did he think that the only way she could learn to deal with her new face was to escape the world she knew?

She could read nothing in his dark, penetrating eyes, and she told herself that it didn't really matter anyway. She couldn't go with him; it would cost her too much and she knew her heart was not yet ready to pay the price. It was too wounded and vulnerable as it was.

She struggled with herself before refusing, recalling all the times she had actually pleaded with him to take her. He had said firmly and unemotionally that these trips were not for her. She had wondered then if he had wanted the time away from her. It made her all the more curious about why he would invite her to go now. But she was too afraid of his answer to ask him.

She lowered her eyes to stare down at the half-finished meal on her plate. "No," she said softly. "I don't think so."

It was the answer he had expected, but still it hurt. He had forgotten for a moment that even though her face had changed, her life had not. She was a stranger to him now as she had been then. Just as she always would be. The two of them were worlds apart.

He was embarrassed that he had asked her, and he felt the need to justify his offer. "I'm only suggesting it as your

143

doctor, Kea," he said brusquely. "I think a change of pace might be good for you."

Kea's smoky eyes lifted to meet his steady, unrevealing gaze. So, she had the answer to why he had invited her, and though she had guessed it, it still hurt. They were back to the doctor and patient relationship; he was only concerned with her mental health.

"No," she repeated, this time more firmly.

Although he had known that she would, Rafe hated to hear her refuse a second time. He watched her expression briefly, then he returned his attention to the meal.

Finally, they had made an attempt at consuming some of the delicious food Mrs. Fortune had cooked, and Kea stood up to remove the plates from the table. She was surprised and delighted when Carmen joined her, working by her side as if it were the most natural thing in the world.

Rafe remained at the table, lost in thought, his brows almost touching. They made a strange pair, the thin, dark Mexican girl, and the tall, voluptuous, fair Caucasian woman. And yet they shared something very real. It wasn't the first time Rafe had known accident victims to feel a bond, despite all their other differences.

He stood up and walked over to an automatic popcorn popper. When he had put the popcorn in the hot-air machine, he touched Carmen on the shoulder. She turned around and watched with amazement in her eyes as the kernals exploded into bits of white fluff, but she didn't make a sound.

"Will you join us for a movie on television?" Rafe asked. Kea turned around to be sure he was talking to her, and when she discovered that he was, she didn't know whether to be pleased or dismayed.

"Yes," she said at last. "I'd like that." It didn't seem to bother Rafe at all that Carmen wouldn't be able to hear the movie. Suddenly Kea realized how grateful she was for Carmen's presence. It obviated the need to make conversation with Rafe or to retire to her room. The girl gave them a mutual ground.

Rafe nodded, then handed a bowl of popcorn to Carmen. Small and silent, she followed the muscular man to the living room. Kea trailed along behind as soon as she had finished the dishes, and to her chagrin she found that a flood of memories from the past filled her mind, memories and dreams that had died when Rafe hadn't married her as she had hoped. She unexpectedly found this time with him and the girl incredibly intimate; it was almost possible for her to imagine what it would be like living in Rafe's house, sharing a child with him. And she was alarmed by the pain that rose up in her, for she knew that the dream had been impossible when she had first dreamed it—and it was even more impossible now.

She experienced an awkward moment when she entered the living room. Carmen had found a spot on the floor, and Rafe was sprawled out on the couch, looking temptingly male in his jeans and casual shirt. Kea longed to snuggle up to him as she had done in the past. With as much nonchalance as she could muster, she sat down on the couch not far from him. He offered her some of the popcorn, and she took a handful.

When the movie came on, Kea was amused to see that it was a Disney special; she told herself that she should have expected no less of Rafe. Soon she and Rafe were laughing heartily at the antics of the protagonist, and Kea thought that even Carmen couldn't resist a smile or two. At an especially humorous incident, Rafe tossed his head back and laughed deeply. Kea glanced at him, laughter in her own eyes, and their eyes met. She had never seen Rafe in quite this same situation, and she had to remind herself that the three of them were not a happy little family. She and Carmen were Rafe's patients, and they were here only because they needed his professional services.

The laughter died on Kea's lips, and she looked back at

145

the screen, the magic of the time gone for her. Even though Carmen couldn't hear, she was clearly intrigued and entertained by the movie. It went on for some time, and Kea sat with her eyes glued to the television set, barely aware when the movie ended.

"Look at Carmen," she heard Rafe whisper, and she glanced down to see the child curled into a ball at Rafe's feet, fast asleep. Bending down, he gently lifted her up in his arms. "Will you come help me put her to bed?" he asked softly, and there was no way Kea could refuse.

Kea helped undress the soundly sleeping girl, and get her into a nightgown. Then she pulled down the sheet and spread before Rafe laid the girl down. Kea felt Rafe's dark eyes on her as she tucked the cover up around Carmen's shoulders, and she thought her heart would break when he murmured low, "You should have a child of your own. You're a natural."

The comment seemed to have surprised him as much as it did Kea, and she lowered her eyes to stare down at the sleeping Carmen. She looked up again when she felt Rafe gently brush her hair back from her right cheek. "Your hair is very becoming this way," he said softly.

Kea was still trying to think of something—anything—to say when he said more firmly, "You're still healing from the accident. You shouldn't be gadding about all over town making yourself beautiful." Then he turned on his heel and left.

Kea closed her eyes and stood very still, grateful that she hadn't responded to his compliment. She would have felt like a fool when he made his last statement. Once again she was harshly reminded that she was his patient and his interest in her was professional.

CHAPTER EIGHT

When Kea awakened the next morning, she was filled with a dreadful sense of foreboding. She hadn't realized how anxious she was about the will. In her vulnerable condition she didn't know how well she would hold up to Shane's hostility.

By the time she had showered, blown her hair dry, dressed in a flattering gold silk dress and practical, yet dainty matching gold shoes with moderate heels, Kea found that Rafe had gone to work and only Carmen and Mrs. Fortune were in the kitchen, the girl silently watching the older woman cook the morning meal.

"Hello."

The ever-effervescent Mrs. Fortune turned around at the sound of Kea's voice. "Good morning. How are you? My, don't you look lovely today."

"Thank you." Kea smiled at Carmen, but the girl stayed in her world, withdrawn and shy. Kea was a little disappointed, for she had felt that she was making some progress last night. "How are you today, Carmen?"

This time the child lowered her gaze so that the long length of her lashes shadowed her dark cheeks.

Refusing to lose ground with the girl, Kea went over to her side and knelt down by her chair. "Friend," she said, signing with her index fingers.

When Carmen raised her dark eyes, Kea was sure she saw the beginning of a sparkle in them. She impulsively rose and returned to her room to search through her belongings. When she found Mickey her good intentions almost failed her. He was about the only friend she had left, but before she could change her mind, she went back to the kitchen and held out the stuffed toy to Carmen.

The girl glanced at it, then snatched at it quickly, holding it in her arms as if it were a baby. Kea realized that Carmen needed Mickey more than she did, and she smiled.

"His name is Mickey," she said gently. "He was a good friend to me and I know he will be to you too." She briefly glimpsed the pleasure on Mrs. Fortune's face, and then she settled in a chair and began to eat her breakfast.

Mickey gave Carmen something to focus on, and both women were pleased to see that she was eating better than she had been. She kept her eyes on the stuffed toy and stroked its fur with her fine-boned hand.

"Where are you off to?" Mrs. Fortune asked.

"My late husband's will is going to be read today," Kea said. Not wanting to dwell on the subject, she rushed on. "Carmen helped me with the dishes last night."

"Good. That's a good sign," Mrs. Fortune said cheerfully. "I'd sure like to think the little thing is going to be all right. I'd give anything to hear her speak."

Kea sighed. "Yes," she agreed. "So would I." She, too, had become involved in Carmen's life.

She finished her breakfast, then called a cab for the trip to the lawyer's office. When she arrived, she braced herself for Shane's hostility, drew a deep breath, and went into the office. Suddenly feeling chilled to the bone, Kea hugged her arms to her body and found a seat behind Shane and a few members of the household staff.

"All right," the lawyer said. "I think we can proceed now. I believe everyone is here." He studied the document before him for a moment while everyone waited expectantly, Kea thought not unlike vultures, to see what their share of the take would be. When the lawyer read the division of property, a collective gasp rose from the little group as they discovered that Kea had been left the majority of the estate, including the house, while Shane had been left a modest monthly allowance.

· No one was more shocked than Kea. The will had been made right before Roxwell's death, and he had clearly spelled out that Shane could earn his own way, as had Roxwell. The household help had been generously provided for, a move that restored some of Kea's faith in Roxwell; however, she was stunned that he had been so generous with her. It was almost as though he had left her the money to spite his son, and Kea found it morbidly ironic that in leaving her a fortune, he had only created another problem for her. Shane would never tolerate it. She had known that before he stood up and announced it.

"I'll contest!" he declared angrily. He turned around to glare at Kea. "I'll take you to court. I know you exerted undue influence, and you won't get away with it. You will not be allowed to strip me of what's rightfully mine."

Kea didn't even want the money, but she had no intention of telling Shane that now. She was still numb with shock, and all she wanted to do was to get out of the office. While the others stared after her, she slipped out the door and asked the secretary at the desk to call a cab for her. Then she went out in the sunshine and drew in several steadying breaths.

She was thankful that her cab appeared quickly, and she hastily climbed in, her mind whirling. Too agitated to return to the house immediately, she directed the driver to take her to Rodeo Drive where she spent the next few hours. Tentatively testing her ankle, she did a little shopping to distract herself from the news she had just heard, and then she whiled away the hours in a restaurant, trying fervently to understand why Roxwell had left her his money. He had seen her as some kind of status symbol that he had just had to have, and maybe he considered this his way of repaying her for her foolishness in marrying him. Or perhaps he saw this as the way to care for her and protect her as he had wanted to do in life. Or maybe he just wanted to teach the ungrateful Shane a lesson. Kea really didn't know—and she realized that she never would.

When she had used up most of the day, she spent a little more time shopping for herself and Carmen, selecting frivolous items—bathing suits, culottes, shorts, tops, and sandals—before returning to the house. Mrs. Fortune was preparing the evening meal, and Kea was sharply reminded of the meal she had shared with Rafe and Carmen last night.

"How did it go?" Mrs. Fortune asked when Kea walked into the room. "My, my," she said teasingly, seeing the bags in Kea's arms, "you must have inherited a bundle."

A flush of guilt raced over Kea's face. She didn't want anyone to think that she was already spending Roxwell's money. "*I* paid for these," she said defensively.

Mrs. Fortune looked at her curiously. "I'm sure you did," she said in a kindly tone.

Kea was immediately contrite. "I'm sorry I spoke so curtly. The fact is that I did inherit a bundle, and I don't want it."

Frowning, Mrs. Fortune murmured, "I wasn't trying to pry, Kea. I was only curious. You seem terribly unhappy about this—hardly the usual attitude for a woman who's just come into a fortune. May I suggest that you talk with Dr. Jordan about it? He's a very good listener."

Kea could feel her cheeks redden. She was sure Mrs. Fortune had heard about Shane's public and private attacks on her, and she didn't want to discuss it with the woman; however, she did recognize that Mrs. Fortune's advice was good. She did need to talk with someone. But Rafe? Dare she impose on him further? Could she talk to

150

him about the money her dead husband had left her? Under the circumstances, it hardly seemed right.

But she didn't have anyone else—no one who might understand. She desperately needed a sounding board in this matter; she wanted to return the estate to Shane, but she didn't know if she would be doing the right thing since Roxwell had explicitly requested that Shane make his own way with only a little help from his father. Would it be wrong to give him all Roxwell's money? Wasn't it too cruel to deprive him of the house *and* the money? She could talk to her lawyer, but she had a suspicion that he would encourage her to keep everything as Roxwell had instructed. It didn't sit well with her at all.

She was distracted all through dinner, and Rafe noticed it. When the meal was over and he was helping her clean up the kitchen while Carmen watched television, he asked her, "What's bothering you? Anything I can help with?"

Kea looked levelly at him, but she could tell nothing from his expression. "Roxwell left me the majority of his estate, Rafe," she said without preliminaries. "He only gave Shane a modest monthly allowance. He didn't even leave his son the house."

Rafe's first thought was that Roxwell must have loved Kea very much, but it would have pained him too much to verbalize it. He was amazed by her next statement.

"I want to give Shane's inheritance back to him."

Rafe's black brows were furrowed. "Why? Did he threaten you?"

Lowering her gaze, Kea recalled the humiliating scene in the lawyer's office. "Only with court, but that's not the reason I want to give it to him."

"Then why? Are you going to let him win so easily after the pain he's caused you?"

"This isn't a game, Rafe," she replied.

"Isn't it?"

She shook her head, and he wondered why she wanted

151

Shane to have Roxwell's fortune after he'd left it to her. Was it guilt? Despair? Or had she wearied of the trials of her life? Why?

Regardless of her reasons he thought she should respect Roxwell's wishes. "Do you think it's fair to turn it all over to Shane when Roxwell specifically gave him only an allowance?" he asked her. "He must have had a reason. Perhaps he saw what a selfish, inconsiderate child he had created, and he wanted him to learn things the hard way— to be forced to grow up."

Kea was thoughtful for a moment. "He did specify that Shane should have to make his own way as he had."

"And you want to make it easy for him, in spite of his father's request? Don't you have more respect for your husband's memory than that, Kea?"

Kea didn't know what to say. She didn't want the burden of the money, and she didn't want to encourage Shane's hatred. But did she owe it to Roxwell to abide by his request? Should she honor his memory with this final request?

"But it seems that Shane has more right to Roxwell's money than I have," she murmured.

"Right?" Rafe questioned. "It was Roxwell's money. He had a right to leave it to whomever he wished. Where is it written that children have a right to their parents' money? That's hogwash! Are you going to give in to the boy's hatred and greed? Don't you think his father knew him better than you do? Don't you think you can make better use of the money than he can?"

Kea immediately thought of Carmen and people like her, people who had a genuine need for the money, and she was staggered by the way her heart pounded and her mind raced at the thought. But still she didn't feel good in her heart about stripping Shane of his inheritance as Shane had so aptly put it.

"Are you afraid of the scandal? The battle with Shane?" Rafe asked gently.

Kea shook her head. "No."

"Why don't you think on it awhile before you make your decision? I coul give you the name of my lawyer if you want to talk to him about it."

"I have a lawyer, but thank you for offering," she said. Somehow she felt better already. "I'll talk to my lawyer about it." She laid down the dishcloth. "In fact, I think I'll call him at home and get it over with."

Rafe watched her as she walked away. She seemed terribly tired, and he wondered if she could take another battle just now. Apparently her marriage to Roxwell had been a lot stronger than he had imagined for the man to leave her so much, and she had to be aching from his death. He wished that she had agreed to go with him to Mexico, not only for his own selfish reasons, but because he honestly felt the trip would be beneficial to her.

He was still standing in the kitchen, leaning against the counter some time later when Kea returned. "What did the lawyer say?"

Kea looked very weary. "He thinks I should keep the money, but he's sure there will be a nasty court case. He suggested I get a court order to get Shane out of his house now. Rafe"—she turned somber gray eyes in his direction —"I'm going to give Shane the house. I couldn't live with myself if I didn't."

Rafe pondered her words for a moment, but he could offer her no additional advice. She had made up her mind, and he wouldn't attempt to interfere. "You'll have to be here for the court battle, won't you?"

"Yes, but it won't come up for some time."

He moved closer to her, making Kea's heartbeats pick up wildly. He put his hands on her shoulders and looked deeply into her eyes. "Why don't you come to Mexico

153

with us? I really think the trip would be good for you. I'm sure Carmen would love to have you along."

Carmen might, Kea told herself, but would Rafe? Why had he asked her again? Did he really want her companionship, or was he feeling sorry for her and doing this in the interest of her health? What would she be letting herself in for going away with him like that? It was hard enough to be around him now and not fall into his arms. How would she manage to hide her feelings for him when she was with him constantly for so many weeks? She *wanted* to go, it was true, but should she?

The simple truth was that she couldn't refuse him a second time, regardless of his reason for wanting her to go. Perhaps she was hoping for some miracle, something that she knew in her heart would never happen, but she nodded. "Perhaps the trip would be a good diversion. Why not go?"

Rafe smiled, but Kea couldn't tell if he was really pleased or not. With him leading the way, they went into the living room to join Carmen, and Kea wondered why she had agreed. Was it for Carmen? For her own sanity? Or for any chance to spend more time with Rafe?

"I'll make the arrangements for the necessary papers," Rafe commented. "You need to take only casual clothes. The country will be very hot this time of year. Be sure to take some comfortable walking shoes." He glanced down at her feet. "Is your ankle still giving you trouble?"

Kea shrugged. "Not much. If I wear sensible shoes and don't press my luck, I find that it actually feels better when I use it some."

"Good. I'm glad to hear it. We'll leave for Mexico on Sunday." His eyes met hers. "I'm taking the day off tomorrow. I want to take Carmen to Disneyland and perhaps eat dinner at Farmers' Market on the way home." He studied her features, letting his eyes roam over her eyes, nose, and mouth, lingering briefly there. "Do you feel like going with us?"

Kea was unreasonably pleased that he had asked. "I'd love to," she replied, unable to contain her pleasure. She smiled at him, and she was dazzled by the brilliant—and most unexpected—smile he gave her in return.

She thought about the clothes she had purchased today, and she wondered if, subsconsciously, she had selected them with the Mexico trip in mind. She shook her head; she hadn't even known that she was going, of course, but she had wanted to. She was thankful she would need to do little additional shopping. Since she hadn't yet given her gifts to Carmen and she was feeling uncomfortable standing there with Rafe, she decided to use Carmen as an excuse to escape. Perhaps there was something the girl would want to wear to Disneyland tomorrow.

Excusing herself, she went into the living room. When she beckoned to Carmen to join her in her room, the girl bowed her head and followed meekly, holding Mickey close to her. Kea had left her bags in a bunch on the floor, and when she began to pile them on the bed, she saw Carmen's eyes widen with anticipation.

"For you," Kea said, holding out a bag.

She could see the excitement building in the girl's sad brown eyes. When Carmen placed her delicate hand on her chest to sign a question asking if the bag was really for her, Kea nodded eagerly. To her knowledge, it was the first time Carmen had signed.

"Yes. Yours," Kea said.

Carmen laid down the prized Mickey to peer into the bag, then she quickly dumped the contents, holding up first one article of clothing, then another. Kea had purchased red shorts and a blue and white sailor top for her, and it was the outfit she apparently loved best.

While Kea watched, she stripped off the dress she wore and tried on the new clothes. Kea smiled, very pleased by

Carmen's enthusiasm. She glanced up in surprise when Rafe spoke from the doorway. "This is a sight worth seeing," he murmured.

When he had watched the thrilled Carmen examine herself in the mirrowed closet doors, he asked Kea, "May I come in?"

"Yes, of course."

"You didn't tell me where you were going, so I didn't know if this was an all-girl party or not," he told her, his gaze holding hers briefly. Although his tone was teasing, Kea could think of nothing to say, and she gazed at him as he walked over to stand behind the happy child. He spoke to her in Spanish, and her dark eyes glowed brightly.

"What did you tell her?" Kea asked.

"That we're taking her to Disneyland tomorrow and home on Sunday. I said she could wear this outfit tomorrow. You don't mind, do you?"

"No, certainly not."

They both enjoyed Carmen's pleasure as she went through the other things Kea had bought for her. The evening was one full of excitement for both Carmen and Kea. The girl was ecstatic about going home, and Kea was looking forward to the trip with more anticipation than she would have wanted to admit to Rafe.

Rafe finally decided that they all should go to bed, for they had to be up early tomorrow to make the drive to Disneyland in Anaheim. Regretting that the special evening was ending, Kea gazed after the dark man and the child as they left, then she sat down on her bed, suddenly feeling very lonely. Finally, she made herself change her clothes for a nightgown and climb into bed.

For some time she lay there, too lost in thought and too excited to sleep, and she wondered if Carmen was having as much trouble getting to sleep as she was. She was filled with the sense of embarking on some tremendous adventure, and she knew that she was excited all out of proportion to the situation. Rafe had felt sorry for her. She knew that, but it didn't diminish her joy.

Mrs. Fortune arrived earlier than usual the next morning to cook breakfast for the little group. Kea, wearing new blue culottes and a tunic top, was a bit embarrassed to find that she was the first one ready. Carmen soon rushed into the kitchen, dressed in her red shorts outfit. Rafe followed immediately, and Kea couldn't keep from staring at him; he was dressed in cords and a brown shirt, and she found him very attractive.

Carmen sat down at the table, but she was almost too excited to eat when the others joined her and Mrs. Fortune served them. She had decided to take Mickey with her to Disneyland, and Kea wondered how the child would react if she saw the Mickey character walking around the amusement park, greeting visitors. She couldn't wait to see what Carmen would do.

By the time they reached Disneyland, all three of them seemed unusually exhilarated. Kea realized that she had never seen Rafe interact with a child before, and, to use his same words—the words that had caused her great pain—he was a natural. Kea was amazed that he could live in his world of suffering and disease and then take such pleasure in something as simple as an outing to an amusement park. But then, she reasoned, perhaps the grim nature of his work was precisely why he found such joy in the simple distractions. He had learned to appreciate each separate moment of happiness as a rare gift.

From the instant they arrived Carmen could hardly keep still. They were walking slowly because of Kea's ankle and Carmen's injury. Rafe's gait was easy and unhurried, but he had to remind the girl time and time again to walk slowly. *"No hay prisa,"* he told her.

Her eyes big and round with undisguised delight, Carmen gazed at everything in the fairyland park of castles and creatures and magic. Rafe knew Carmen and Kea had the stamina for only a few of the less-strenuous attractions, and he had selected them carefully. They all had just finished eating a chocolate-covered banana purchased from a strolling vendor with a pushcart when Mickey Mouse stepped out into their path.

Carmen let out a wild giggle of delight as the huge caricature bent down over her, pointing to her stuffed toy. *"Mira! Mira!"* she cried gleefully, turning first to Rafe, then to Kea.

Kea's eyes filled with tears as she met Rafe's over the girl's head. How she had longed for this moment! She was then astonished to hear the girl break into an excited stream of Spanish, as though she had been talking all along.

"Listen, Rafe," Kea exclaimed. "Listen to her talk!"

Rafe smiled, but Kea could tell that he was no less excited than she. "That's how elective mutism is," he explained. "Once the first word is spoken, the victim is as articulate as if he had never been afflicted at all."

Rafe had brought his Polaroid camera along to record this time for Carmen so that she would always have memories of a day not likely to come again once she was home in Mexico. When the real-life Mickey hugged her, Rafe took a picture.

Soon Mickey Mouse resumed his rounds, and a thrilled Carmen clutched the picture Rafe had taken as she stared after the character. It was a day for miracles, and the mood was heightened even further as Rafe, Kea, and Carmen boarded a train.

Carmen's face was wreathed in smiles, and though she was enchanted with her photograph and the ride, she soon forgot about both as the three of them seated themselves to be entertained by the bears at the Bear Country Jamboree. Carmen clapped and laughed and had as much fun

158

as anyone despite her lack of hearing. Rafe and Kea exchanged smiles over the child's head, and Kea was moved by the tenderness she saw in Rafe's eyes. She looked away when his gaze continued to hold hers. She reminded herself that this was a special day, and that the smiles and fond looks were caused by the occasion and by Carmen.

After a rest stop they worked their way through the crowds to the Jungle Cruise. *"Mira!"* Carmen cried time and again as the low, wide boat moved through the water and mechanical hippopottamuses made their appearances. When the guide pretended to shoot a threatening one, Carmen tensed, but she soon realized that it was all in fun, and her eyes sparkled with merriment.

Kea glanced over at Rafe and smiled; she could not help but be affected by Carmen's enthusiasm. "She's like a different person," Kea observed. "It's almost as if she's forgotten her misfortune completely."

Rafe's lips curved into a half-smile, but there was a glint of seriousness in his eyes when he said, "It *is* possible to forget, you know. For Carmen, it's as if a new world has opened up, despite her deafness. Her physical appearance was more of a trauma to her than her loss of hearing. You can see how happy she is." *And you can be, too,* his silent gaze seemed to say. *If Carmen can learn to live with her injuries, so can you. Life can still be good.*

Unexpectedly, he reached out to trace one of Kea's scars with a gentle movement. "Some pain is harder to forget than others," he commented soberly. "You learn to live with some of it, but you don't forget."

Kea studied his features curiously, sensing that he was not talking about her accident or Carmen's. His statement had been too introspective, too pensive. Was he referring to the past—his and hers? No, she told herself harshly; she was engaging in wishful thinking again. He had made it clear that he didn't care about their past; he was here with her today because he was concerned for her as his patient.

Hadn't he told her that often enough for her to understand?

He looked as if he might say something more, but then Carmen grasped his arm, chattering to him in Spanish. By the time he returned his attention to Kea, the solemnness had left his expression, and he was laughing once more.

"Carmen wanted to know if she could take a hippo home to show her parents, but I told her he would be too uncomfortable in the backseat of the car. She suggested that we could fill the trunk with water and the animal could ride there."

He laughed, genuinely amused, and Kea could not resist joining in. She gazed fondly at Carmen and she grew thoughtful. Strange, she mused, she had wanted to help the girl, but it seemed that, somehow, the girl was helping *her*. If there was one thing that Carmen had shown her in the past two days, it was that there was still joy and spontaneity in the world.

Looking at Rafe with shining eyes, Kea felt her heart turn over when his smiling gaze met hers. And for a moment, with Carmen's laughter ringing in their ears, it was as if the past didn't exist and time had not cruelly dragged them apart. In that instant the old understanding and easy camaraderie was there, and when Rafe took her hand, she did not pull away.

When the ride was over, the spell lingered as the three of them moved on to a Polynesian restaurant for lunch. Kea was feeling quite well and her ankle wasn't giving her any trouble. Carmen seemed to have forgotten all about the hated helmet. Kea marveled at how relaxed and happy they all were. Carmen chattered nonstop, mostly to Rafe, occasionally using some signs she knew. Rafe would interpret for Kea, and she had to caution herself against enjoying this time too much. Her careless heart was fluttering and excited, all too easily forgetting the unwelcome past;

she had to tie a mental string to her spirit to keep it from soaring too high.

It would have been very easy to believe that all was right between her and Rafe again, but in reality, this was only one day—one magical and wonderful day—and she allowed herself to enjoy it to the fullest. It was a day of miracles, for Carmen had spoken. And it was a day of magic because Rafe was here, charming and delightful. And it was a day of joy because Kea was able to forget everything but the sheer delight of this place and these two people she shared it with.

In the afternoon they visited the Tiki Room, with its enchanting birds and flowers and fountain, and then it was time to start back home. "Do you think we should pass on Farmers' Market?" Rafe asked, glancing at Kea as he drove. "It's been a big day."

"No, let's go there. We've taken it easy all day, and I think Carmen will love to see the tremendous food selection."

"Is it Carmen or Kea you're thinking of?" he teased lightly. "If I remember correctly, it's one of your favorite places."

Kea laughed. It was true. She and Rafe had gone there often those many months ago; Farmers' Market was fascinating and the food was delicious. Rafe winked at her, and she settled back against the seat. "Well, maybe I'm just a little interested myself." She looked away, knowing that she was enjoying this time—and this man—too much. When she glanced back at Carmen, she saw that the girl was fast asleep, the stuffed toy held tightly to her breast.

Farmers' Market was fun. Carmen had never seen so much food—or selection—in one place. Before they made a decision, the three of them wandered from one food stand to another, considering the Chinese kitchen, then the hamburger stand, then the French station, and on

161

through the marketplace, pausing by each stand. They all finally settled on food from the fish stand, and then they found a colorful table near a huge tree and ate scallops and fries.

Finally they made their way back to the car and headed home. There would be only one day of rest before leaving for Mexico on Sunday. Once again Carmen fell asleep as soon as she had snuggled back down in the rear seat with Mickey.

"Tomorrow we can go to a department store and do any last-minute shopping you need to do for the trip," Rafe told Kea. "We'll leave early Sunday morning."

Kea nodded, although she really had little left to do other than buying a piece of luggage. When Rafe had parked the car in the garage, he carried the sleeping Carmen into the house and again Kea helped him undress her and put her to bed. Kea and Rafe were walking down the hall toward their respective bedrooms when Kea glanced at him.

"Thank you, Rafe," she murmured. "It was a most special and wondrous day, and I appreciate you letting me share it with you and Carmen."

His eyes held hers, and for a brief and foolish moment Kea honestly thought he was going to kiss her. Instead he smiled. "You're welcome. I'm glad you decided to come with us. Good night."

"Good night," she whispered, turning toward her room.

Rafe stared after her, aware of the faint hint of lilacs lingering from the perfume she wore. He had been tempted to kiss her a moment ago, but he had caught himself in time. He had tried to convince himself that they could start again, as in the old days, but he knew it was only a dream. Too much had happened and he had learned his lesson well when Kea married Roxwell. But he had to admit that he hadn't enjoyed himself so much since Kea had left him. He had missed her terribly, and it would be so easy to fall into the old patterns with her—so easy until she walked out on him again.

Kea slipped into her nightgown, then snuggled under the sheet, letting her mind review the day. The time she had spent with Rafe had been wonderful, and she had to make herself remember that it had been only one day—Carmen's day. It had truly altered nothing in her own life. Certainly not her relationship with Rafe. Still, as she slipped into sleep, she couldn't help but dream the dreams she wanted to dream. And they were of a new beginning with Rafe.

CHAPTER NINE

Kea was glad when Sunday morning finally dawned; she felt as if she hadn't slept a wink, but she knew she had dozed. She was so thrilled about the trip that she wondered how she had ever refused Rafe's offer in the first place.

Before anyone else got up, she had showered and washed her hair, dressed in flattering green culottes and a white blouse with tiny green flowers, and had dragged her suitcase halfway down the hall.

She gasped when Rafe's door opened unexpectedly and he stepped out to stare at her. "What are you doing?" he drawled, seeing the obvious.

Kea's gaze skimmed down his appealing body, clad only in a short brown robe. "Taking my suitcase to the front room," she explained.

"Why don't you take it out to the car and load it?" he asked, and it was a moment before Kea realized that he was teasing her.

"It's heavy," she retorted.

"No kidding?" He reached down to lift the suitcase, and when he moaned in false pain, Kea slapped playfully at his shoulder. She drew back as if she had struck him in earnest; she had no right to behave with him in such a manner. He had neither invited nor encouraged such familiarity. For a moment she had forgotten all that separated them.

164

"I'll get my overnight bag," she said hastily, and she had vanished before Rafe could reply.

Mrs. Fortune arrived, and though Kea protested that she could cook the breakfast, she soon had the meal done. Rafe came into the kitchen dressed in a well-worn pair of blue jeans that hugged his muscled legs, and a casual blue work shirt with the two top buttons opened. Kea didn't think she had ever seen him look more rugged or masculine, and she quickly averted her gaze when he caught her staring at the dark hair curling over the open edge of his shirt.

When Carmen came in, they all sat down to breakfast, and Kea could contain the news of Carmen talking no longer. "Say something to Carmen," she urged Mrs. Fortune.

"Buenos días." The woman complied cautiously, suspecting something from Kea's animated face.

"Buenos días," the girl responded a little shyly, conscious that she had never before spoken to Mrs. Fortune.

"Praise God!" the older woman cried. Then she rushed over to hug Carmen. "Bless you! Bless you!" she exclaimed. "I knew you could do it." She turned around to look at Rafe. "Won't Trena be pleased? She's worked so hard with Carmen."

Kea experienced a sudden and painful burning deep in her stomach. Trena. She had forgotten about Trena, Rafe's nurse; she had wanted to forget about her. Of course she would have worked with Carmen too.

"I'm not going to tell her until she joins us in Mexico," Rafe said, smiling at the thought. "She'll be shocked."

Kea's breath stuck in her throat as she experienced a shock of her own. So Trena was going to Mexico too. Kea hadn't even suspected it, and that had been foolish, for she had known in the past that Trena always went with Rafe. Hadn't she been tormented often enough with questions about the two of them when they were away?

165

"Is she driving down with us?" she asked as lightly as she could manage. She had to know, but the question had almost choked her.

Rafe shook his head. "She'll fly in with the anesthetist later on. She wants to visit with her own family, and it so happens that she and the anesthetist are from the same village."

"I see," Kea murmured. And she was ashamed of the relief she felt upon hearing that she and Rafe would spend a few days without the other woman. She didn't know what it could possibly matter, or why she was so upset at the thought of Trena joining them. She had known nothing could come of this trip. But she hadn't expected to have the fact confirmed beforehand.

Carmen could hardly contain her eagerness, and Rafe had to be firm with her to get her to eat any breakfast at all. She was as thrilled about the actual trip as she was about seeing her family again, and all through breakfast she squirmed in her chair. Finally Rafe stood up.

"Ready to go?"

Kea and Carmen both pushed back their chairs, but Kea found herself doing so with considerably less enthusiasm than she had been feeling. The luggage had been loaded into Rafe's station wagon along with many of his supplies, and Kea was soon settled in the front seat beside him.

Unexpectedly, Rafe became more and more withdrawn as they rode toward Chula Vista, where his parents now lived. Although he answered Carmen's questions and responded to her pleasant chatter, Kea could tell that his thoughts were elsewhere. Kea didn't know what to make of his change in attitude, and she found herself imagining all kinds of reasons. Hadn't he changed since Mrs. Fortune mentioned Trena? Did he realize how much he would miss her until they met in Mexico? Kea tensed at the thought, and she gazed out at the scenery as the miles moved past; her only respite from her thoughts was her responses to Carmen's happy chatter when she could understand what the girl said.

Much to Kea's chagrin, she began to feel nervous as they approached the border town. She was reminded of all the times she had prayed, hoped, and dreamed that Rafe would bring her here—and all the times he never had.

Rafe had grown increasingly more quiet, and Kea was puzzled over his mood. She didn't know what to make of it, or what to do about it. Did he regret bringing her after all? When Rafe had parked the car in front of a big two-story house, he gazed at Kea thoughtfully, and she sensed that he had something he wished to say to her. She felt her palms growing moist in anticipation as she turned her attention to the house.

Rafe sat at her side, knowing he should speak to her about his family before she went in, but too proud to do so. He knew she wouldn't be expecting what she would find. He felt a flush of embarrassment at what he was contemplating; he wasn't ashamed of his family—he just knew that they were different from what Kea was used to, different from what he knew her image of him was. But how could he prepare her without sounding as though he *were* ashamed of them?

Sighing in defeat, he said nothing. He reached across her to open her car door, then his own. He could see that Carmen was suddenly cowering in the backseat, and he knew that she had a real fear of strangers.

He spoke consolingly in Spanish, assuring her that she had nothing to be afraid of. When Kea was out of the car, she looked back and saw that Rafe was having to coax the frightened Carmen out.

Instinctively, Kea held out her hand to the girl. Carmen clung tightly to it as if it were a lifeline, and when she was out of the vehicle, Kea wrapped her other arm around the child. The anguish in Carmen's soulful eyes almost

167

brought tears to Kea's, and she held the girl's hand as they made their way up the walkway to the lovely home of Rafe's parents. In truth, Kea didn't know which of them was more frightened, she or Carmen. After all this time Kea had convinced herself that there must be some very real reason why Rafe had never brought her here. And she was afraid she was going to learn why now.

She was taken aback by the woman who answered the door. Tired and faded-looking, the heavy Mexican woman was probably in her fifties and looked much older.

Stepping forward, Rafe embraced her warmly. *"Madre, Madre,"* he murmured gently, *"como estás?"*

There were tears in the woman's eyes when Rafe turned her around to introduce her to Kea and Carmen. "This is my mother, Señora Deluca. My friends, Kea Montgomery and Carmen. Carmen is deaf, but she reads lips," he added.

The weary woman smiled hesitantly at Kea, and it was all Kea could do to hide her shock at finding out this was Rafe's mother. She had uncovered many secrets in her line of work, but that this humble, unassuming woman could be Rafe Jordan's mother was one of those things she had never expected.

Señora Deluca's smile broadened when she gave her attention to Carmen. She spoke low and sweetly to the young girl, and immediately Carmen broke into a big grin, her shyness and fear evaporating like magic. Kea wondered what Rafe's mother had said to her, but no one translated. Carmen released Kea's hand and took that of the other woman, and Kea couldn't help but feel a little bit abandoned.

Then Señora Deluca looked at Kea again. "Please, come into my *casa.*" She started to lead the way, then glanced back proudly at Rafe, her black eyes glowing. "My son the doctor paid for it," she added, bestowing a beautiful smile on him.

168

When Rafe murmured something in Spanish, Señora Deluca responded softly before continuing down the hall. The house had obviously been magnificently appointed at one time, but the furniture and walls were showing signs of neglect and slovenliness now. Rafe's eyes met Kea's for a single moment when he glanced obliquely at her, and Kea had the unpleasant sensation that he was daring her to be critical of his mother and her life-style.

A balding, stoop-shouldered man wearing a T-shirt and baggy trousers met them as they walked into the huge kitchen where a number of adults and small children were working and playing. Kea wondered about the difference in Rafe's last name and his mother's, and she knew that Rafe's resemblance to this man was too strong to be other than that of father and son. Rafe confirmed her suspicions when he made the introductions.

"Kea Montgomery, Carmen Mendoza, this is my father, Antonio Deluca, my sisters Julia, Maria, Josephina . . ." Rafe continued with the list of names until his sisters and their husbands and children had all been introduced, a formidable task to say the least.

Kea kept her silence except for a general acknowledgment of the names, but she wondered how many of these people lived in the house and how many of them were supported by Rafe. She guessed that the house had six or seven bedrooms, but there were hardly enough to house all these people.

"I have four other sisters who do not live here," Rafe answered as if reading her mind. "It's such a big house that these felt comfortable here and Mother and Father were happy to share what they have with them."

Kea could read no animosity or dissatisfaction in Rafe's words or tone. He made no excuses for his family. One sister, Maria, came forward to kiss him on the mouth and hug him before holding out her young son to him.

"This is my nephew, Rafe," he said, and Kea could see

169

his dark eyes glisten with pride. Yes, she decided, he loved these people.

He motioned Carmen forward, and spoke to her in Spanish, obviously saying something about Maria. Carmen raised her hand and traced Maria's face with it, touching several fine scars on the woman's cheeks and neck. She seemed in awe at first, and then she looked at Kea as if to confirm whatever Rafe had told her. Since Kea had understood very little of Rafe's words, she could only gaze at the child blankly. Señora Deluca stepped forward to verify the tale, whatever it was, and Carmen's face was wreathed in smiles.

"Please," Señora Deluca said to Kea, "please be seated at the table. Make my house your house."

"Thank you," Kea replied, and she sat down in the chair indicated. Once she had been seated, all the others joined her.

Lunch was chaotic, at best, with so many people eating, even though the well-used table was long and seated many. Antonio Deluca presided over the head of the table, and Kea soon discovered that he spoke a mixture of English, Spanish and Italian. The children and grandchildren were all multilingual, and the result was highly entertaining.

Despite their frazzled and weary appearance, the Deluca parents were jovial and full of life. They obviously loved being able to share the meal with their offspring, and though Rafe, Kea, and Carmen were served first, throughout the meal there were urgings of, "Eat some of this, try that," for all the participants. Much to Carmen's delight there were enchiladas, eggs, and huge bowls of beans and rice.

Kea was unable to miss the special bond between Rafe and Maria, and she wondered why this sister was the chosen one out of so many. Had it something to do with

170

the scars on Maria's face and neck, or was Kea being overly imaginative?

The meal ended with sweet bread covered with syrup, and all too quickly, in spite of Señora Deluca's pleas for them to stay, Rafe, Kea, and Carmen were again en route to the Mexican interior. The border requirements were handled smoothly and quickly by Rafe, and the threesome were soon traveling along isolated Mexican roads that seemed to stretch and wind aimlessly around the countryside. As the hours wore on, Kea searched for the right time to ask Rafe some of the many questions on her mind. Glancing back into the rear seat, she saw that Carmen had curled up in a ball with Mickey and was fast asleep. She smiled at the girl; this all had been quite an adventure for her. A scene of Carmen caressing Maria's face flashed into her mind, and she turned to Rafe again. Suddenly she realized that she knew nothing about him—his past, his griefs, the force that drove him to do the things he did. She had seen only one side of him before, and it had taken the shock of his family to make her realize how complex he was. She sensed that he had never taken her to meet his family because he had felt that she wouldn't understand. Now she wanted to desperately.

"I couldn't help but notice Maria's scars," she said tentatively. "How was she injured?"

Rafe glanced at her, and in that brief moment Kea saw that his eyes had darkened with shadows of the past. There was a long pause before he responded, and Kea was very much afraid that she had stepped in where she had no business treading. She felt sure that he wasn't even going to acknowledge her question, but finally he did.

"Maria was scalded when she was just a little girl," he said very quietly, as though the memory still pained him. "She pulled a pot of boiling water off the stove onto her head."

"Oh, how terrible," Kea murmured, disturbed by the

story. No wonder the woman still bore scars, and Kea suspected she was very fortunate at that, for they were hardly noticeable. Rafe fell silent again, but Kea couldn't leave the subject alone. She longed to know more about him, about his family now that she had met them, so that she could understand Rafe better.

"Did you become a plastic surgeon because of Maria?" she asked softly.

When Rafe looked at her again, his dark eyes were veiled, and Kea was sure he resented this intrusion into his past, but she couldn't let it alone. She had to know and gradually he began to tell her.

"Yes. Maria was tormented by the neighborhood children. We had neither the money or the knowledge to know what to do for her. I couldn't stand to see her weep." The words were spoken with such anguish that Kea realized he still harbored resentment because of his sister's pain, and the knowledge gave her a much-needed clue to his dedication to the injured and maimed.

"I was fourteen at the time. I heard about a plastic surgeon in the city who worked miracles, and naively, I went to see him to get a miracle for my sister. Much to my astonishment, he gave me one."

Rafe seemed to retreat somewhere into his memories, and Kea asked another question before she lost him entirely to the past. "Is Antonio your natural father? You favor him remarkably."

Again the pause, and still Kea couldn't hold back her questions. "Is he your stepfather?" Years of questioning stood her in good stead now, and Rafe slowly opened up to her with the information she needed to hear.

"No, he's my natural father. I was adopted by Hadley Jordan, the plastic surgeon who worked on Maria. He gave me a new life. He taught me so much." His dark eyes met Kea's briefly. "I wish you could have interviewed him, Kea. He was the most remarkable man I've ever known. He gave so generously and he cared so deeply. He's dead now, but he lived long enough to tell me he was proud of me. His words have meant more to me than any I've ever heard."

Now it was Kea's turn to be at a loss for words. In all the years she had known Rafe, in all the times she had questioned him, and interviewed him, she had never even suspected that he was adopted. She felt that he had just shared something precious with her, and she was deeply moved. She had never felt closer to him than she did at that moment, and she wanted to touch him, to move nearer to him, but she didn't dare.

How she wished he had shared some of his past with her sooner; she could have understood him so much better. Perhaps it would have changed her life to have known then what she knew now. But Rafe had chosen not to disclose anything so personal and private.

And perhaps he had been right, she admitted. Maybe she wouldn't have understood any better then. How selfish she had been to want him all to herself!

Suddenly she understood a great deal that had previously eluded her. She could see now why he went around the world doing good; he was trying to repay a debt to Dr. Jordan—and it was a wondrous and admirable thing that he was doing.

"I wish I could have talked with your Dr. Jordan too," she finally murmured. "I'm sure he was very special." She gazed solemnly at Rafe, and her words came unbidden. "You're very special too, Rafe. I know that Dr. Jordan would be tremendously proud of you today. You give hope and life to people who might otherwise live out their days in private torment and desperation."

Rafe's eyes met hers again, and for a short, special time Kea was sure that they looked into each other's souls. And they both understood. It was a rare and naked moment. But they both knew, too, that it did not alter the past, and it could not change the future. They had missed this moment when they had belonged to each other. That couldn't be changed now. There had been too much water over the dam, too much of each other spilled and stripped away.

They both were lost to their separate thoughts, and as the miles wore on, Kea found her own eyes growing heavy. She was still recovering from her traumas, and, overwhelmed by all she had learned about Rafe, at last she gave in to the drowsiness the miles and the heavy meal had wrought. Following Carmen's example, she closed her eyes and edged into a remarkably pleasant and dreamless sleep.

As Rafe gazed over at the sleeping woman beside him, he found it painfully ironic that only after he had lost her had he been willing to share the private side of himself. He smiled bitterly; before he had been too afraid that she would be disappointed in him if she discovered his weaknesses—his family, the fact that he was adopted, his obsession with repaying the debt to Dr. Jordan. Then, too, he had figured that it wouldn't matter in the long run; she would never be his. Now he knew it for a fact. And still he had wanted her to understand him. He glanced at her again, seeing how uncomfortable she must be with her head thrown back on the seat, and he was unable to resist having her near him, for just a short time.

When Kea awoke some time later, she was surprised to find her head nestled against Rafe's shoulder, his hand gently caressing the side of her face. A warmth washed over her, and she longed to hold his hand against her lips and kiss it, but she didn't. She felt so secure and cared for that she was reluctant to let him know she had awakened. It seemed so right, somehow, that she should be here. And for one wild magic moment she felt that this was where she belonged—where she had always belonged. But she knew she was only fooling herself; what she had learned about Rafe changed nothing, except to make her love him more.

A contented sigh betrayed her, and she was disappointed when Rafe put his hand back on the wheel, presumably to maneuver a sharp turn. Moving a little away from him, Kea yawned and pretended to be waking for the first time.

"How was your rest?" he asked her, his eyes unreadable when they met hers.

"It was wonderful," Kea murmured, her voice still thick with sleep. "Are you tired? Would you like me to drive for a while?"

He shook his head. "No, I don't think so." He laughed a little. "I never did trust your driving, remember?"

Kea giggled. Once when she had been driving, she had been so excited about a guest she had interviewed that she had almost rear-ended another car. Rafe had never forgotten, and he hadn't let her forget either.

"Now that you mention it, I can't say that I blame you," she agreed, loving the shared laughter and wanting to make the most of it. "However, there are so few cars on this road that I don't think we're in danger of a repeat performance. Besides, you're the only person I've interviewed recently."

He smiled and she knew he was remembering that moment earlier when they had understood each other so well. "You haven't lost your technique. Did you learn anything?"

She nodded. "Far more than I ever thought possible." She kept her eyes on the highway, and she nervously clasped her hands together. "Why didn't you ever tell me about your family and your past before?"

He shrugged with pretended carelessness, but Kea saw his hands tighten on the wheel. She knew he wasn't comfortable with the subject, but she had to explore it as far as she could, for she was afraid she would never have another chance. "What would it have mattered?" he asked.

"A good point," she conceded with some bitterness. It wouldn't have mattered, she was reminded, for he never had intended to make her a permanent part of his life. His comment caused her to lapse into introspection, and it wasn't until minutes later that he spoke again.

"You intend to go back into television if you can, don't you?"

Kea was surprised by the unexpected question. What had made him ask that now? For a while it had seemed to her that the future had become unimportant, especially since her discoveries about him. The problems of the past were nothing compared to the frustration, the agony of sitting so close to Rafe and knowing he might as well be miles away.

But now he had brought the memory of her other troubles rushing back, and she found that she was more determined than ever to succeed in the one thing she knew best. "I don't just *intend* to get my job back, I *will* get it back!" Her eyes glittered with silver fire, and she was startled by the fierceness of her response. "I have to," she added with quiet conviction.

Rafe nodded, but didn't remark on her announcement. He had expected no less, despite the changes in her that were surfacing. However, he admitted to himself, he had hoped things would be different this time. And he wondered if she knew what a battle she had ahead of her. Even as she sat so closely by his side, learning about his world, seeing him as never before, he knew that he was losing her again. She needed him now to get over the most immediate hurdle, and she would need him—briefly—in the future to revise her scars. Then she would be ready to go back to her world, and he would be left to his. Nothing would have changed. Not really. Except that for one brief moment she had brightened his world again. But when she left it, it would be darker than ever before. And she would leave behind her fresh and painful scars. Scars that no doctor could ever alter.

Neither of them spoke again until Rafe turned off the main road into a sleepy little Mexican town filled with an assortment of adobe houses with red-tiled roofs.

"We'll have dinner here," Rafe said, breaking into Kea's reverie. "I know a family who will feed us."

He drove down a narrow dirt road and turned into the barren yard of a house where several small children were playing out in the dirt with an old cart and a piece of rope. They looked up curiously as the station wagon approached, and suddenly one of the little boys ran toward the vehicle, calling out, "¡Médico! ¡Médico!"

Smiling broadly, Rafe stepped outside and lifted the gleeful child high into the air. "Como está usted, Armando?" he asked, giving the boy a playful shake before he put him on the ground.

"Bien," the boy replied, grinning from ear to ear.

"I once operated on him," he explained matter-of-factly, "and his family couldn't afford the surgery."

The boy scurried in through the open door of the house, calling, "Mama! Mama!"

Carmen was stirring from her deep sleep in the backseat, and seeing that she was perspiring in the helmet, Rafe unstrapped it. When he had examined her ear, he removed the helmet, apparently explaining to Carmen that she could leave it off for a while. The sleepy girl murmured, "Gracias," and she stumbled from the car to gaze around.

A tall, handsome Mexican woman came out of the house, drying her hands on a plain white apron. She spoke softly and swiftly in Spanish and then smiled at Kea and Carmen when Rafe introduced them.

"¡Adelante!" she said warmly, indicating the open doorway.

The children were gazing at Carmen with interest. Her

newly formed ear was clearly visible now without the helmet, for her hair had been plaited into a single braid. The girl glanced apprehensively at Rafe, probably expecting to be tormented, and when the others merely invited her to join them in their play, she looked as if she could hardly believe it. Getting used to not being the target of cruel comments was going to take some time. She happily went over to join them while Kea and Rafe followed the woman into the building.

The house was quite simple and the furnishings humble, but the warmth of the family quickly made Kea forget how poor they were. The table was set and all the children were summoned inside. The meal consisted of large triangular tamales wrapped in green corn leaves called *corundas,* fried pork, sour cream, tender pieces of boiled corn, and beans.

Kea accepted a beer, and Rafe had a drink called *pulque,* made from the maguey plant. There was much laughter and joking, some of which Kea could understand without words or with her limited Spanish, and some Rafe explained. The air was stifling with the summer heat, and the travelers welcomed the liquid refreshments.

After the meal the children scampered back outside to play in the last rays of daylight, and the adults lingered over the remains of the food, drinking and talking as the day slowly slipped into night. The small, cramped house afforded little in the way of coolness despite its adobe walls, but as the sun went down, a tiny breeze danced in through the open door and windows. Kea felt as if she had been taken back in time in this house with these people. Here there were none of the pressures—or conveniences— she had always had.

She was surprised when Rafe spoke to the hosts, then turned to her. "I'm going to visit with some old friends for a little while. Would you like to come? Carmen is going to stay here."

"Yes, I would like to," she answered, pleased that he had asked her. She thanked her hosts for their hospitality in her broken Spanish, then she and Rafe excused themselves.

"Armando's parents are very nice. I like them," she said, seeking conversation as she and Rafe walked up the street.

"Yes," he replied. "I would have preferred to stay with my friends, but these people have a lot of pride and they want to do something to repay me for treating their nephew. It would be wrong of me to refuse their hospitality."

"Yes, I'm sure it would," she agreed.

The house they went to was much nicer than Armando's, and Kea gazed at it with interest. There was a note on the door, and she suspected before Rafe read it that it was for him since he didn't bother to knock on the door.

"That's too bad," he murmured. "They've gone to another town to see a sick relative. However, I know where a door key is hidden, and they insist that we go in and sample the treat the Señora has left for us." He smiled at her. "How can we refuse?"

Kea laughed. She had a feeling that she would gain considerable weight if the entire trip went like this. Everywhere they had stopped, people had prepared food for them. "How can we?" she repeated, stepping inside when Rafe had opened the door.

The house was very attractively decorated with baskets and rugs, the effect being cozy and comfortable, and Kea felt right at home as Rafe led her to the kitchen where the Señora had left a beautiful sponge cake and a coffee pot and a can of coffee.

"This was a wonderful idea," Kea told Rafe. "That cake looks delicious, and I could use a good cup of coffee."

"Manuel and Pila are marvelous. I'm sorry you didn't get to meet them. Pila's a fantastic cook, and I can tell you

179

the *bizcocho*—the sponge cake—*will be* delicious. I'll make the coffee, you serve the cake," he suggested.

Kea smiled at him as he put on coffee water and then she opened a cupboard to hunt for dishes. When she reached for the dessert plates, a bowl suddenly shifted from its precarious perch and plunged toward her. "Oh!" she cried in alarm, trying desperately to keep it from crashing to the floor.

Rafe spun around and bent down to catch the heavy piece of pottery just as it slipped through Kea's fingers. He grinned triumphantly as he managed to avert breakage just in the nick of time.

Kea reached out to touch his arm as he set the bowl on the counter. "Thank heavens," she exclaimed. "I don't want to break the Señora's dishes." She was laughing in relief, but when her eyes met Rafe's, she saw his expression change from laughter to something more serious.

Abruptly, he drew her into his arms and his mouth claimed hers in a hungry kiss. Kea's lips automatically parted under the pressure of his, and she moaned in sweet surrender, giving in to him as if it were the most natural thing in the world.

His arms locked around her, pressing her so close to him that she thought he intended to become one with her forever, but she didn't object. Arching her back, she moved closer to him, loving the feel of his hard body against hers. His kiss intensified; his mouth moved passionately against hers. And Kea met the fire in his kiss, her lips burning with her eagerness. She was hungry to know the power of his touch after being so near, yet so far these past few days.

She had desired him with everything in her since the night he had claimed her in the pool, and she would not deny herself the pleasure once again, no matter the outcome or its effect on the future. She wanted him. She loved him. She needed him as a bird needs the freedom of the

180

sky and the food of the earth. He was all that had ever been or would ever be to her, and this moment was all that meant anything.

Whisking her up in his arms, Rafe strode to a bedroom, his mouth playing wildly over Kea's and down her throat, scattering feverish kisses and sending her temperature soaring. There was an urgency about him that made her senses whirl and her body flush with mounting desire. He lay her down on the bed and then began to take off his jeans. Kea didn't wait for him to help her undress. Their eyes locked as they took off their clothing, and Kea held out her arms to Rafe when he walked toward her. As he lowered his lean, muscled body to her soft curves, her heart beat in wild anticipation.

He invaded her mouth as a starving man would, plundering, thirsty, greedy, taking what he wanted, what he needed from her, and his possessiveness sent rivers of thrills racing through Kea's blood. Opening her mouth wider, she received his searching tongue, meeting it with her own to taste and tease. Rafe's hands left burning circles over her body as they explored and embraced, touching, caressing everywhere, branding her with his eagerness.

When Kea was sure she would burn up from his fire, he placed his hands beneath her hips and made her his as only Rafe could do. She felt wave after wave of pleasure assault her body until she was lost in the glorious wonder of his loving.

Somewhere beyond the here and now, in another time and place, a place of incomparable ecstasy and joy, Kea let her mind and soul and body become one with Rafe's as their enchantment and fulfillment in each other transcended the pain and disappointment of the world and the past. He was hers, and she was his—if only for this splendid moment.

Matching perfectly in movement, their bodies merged

with an ancient and powerful rhythm that took them endlessly on that exquisite journey filled with the provocatively tantalizing pleasures of flesh and spirit.

"*Now*, Kea," Rafe whispered urgently, arching over her. "Come fly with me."

"Yes," she cried breathlessly. "Yes," as she was borne away by his magic. And, at last, she was set free once again—free as she could only be in the arms of the man she loved.

When sanity returned, Rafe and Kea lay side by side, letting the last waves of their strong loving subside into warm contentment. Rafe stroked Kea's skin with sensitive fingertips, and when she clasped his fingers to her lips, he raised himself up on his elbow to gaze into her eyes in the semidarkness.

Kea was sure Rafe was as surprised as she by their sudden all-consuming passion; he had no more expected it than she, and now both seemed a little embarrassed. Kea certainly hadn't intended to let him make love to her again, and she hadn't thought he had wanted to. It was just that she couldn't seem to stay out of his arms, no matter how fiercely she promised her heart that she would guard it from more pain.

Rafe was the one to speak finally. "We should be getting back," he said in a thick voice. "I have to put Carmen's helmet back on so that she can go to bed. We'll get an early start tomorrow."

Kea wasn't sorry that she had given herself to him, but she couldn't stop the disappointment she felt at his words. He had said nothing about them, about what had happened between them, and she made herself speak as rationally as he. "Yes, it's late."

He lay by her side for another few minutes, then he eased off the bed and began to dress. Kea was glad the only light in the room came from the hall; she didn't want Rafe to see her face right now. She dressed as quickly as he and they were soon on their way, remembering only at the last minute to turn off the coffee water, which had almost boiled away.

Kea fleetingly wondered what the Señora would say about her cake being uncut, but perhaps she would think they hadn't been able to come by at all. They hadn't used any coffee, and they had put the coffee pot back where they had found it.

When they reached Armando's house, Carmen was sent for, and after Rafe had again put on her protective helmet, she was bedded down in a room with two other girls on a simple straw pallet.

A moment of embarrassment came when the Señora directed Rafe and Kea to another bedroom. Obviously it was her own, and Rafe looked at Kea for a brief time before he shook his head.

"No, *gracias*," he murmured. He explained that Kea would sleep with the girls, and he would sleep with the family's sons.

The woman glanced from one to the other, and Kea blushed, sure the woman could see the glow of love still on her cheeks. Even Kea understood the woman's disbelieving question when she asked it. "*¿Ella no es su esposa?*"

Kea expected to see amusement in Rafe's eyes, but to her chagrin, when she laughed gently at the mistake, he looked at her with what she could only describe as regret.

"*No,*" he said firmly, "*no es mi esposa.*"

The embarrassed hostess laughed with Kea about the incident and directed her back to the room where Carmen was sleeping. Kea glanced at Rafe once and saw that he was staring after her, the memory of their lovemaking burning in his eyes. And his gaze was somehow accusing. She didn't understand his anger; she could only think that he was sorry he had succumbed to her loving once again. Hurt, she directed her attention to the woman with her, and she was soon dressed in her nightgown and had settled down on a pallet. Much to her amazement, though the pallet was hard, the room was stuffy, and her thoughts of Rafe confusing, she was quickly overtaken by sleep. Her last memory was that of Rafe's deep, low voice as he talked with the host of the house.

The morning dawned much too early as Carmen and Kea roused to the hostess's call to breakfast. They washed up in the small bathroom, then donned the day's clothing and went in to eat. There were eggs, sausage, and tortillas with butter, and thick mugs of steaming coffee to help awaken them. Most of the children were still sleeping, so there was little fanfare as the three travelers got underway.

The morning was already warm, and Rafe allowed Carmen to go without the helmet. He had decided she would only need to wear it when she slept at night; the girl was so pleased that she grinned constantly and smoothed back her hair, as if she had had forgotten what it felt like to be free of her burden.

Kea offered to drive again, but Rafe refused. She saw that he was subdued this morning, and again she wondered if he was regretting their intimacy last night. The thought haunted her and silence lay heavy in the car. Soon Carmen lapsed into sleep, and Kea followed suit to escape the thoughts that plagued her. How could Rafe regret their lovemaking when it had been so splendid, so fulfilling? Or had it only been so for her? Her dreams were filled with the man at her side, and she couldn't know that his mind was filled with dreams of her.

Rafe glanced back in the rearview mirror and saw that Carmen had stretched out in the backseat and was sleeping soundly. He smiled at the vision of the small girl in her new blue shorts and white top. She looked like any other contented child now, and he was pleased that he had been able to share this small part of her life. When his gaze returned to the woman at his side and he saw that her head had fallen forward on her chest in her sleep, he was unable to resist gently drawing her against him so that she could sleep on his shoulder. She smelled so sweet and clean. Her nearness caused his heart to race this morning, and he was reminded of the incident in the house last night.

For a single crazy moment he had been tempted to accept the host's and hostess's bedroom so that he could spend the night with Kea by his side. It had been a crazy and unrealistic thought, but it had occurred to him all the same. He had just made love to her in a wild moment of passion, it was true, and he shouldn't have been that weak, but he had still been hungry for more. He had wanted to lie beside her hour after hour, to find her in his bed when he awoke.

But she had laughed at the hostess's offer. And her laughter had reminded him that she was not his wife. She had chosen to give Roxwell Mason that priviledge. And that was as it should have been, he reminded himself brutally, but it didn't make the pain any less.

He sighed tiredly; being with her day and night was driving him a little crazy, and he would be glad when they arrived at their destination so that he could get some breathing space. Her constant nearness drove him to the brink of madness.

He glanced at her again as she slept peacefully on his shoulder. Although the morning was warm, he had not yet turned the air conditioning on. The windows were open and a breeze danced across Kea, ruffling her pale blue blouse, and Rafe's gaze was drawn to her high, full breasts, outlined now by the thin material. He relished the sight of her long legs displayed in the sky-blue culottes she wore.

When the breeze lightly kissed her cheek, gently teasing her red hair, Rafe studied her features. He knew that her beauty would always be marred by the scars that surrounded her right eye, and his heart contracted in sympathy over the battle she would have to fight to regain her job. He hoped she succeeded, even though it would mean leaving him behind again. For although her celebrity lifestyle had kept them apart, he knew she would not feel whole and happy if she had to give it up. Just as he could not be happy if he gave up his work here in Mexico and all over the world. Kea was lost to him now as surely as she had been the day Roxwell Mason had made her his wife.

At mid-morning he pulled off the main road for a rest stop at a small café. They all decided on ice cream and although it began to melt the moment they stepped back out in the relentless sun, it was refreshing. Kea laughed at Rafe when a glob of ice cream dripped onto his white shirt, and he got his revenge when hers suddenly fell away from the stick and landed on her foot.

"Oh, Rafe," she moaned, staring down at the sticky mess coating her shoe and toes. "Look at this."

"If I'd known you were going to throw it away, I wouldn't have bought it for you," he teased.

"It melted around the stick and you know it," she cried.

He only laughed at her. "Go clean up and let's be on our way."

While she and Carmen went back into the building to wash with wet cloths, Rafe waited outside, enjoying the freedom from the confining car. Kea was eager to return to its air-conditioned comfort, and she hurried toward it the minute she walked back into the heat.

"Hey, señora," Rafe teased, "you'd better get used to this sun. You're going to be seeing a lot of it."

Kea made a face at him and climbed into the car, grateful that the earlier tension of the day had dissipated. Once again they were on their way. They stopped briefly in a nameless little village where Rafe checked on a former patient, and Kea began to realize how many people he had helped. And it must have been the same in other countries. What a legacy this man had left for the world.

As they grew nearer Carmen's town, the girl grew increasingly restless. The roads, which had never been very smooth, became rougher as they completed the last leg of their journey.

The countryside was changing a little, but the buildings looked like those in places they had passed along the way. As they approached the town, Kea saw the familiar small houses with tin roofs, and as they traveled closer, she saw rows of adobe houses with tile roofs, and pretty churches and shops lining cobblestone streets. Brightly colored plants bloomed in the hot sun, and animals roamed freely by the side of the road. An old man was selling tamales on the street corner, and a marketplace was filled with people shopping for an assortment of fruits and vegetables.

Carmen's house, Kea was relieved to see, was somewhere in between the shacks they had passed and the more attractive homes. She had been afraid that Carmen lived in utter poverty, and she had thought she wouldn't be able to bear the girl's misfortune had that been the case.

White garments fluttered halfheartedly in the heat on a line in the front yard, and a number of chairs lined a stone patio. The house was small, but neat. As though word had spread before them, several people were already gathering in front of the building, and with the appearance of the station wagon the occupants of the house spilled out, waving their hands excitedly and chattering rapidly in Spanish.

"*¡Madre! ¡Padre!*" Carmen called out, scrambling out of the car before Rafe had managed to park it.

The objects of Carmen's affection stopped dead still at the sound of their daughter's voice, and Kea was reminded that the girl hadn't spoken for two years. The entire crowd was hushed for a moment, then there arose a humming like the droning of bees as they discussed the miracle that had occurred. Some of the women were crossing themselves, and Carmen's mother burst into tears as she hugged her child.

Rafe opened the door for Kea, then stood back and waited for the reunion to play itself out. Kea met his eyes, and they smiled proudly at each other, both pleased to have been a part of Carmen's recovery. The group surged forward, engulfing the girl and her mother as they boldly examined Carmen's new ear and marveled at it. There were a lot of wide-eyed stares and low, amazed voices before someone sent up a cheer, and Carmen was lifted up onto her father's shoulders.

Suddenly Rafe became the center of attention as the crowd gathered around him with good wishes and questions. When the people had satisfied their curiosity and given their praise, they finally began to drift away, leaving Carmen and her family alone. Rafe took the opportunity to make the introductions. Kea, caught up in the gaiety and joy of the moment, smiled as she walked by Rafe's side onto the Mendoza patio.

She felt as if she, too, were coming home, and she knew that she was as much a part of the celebration as were Rafe and Carmen. She was overwhelmed by the affection and good wishes of these people who did not know her. They chattered happily, and though she couldn't understand a word, she felt their warmth and genuine liking and returned it with her own wide smile.

Her eyes glistened with pleasure when Rafe touched her arm, and she looked up to meet his intent gaze. Their eyes met and locked for an instant and a sense of quiet triumph passed between them. They both knew they had helped bring this happy reunion about, and somehow the knowledge drew them together, forging another fragile bond between them.

Kea smiled and Rafe answered her with a smile of his own, and she knew that for this moment alone she was glad she had come to Mexico. This was her own little miracle, as real and wonderful as the sound of Carmen's laughing voice.

And then a new voice drifted through the relatives still admiring Carmen, and Kea looked up to find Trena coming toward them. Her dark eyes held stormy questions, but she could not disguise her joy at seeing Rafe again.

Leaving Kea to stand as if turned to stone, Rafe went to embrace his nurse fondly. Kea closed her eyes for a moment, trying to erase the image from her memory. She had forgotten Trena was coming to join them, but her arrival had brought the bitter realities of Kea's life rushing back to her. And the oncoming tide of painful thoughts washed away that single magic instant of wonder she had shared with Rafe as if it had never been.

CHAPTER TEN

Kea took a deep breath and forced the angry thoughts from her mind. She must not let them see how shaken she was. Averting her eyes, she found herself gazing at a young Mexican standing near her.

"Hello," he said, extending his hand. "I'm Joe, the anesthetist. You must be Kea."

Somehow she managed to smile at him. "Yes." She shook his hand firmly. "It's nice to meet you. I'm glad to find someone else who can speak English so I'll know what's going on."

He smiled, showing very white teeth. "Before we leave here, you'll be speaking Spanish like a native."

She laughed lightly. "I doubt it," she said, but she liked his warmth. She needed a friend just now. He was very young, hardly more than twenty-five, she guessed, stocky and attractive with dark brown hair and almost black eyes.

"Is there a hospital here?" Kea asked, wanting desperately to make conversation so that she wouldn't have to concentrate on Trena and Rafe.

Joe nodded. "A reasonable facsimile, old and obsolete, to be sure, but a hospital all the same."

Glancing around, Kea saw that there were other people now who had arrived at the Mendoza home. "Carmen has a lot of friends," she commented.

Joe looked out over the group assembling. "Most of

these are strangers who have heard about the doctor. They've come, hoping that he will heal their wounds."

Before Kea could comment, Rafe came back to her side, shook hands with Joe, and ushered her forward. They were just stepping into the house when a young woman, not more than seventeen or eighteen, rushed up behind Rafe and tugged at his shirt. She had a small boy in her arms, and when Kea looked at the child, clad only in a piece of white cloth, her heart went out to the mother and child. The boy had a cleft lip and palate.

"Por favor, Médico," the young woman pleaded, *"¿Puede curar mi niño?"*

Kea watched in admiration as Rafe tenderly took the child from the woman's arms and gazed into his face. The boy obligingly began to cry and Rafe examined his mouth with a finger.

"Mañana," Rafe told her. *"Haré lo que puedo hacer."*

Others tried to reach out to him, but Carmen's father spoke sharply to them and they fell back from the door amid disappointed sighs, their eyes full of sorrow.

At the door Rafe turned back and gently instructed them to go to the hospital the next day where he would see them all eventually. Kea was so moved by his compassion that she felt like weeping. Rafe was like a god to these people; he had the power to set their worlds right again to some degree, and they clearly had the faith that he would do so.

A new wave of affection for him washed over Kea, and it pained her heart to realize that her love for him was even stronger now. If he had just once taken her to a place like this in the three years they had been together, perhaps she never would have ruined her life as she had, or found herself in the position she was in today.

She saw how humble Rafe was, embarrassed, in fact, in the face of all the adulation, and she was impressed by the kind of man he was. He gave so much of himself, and she

191

had so selfishly wanted him all for her own. She marveled that he had made as much time for her and her frivolous pursuits as he had. For truly his heart was here with these people and others like them. They needed him and he answered their need. This was his life's work, his very essence; Kea saw it in his eyes, in the way he moved among the people, and her heart wept because she hadn't known.

When she looked over at Trena, standing at Rafe's other side, Kea realized that the other woman *had* known, had always understood Rafe's need to treat the unfortunate people of the world. While Kea herself had been ignorant, Trena had shared Rafe's most precious secret. And that was what hurt most of all.

Carmen's parents led them all inside, and Kea saw that they had prepared a feast, with the help of other townspeople, she suspected. There were fresh fruit and vegetables, tamales, enchiladas, beans, rice, pork chops, and bottled orange drink, which had been obtained especially for the Americans.

The meal proved to be a pleasant time for all; Kea enjoyed Carmen's parents, and to her chagrin she even enjoyed talking with Trena. But she couldn't forget what the other woman's presence meant. And Trena herself seemed restless, as if her thoughts would not let her be still. Several times she looked at Kea with a question in her dark eyes, but apparently she could not bring herself to ask it.

Kea was glad. She had seen the way the nurse's gaze sought Rafe time and again. Each time Rafe sensed Trena looking at him, he glanced up and smiled, and each smile was like the twist of a knife in Kea's heart. She was grateful that Joe sat beside her, chatting gaily with everyone. Often he translated the humerous stories for her, and though at first she had to force herself to laugh, soon the food and the warmth of the people made her amusement genuine.

When all had finished eating, Carmen was sent to bed to rest after all the commotion. Kea and Trena offered to do the dishes, but the hosts wouldn't hear of it.

Kea turned to gaze out a window and saw that night was falling on the town, which had few lights to hold back the darkness. After the long ride and finally reaching her destination, she was eager to explore the area. She was too excited to feel like resting, and her emotions were turbulent. It was still almost unbearably hot, although the sun had been driven down by the descending darkness, and she unconsciously fanned herself with her hand.

"Too warm?" Rafe asked.

Kea met his eyes across the expanse of the table. "No, not really," she murmured, not wanting her hosts to think she was uncomfortable.

"We could go for a walk if you're interested," he said.

Kea's breath caught in her throat as she remembered how their walk to Rafe's friends' house last night had ended, but she nodded, "That would be fine."

Standing up, they excused themselves to the others, and Kea caught Trena's eyes briefly; she quickly looked away when she saw the naked pain in the other woman's gaze. She was ashamed for herself and for Trena when she saw how much in love with Rafe the woman was. But then so was she. And she saw little hope for either of them.

"Let's walk down by the river," Rafe suggested when they were outside. "It's almost dark, and no one will bother us there."

"Where is it?" Kea asked, delighted with the idea, but clearly thinking he had lost his mind. The town was hot, dry, and dusty, and she hadn't seen any sign of water anywhere. Despite the civilization, the town was only a step away from the desert.

"At the edge of town," he explained. "It's a source of

great pleasure to these people. A few of the houses still don't have running water in them, and those families depend heavily on the river."

"How do these people make a living?" she asked.

"This once was a town noted for its copper, but now the people do whatever they can to exist—a little farming when they can irrigate with river water, and raising cattle. The mine is still being worked, but it hardly yields any precious minerals these days."

Kea considered the narrow streets and assortment of houses as she and Rafe worked their way through the town. "Why don't the people move?" she asked.

"And go where?" he returned realistically. "Times are bad in Mexico now. Here at least the people have their homes and family and land. They get by. That's all most of them ask. Their families have been here for scores of years."

"I see," Kea murmured, and she reminded herself that this wasn't the fast-paced, money-conscious world she inhabited. The town was settling in for the evening, and the smell of peppers and spices filled the air with a rich aroma. Most of the streets were deserted, but Kea saw an occasional adult or child as they walked along.

"How does a town this size rate a hospital?" she asked.

"It was built when the mine was booming."

"Thank God for small favors," she murmured.

At last they came to the river, a wide, winding oasis in the middle of a desert. Trees clung to the sandy banks, seeking water for their thirsty roots, and shading sections of the river as it whispered over rocks and gurgled nonsense to the pebbles and stones. Some children were playing nearby, and Kea and Rafe walked down farther to find a more secluded spot.

They found a place on the sandy bank and sat down, both pretending to be absorbed in the water running so

194

close to them. Kea used the moment to slip off her sandal, and Rafe looked at her with concern.

"Is your ankle hurting?"

She shook her head. "No, I think I have a blister. These are new sandals."

Reaching down, Rafe raised her foot so that he could examine her heel, and as he bent over her, Kea had the strongest urge to run her fingers through his hair.

"Yes, a small one," he agreed. "When we get back, I'll give you some ointment for it." He looked up into her eyes as he freed her foot, and for a moment time stood still for her.

Then Rafe settled back against a tree trunk and spoke, shattering the moment. "What do you think of Mexico?" he asked, his eyes glowing curiously in the dusk. "It's a world apart from what you've always known, isn't it?"

She nodded. "Life here seems so much more urgent, and yet the pace is slower," she mused. Suddenly she was shy with him, unable to meet his eyes, uncertain why he had brought her here and how she was expected to respond. Did he really care what she thought about these people? About him? Last night he had made love to her, and today he had seemed to regret it. She didn't know what to think now.

"The people need so much," he commented, and Kea could still feel his dark gaze burning into her. "Things are bad all over Mexico right now. The world situation changed right when the government thought they had a godsend with their oil discoveries. It has affected everyone."

"Yes," Kea acknowledged softly, "I'm sure it has."

"But the people are still basically happy," Rafe said. "They still feel they have much to be thankful for. They have houses, and the river still flows."

Kea looked at the reds and pinks of the evening sky as

the sun slowly sank into the earth. "This area is beautiful," she said.

"Yes," he agreed. "Very beautiful." But as he looked at Kea, he was sure nothing was more beautiful than she. Never had he expected to be sharing this time with her in this place. Mesmerized by her presence and the unreality of the moment, he struggled to resist asking the question that had haunted him so relentlessly. He did not know what had brought it to mind now, but he needed to know the answer. He wanted to know if she had loved Roxwell very much, but he asked a different question instead.

His voice softened. "How are you adjusting to Roxwell's death?" His eyes were unreadable in the falling darkness. He ached to ask her how much it had hurt her, and how much she had cared for Jon, and how many other men she had known, but he didn't. He wanted to talk about the past, the reasons that had driven them apart, but he knew he had no right. Kea had made her decision long ago.

Here in the country he loved as much as his own, by the river he had come to treasure in recent years, alone with the woman he loved, he longed to empty his heart of the questions that had plagued him for so many tormenting months.

Suddenly he realized a painful truth: He had wanted her to come here with him in the hope that she would understand him better, perhaps even see that she had once cared for him, and maybe give him a chance to be a part of her new future.

The silence hung heavy between them until the quiet murmurings of the water seemed to turn into a wild roaring. Kea wondered if Rafe were asking for himself, or was this more of his concern for her mental health—the concern of a doctor? She didn't want to talk about Roxwell. She was trying very hard to forget, and so far it had been impossible. Shrugging in the darkness with a carelessness

196

she was far from feeling, she replied, "It's very difficult for me."

Rafe realized when she gave the answer that he hadn't wanted to hear it. There was another pause, and she said, "I feel very guilty about his death."

"Why?"

"We had quarreled before the accident. Roxwell shouldn't have been at the controls of the plane under those circumstances."

Rafe was sorry he had begun this discussion, but he couldn't ignore her pain. "Was it the first time you had ever quarreled when he was piloting?" he made himself ask.

Kea shook her head, but Rafe couldn't see the motion. She thought of the many times she and Roxwell had battled high above the cities and fields, times when he had become much more angry than the final time. Times when he had become livid with rage because she wouldn't give up her career. "No."

"You weren't responsible for his death, Kea," he said softly.

This was the first time Kea had recalled that she and Roxwell *had* quarreled over matters he considered more serious. She realized suddenly that she had felt such intense guilt this time because Roxwell had told her about his mistress, and she had known then that her marriage was over.

But she hadn't told him that. They had fought, but he had shrugged off her objections to his mistress as if she were out of her mind to expect him to give the woman up. Kea fell silent again, and there in the darkness by Rafe's side, she finally admitted to herself that part of the guilt she felt over Roxwell's death was because she had never stopped loving Rafe, had never really given herself completely to her husband, for her heart had still belonged to another man.

Suddenly she was unable to hold back the tears that unexpectedly filled her eyes. Everything had gone so wrong. The tears slipped down her cheeks and she began to sob softly.

Hearing her heartache, Rafe drew her into his arms and held her to his chest. The woman he loved was crying for another man, and he couldn't bear to hear her grieve for another lover when he loved her so desperately himself.

But still he held her, because he knew she needed him. He sensed that she was just now releasing the burden of pain that had rested inside her since the accident. He could no more turn away from her now than he could stop loving her altogether.

Rafe could feel her tears soaking into his shirt—violent, healing tears that would dim the edges of her agony just a little—and he felt suddenly as if this were where they both belonged, clinging together to share the misfortunes and triumphs of an uncertain world.

His arms circling her shoulders felt infinitely right, and when at last she lifted her head, his mouth sought hers in the darkness. Unthinkingly, Kea parted her lips in response, and the kiss she shared with Rafe was one of utmost tenderness, their lips touching gently and sweetly. When he drew away from her, Rafe brushed at the strands of hair that clung to Kea's damp face, then his fingers traced the trembling outline of her mouth.

His touch was light and soothing, and Kea held his hand to her mouth for a moment before Rafe lowered his head to trail kisses over her eyes and nose. When his mouth again found hers, she wrapped her arms around him, holding him close, savoring the precious moment.

Kea drew comfort from his soft, caressing kisses and warm lips as he tasted the salty outline of her mouth, spilling tiny kisses along it, kisses that reassured and demanded nothing in return. And Kea held Rafe so very near her heart, wishing that things were different between them, wishing that she had no past or future that didn't include him.

At last his kisses ceased, and for a moment longer he held her close, letting her rest her head on his shoulder. Then he announced the inevitable: "We should go back."

Kea stood up and brushed the sand from her clothes. She had learned something else from Rafe today, and she felt that the river was carrying away one of the burdens that had weighed so heavily on her soul: She wasn't to blame for Roxwell's death. He had had his mistress, and she had had Rafe. But she had cheated only in her heart, and no one had known.

They said nothing to each other as they made their way back to the Mendoza home in the scant brightness afforded by the streetlights and a remote and indifferent moon. Kea felt closer to Rafe than she ever had, but she knew that it would not alter the future—the sharing of their private and personal sorrows wouldn't bind them to tomorrow and yesterday had passed. She stared at the houses, wondering what the people who lived in them were like, if they were happy or sad, burdened down by their troubles, or loving each joyous day.

When they reached the Mendoza home, they found that their sleeping arrangements were much the same as they had been the previous night. Kea was to sleep in Carmen's tiny room, and she was grateful that she and Carmen would have it all to themselves.

Rafe was given a room alone; the two cousins who had shared it had been sent to stay with another family for the duration of Rafe's visit. Although he protested that they shouldn't have been turned out of their room, the host insisted that everyone was pleased with the arrangement.

Much to Kea's relief she was told that Trena and Joe, the anesthetist, were living in a house on the next block with people Trena knew. Kea honestly liked the woman, but it pained her to be around her. Living with her, seeing her with Rafe, would have been too much of a punishment.

To Kea's surprise Rafe returned to Carmen's room a few moments after the host's departure, and knocked softly on the door. "Kea," he murmured.

Her heart beating in anticipation of she knew not what, she quietly slipped over to the door and opened it. The scant light from the hall framed Rafe's face and Kea was breathless as she whispered, "Yes?"

He held out a small tube. "Here's the ointment for your foot," he murmured low, gazing at her levelly.

She released her breath in a sigh; she had forgotten all about her blister. "Thank you," she said softly. Her fingers felt as if they were on fire when she took the tube from Rafe's hand.

"Good night," he whispered, turning on his heel.

Kea watched as he walked down the hall, then she quietly closed the door, and she wondered why the loud hammering of her heart hadn't awakened the sleeping Carmen.

The days began to become routine in the small Mexican town, and for Kea it was an idyllic time, a time for exploration of herself and the area, a time for learning and healing. She bought herself a big sombrero to keep the sun off her face and set about to discover whatever the town had to offer—and it offered a multitude of sights, sounds, and enchantments.

Rafe went to the ancient hospital each day, and, with Trena at his side, he examined patients and discussed their conditions—and sometimes he invited Kea to come with him.

She went along, but usually she stayed outside. She would sit out in the hot sun in the courtyard and watch the line of patients, some of whom would wait for hours to talk to Rafe. She began to take her flute with her to entertain the children who grew restless and weary, and she soon became a favorite with the people. Enthralled, the children would listen and be lured into drowsiness by Kea's lullabies, and she felt that, in her own small way, she was helping.

She loved to see how much happier people seemed once they had talked with Rafe and had either been given a surgery time or been treated. They would walk out of the dingy hospital with a new perspective on life, and Kea was pleased that Rafe had been the one to help them.

Often she would practice her limited Spanish with them, haltingly at first, embarrassed by her scant vocabulary, but growing more confident as the sun-baked days passed. She generally wore culottes and a plain sleeveless blouse and sandals, and her body began to turn berry brown under the hot sun and wind.

Kea felt oddly at home with these people. They didn't judge her and she didn't judge them. She didn't have to be on display every day with her makeup and her demeanor perfect. No one discussed the shops on Rodeo Drive or who was giving a party for whom, and no one cared which designer's label was the hottest this year. The doctor and the weather were the most popular topics.

Kea spent some part of each day wandering through the town's shopping areas, sometimes with the exuberant Carmen, and sometimes alone, buying huaraches, sarapes, and hats, or sitting in the coolness of quiet churches, thinking about her place in the scheme of things. And somehow her own problems ceased to be urgent.

She grew stronger mentally, and she grew stronger about her convictions. She was preparing herself to return to Beverly Hills and the challenges the television station presented. Her show was the one thing she truly did miss: the excitement of interviewing a new guest, the pleasure she had found when her show would be done in another city, even the anxiety when she had a guest who would clam up, or one who panicked at the last moment and couldn't go on at all. The talk-show business was a part of her, in her blood, and she would not abandon it because of a few scars. Besides, she reminded herself, it was all she had now.

That fact was brought home to her as she sat outside the hospital playing her flute. Trena stepped outside for a break and breath of fresh air, and Kea could feel the woman's dark eyes upon her even though she didn't look up. When she finished the tune, Trena walked up to her.

"You play very well," Trena said. "It's good of you to share your music with those waiting. It has a very calming effect on them."

"Thank you," Kea responded pleasantly. "I enjoy it."

"It would be nice if their injuries could be healed by such a simple thing as your music," Trena commented.

Kea looked up into the woman's eyes, and though she honestly didn't think that Trena meant to be cruel, she had certainly let Kea know that she really contributed very little. The healing was done by Rafe and his nurse.

Kea was all too aware of that, and though she didn't want Trena to know it, she was a little hurt. She had seen how exhausted Rafe, Trena, and Joe were at the end of each day, while she, herself, was still full of energy. She studied Trena's face and saw that Trena realized she had hit a sensitive spot, but was not sorry.

The tension became heightened between the two of them as the silence stretched with the unspoken knowledge that each had the power to hurt the other; until now they had coexisted, inevitably sharing part of their days, seeing each other here and at the homes of the different families who invited them to dinner. Because Trena was near Kea's age and spoke English, Kea had found herself more and more in the company of the woman, and to her dismay she had grown to both admire and respect her.

Unexpectedly, Joe strolled out into the courtyard and

began to make jokes about the heat. His welcome appearance dissipated the unease growing inside Kea, and she chatted with him for a moment, then decided to go shopping for the rest of the afternoon.

Her thoughts turned to Jon and Ellen as they so often did, and she was reminded of how badly she missed them. The town had a jewelry factory, and Kea went to it. Even in the pounding heat of the sun, the men labored, creating magnificent works of art, as had their fathers and grandfathers before them. Kea often came to watch them. She had seen one craftsman working for days on a magnificent, yet simple, gold ring, and she had admired it tremendously. She finally decided to buy a copper clown for Ellen, who had always loved clowns of any kind; the purchase saddened her for she didn't know if she would ever again be permitted to share Ellen's joys.

That evening after dinner Rafe invited Kea to take a walk with him, as he sometimes did. They usually strolled down to the river, but Rafe never again took her in his arms. Still, she felt close to him somehow. They talked a lot, as they never had before, sharing, for the first time, a common life-style.

Rafe was talking about a little boy they had almost lost on the operating table, and Kea was reminded again that this man held the power of life and death in his hands. Trena's words were still ringing inside her head, and she touched Rafe's arm.

"Isn't there something I can do to help out at the hospital, Rafe?"

He studied her face, and Kea saw the hesitation in his eyes. "I don't think there's a job at the hospital for you," he finally said carefully.

His tone hurt, and she demanded, "What do you mean?" Did both he and Trena see her as a socialite out of her element here with these people?

His voice became gentle. "I don't think you're ready to see the . . . suffering."

"Oh, let me help, Rafe," she pleaded. "I see these people out in the courtyard every day." Although her determination was spurred on by Trena's remark, she wanted deeply to do all she could to help.

He hesitated again, but at last he agreed to let her try. Kea smiled her gratitude, and she settled down to enjoy the all-too-brief time with him.

The next day Kea marched forth with new purpose. She hadn't often been inside the rundown hospital, and she was unexpectedly appalled by the odors that had accumulated over the years there; she had to force herself not to flinch or to recoil as the unpleasantness washed over her. She was shown into a room where Trena was changing a bandage on a woman's arm. The sight was unpleasant, and even though Kea had seen her own injuries, she looked away. Feeling as if she were going to be sick, she tried to distract herself by straightening some instruments on a table.

"How many patients do you see a day?" she asked in a trembling voice, attempting to carry on when all she wanted to do was run from this room.

Trena glanced over at her, and as their eyes met, Kea saw compassion for her in those dark eyes. Trena quickly bandaged the patient's arm, gave her some instructions in a warm and caring voice, then sent her on her way.

When she walked over to Kea, she studied the redhead's pale face and trembling hands. "You don't have to do this, Kea."

"But I want to," Kea insisted. "I want to help."

"You have been helping in your own way."

"It's been insignificant compared to what the rest of you are doing."

"But this is our job," Trena said simply.

"I'll get used to it," Kea vowed. "That was just the first time."

Trena smiled, but Kea knew that it was with understanding. "Some people can get used to it, and some can't. It's nothing to be ashamed of. We're all different."

Kea wondered if Trena was being genuinely kind as she seemed to be, or did she not want Kea here? Regardless, perhaps the woman was right. Kea was still feeling very nauseated, but she wanted so much to try to fit into Rafe's world, and to be truly useful there.

"Give me a little more time," Kea suggested. "I can do it."

Trena shrugged. "If that's what you want, but, Kea, some people really can't do it. I couldn't go on your television show. I'd die of fright. It's just not in me to do that kind of thing, and perhaps medicine and healing aren't in you. There's no shame in it."

Again Kea had to admire Trena, and she felt a new bond with this woman. Under the circumstances the nurse could have belittled her for her weakness. Kea nodded. "Let's try the next patient."

Trena went down the hall and returned with a small child, and when Kea saw the problem, she was certain she would faint. She could feel the color drain from her face and the tears fill her eyes, and she had to sit down quickly to keep from falling. Trena called out to someone, and a heavy woman came into the room to help Kea walk outside.

Standing out in the courtyard, she drew in several steadying breaths and soon she was feeling all right again —except for the nagging feeling that she had failed herself and Rafe. She smiled at the concerned woman and assured her she was just fine, then she wandered over to a stone bench and sat down.

Only minutes later Rafe came out. When she heard his voice, Kea felt her heart sinking. She didn't want to admit to him that she had failed, but she suspected he knew anyway.

"It didn't go well?" he questioned, perching on the edge of the bench and gazing into her still pale face.

She shook her head and her lips quivered as she spoke. "I tried, but I couldn't, Rafe."

He patted her hand. "I didn't expect you to, Kea. It doesn't matter."

At that moment Joe came out. "Doctor, you're needed inside."

Rafe frowned, then stood up. "I'll talk to you later, Kea."

"Yes," she said. "Later." Then she hurried away, filled with embarrassment.

Rafe gazed after her and he realized that it had mattered very much. He had seen how much she wanted to help, and he had been sure that she couldn't. This was not her world, she was only here temporarily, and when her own injuries had healed, she would return to her bright and glittering circle. As he stared after her, he began to question the time he devoted to strangers in faraway lands. How much did he owe to mankind and how selfish could he be with his time? Perhaps if he had tried harder to fit into Kea's world instead of bringing her here to see if she could fit into his, things might be different.

But then if every man put his own pleasure and passion before anything else, who would be left to care for the less fortunate? He looked around the courtyard, and when he saw that the people were giving him their rapt attention, he was filled with a black rage because he wanted Kea to the exclusion of all else. And he knew it was never to be. He swore softly as he strode back into the hospital.

One of the community leaders had announced a party in his home, and Kea and Trena had planned to go shopping together for dresses that afternoon. Kea hid her misery as the two women walked side by side down the narrow streets talking about the party. All the women were instructed to wear native costumes, and Trena's enthusiasm for the idea was contagious.

"I know just the shop," she said. "It has wonderful dresses. I've had my eye on one ever since we've been here."

Kea was only mildly surprised that Trena hadn't already purchased it. She knew that the woman was very frugal, for she had commented that she saved a third of her salary, and Kea also knew that she helped support family members still living in Mexico.

"What does it look like?" Kea asked.

Trena smiled with pleasure. "Wait until you see it. I'm sure it will attract—attract—" She stopped abruptly, then continued. "Everyone's attention."

Kea wondered if she had meant to say Rafe's. "It must be very beautiful."

"It is."

When they stopped before a shop with a number of dresses hanging on a line outside, Kea remembered the place. She, too, had seen many beautiful dresses here, and she knew they would both find something to please.

She smiled when she saw Trena select a red dress with a black border and a delicate lace shawl. It was stunning, and one of the more expensive dresses in the shop. "Isn't it exquisite?" she asked almost reverently, her dark eyes glowing.

"Yes, it is," Kea told her in sincere admiration. "I know it will look splendid on you."

"Which one do you want?" Trena asked.

Kea began to thumb through the racks while the other woman waited for her. At last she settled on a gorgeous white lace dress with shawllike collar trimmed in red and black, and a frilly apron-type overskirt. She knew her tan would be displayed to advantage in the white dress, and she fell in love with it.

"Aren't you going to try yours on?" she asked Trena. The woman shook her head. "I know it's perfect."

Kea smiled, and she wondered if Trena had come here many times and dreamed of this dress. "Is there some place where I can try this?" she asked.

The shop owner led her to a small section of the shop that had been partitioned off by a piece of cloth. When she had slipped the dress on, she stepped outside in search of a mirror.

"Oh, Kea, you look so beautiful," Trena murmured.

Kea laughed a little nervously at the comment. "No one has called me beautiful since the accident," she admitted. "I certainly no longer see myself that way." She looked into Trena's brown eyes. "And do you know something? It doesn't matter to me so much anymore."

"But you are *beautiful*," Trena said solemnly. "Your scars are inconsequential in the overall picture. I've always thought you were one of the most gorgeous women I've ever seen." She was thoughtful for a moment. "You've blossomed here in my home country, Kea. Your tan sets off your magnificent gray eyes and your red hair. The cut you have now is actually more flattering than when your hair was long."

Kea's eyes met Trena's. "Thank you. That's very kind of you. I certainly haven't felt beautiful for a long time now, but I've changed. It's funny, I hadn't thought about it, but my priorities aren't the same now."

As she gazed pensively at the nurse, she realized she was developing a very real affection for the woman. And she could see why Rafe cared so deeply for her.

The thought made her heart sink, and though she chattered animatedly as she purchased the dress and walked home beside Trena, her gaiety was forced.

Everyone in the Mendoza household was in a state of upheaval as the time of the party arrived. The women ran back and forth to the only bath, checking their costumes and makeup, and enjoying every moment of the excitement, while the men waited patiently for their turn.

Not until Kea was dressed did she see how provocative her dress was, and she remembered that she hadn't seen it in the mirror at the shop as she had intended. She had become distracted by Trena's words, and now as she looked at herself in the mirror, seeing how snugly the low-cut bodice hugged her full breasts, which displayed ample cleavage, she wondered if she dared wear it. But it was too late to change now, and anyway, she felt very attractive and womanly, and she found herself hoping that Rafe would like it. When she went to the living room, Señora Mendoza gave her a flower for her hair, and she slipped it behind her ear, then eagerly waited for the men to get dressed.

She laughed softly when Rafe walked into the room a few minutes later. He was dressed completely in white, wearing a peasant shirt over flared-leg trousers, with only a vivid red tie to offset the white, and a wide straw hat was on his head. He looked quite attractive.

Smiling at her, he asked, "What's so amusing? Don't you like my outfit?"

"Yes. I love it." She stood up. "Look! We're a matched pair."

"So we are," he mused, his gaze moving slowly over her costume, lingering on her bosom before returning to her face. "You look lovely."

She was touched by the sincerity of the compliment. "So do you," she murmured, oblivious to the other women in the room.

The moment was shattered when the host entered, and to everyone's amusement he was dressed entirely in black, just as his wife was. They, too, were a matched pair. There was much laughter and joking as the little group walked the distance to the house where the party was being held.

The home, a lavish two-story structure decorated with

wrought iron and red tile, was hidden behind tall walls with a wrought-iron gate. It was magnificent, and Kea was eager to see the inside. She wasn't disappointed; sunny, expansive rooms employed beautiful ornamental brick, tile, and ironwork. The tile floors gleamed under rich wooden-beamed ceilings.

The group was led through the house and out into a large courtyard filled with several patios, fountains, and gardens. Many of the guests had already arrived and they had gathered on the central patio, sitting at tables under tall trees. Drinks were being dispensed from a bar off to one side, and a pig was being roasted over an open pit. Brightly colored lanterns were suspended overhead and around the patio walls. The night was alive with the chatter of the merrymakers and the appealing music of roving mariachis.

Trena was already there with Joe, sitting at a small table, sipping a margarita. Kea had never seen the other woman look more attractive. The red dress seemed to have been made for her, and with her long straight hair, which she wore down tonight, and her big brown eyes, she was in her element here in her country, in this easy atmosphere. Kea felt all too much like the intruder, the gringo, because she was the only one without a drop of Mexican blood.

Joe, dressed as a bandit, looked more Mexican than ever, and, dressed in the Mexican peasant costume, Rafe seemed to have lost his strong Italian heritage. When he saw Joe and Trena, he crossed the red stones to speak to them, and even thought he guided Kea along with him, she felt terribly out of place.

The mariachis, dressed in their somber black suits and big black sombreros, began to play a soft love song, and Joe stood up. "May I have this dance, Kea?" he asked with such a formal air that she had to smile.

With a swift glance at Rafe she murmured, "I'd love it."

She had had time to see the spark in his dark eyes as he appraised Trena in her lovely dress, and she was feeling hurt. She had no way of knowing how lovely she looked, standing out from the dark beauties, with her pale skin, despite her tan. She couldn't see the advantages to being different, but the others did, and she received much attention in her stunning white dress. The pale lamplight gave her red hair fiery highlights and her skin a smooth, golden cast. She was the center of attraction as she went into the anesthetist's arms, but she was only aware that she was leaving Trena alone with Rafe.

Joe was smiling at her as he moved her to the music, and Kea felt a little sorry for him because tonight he had lost his boyish humor and was obviously trying very hard to impress her. She could feel his body tremble nervously against hers; he was a nice man, and she regretted that he wasn't enjoying the dance more.

"You look more beautiful than ever tonight," he said too brightly, and she smiled, wanting him to relax.

"You look good yourself, Joe. Tell me why a handsome fellow like you isn't married already," she teased.

Flushing, he retorted, "Why aren't you?" He realized his mistake immediately when he remembered that she was recently widowed and why, and he blurted, "I'm sorry. I didn't mean to say that."

Kea was embarrassed, but she managed a weak smile. "That's what I get for joking about things that are none of my business," she said with a lightness she was far from feeling. She wondered if she could ever again resume her past life without going on the defensive every time someone asked her a question like that.

"In answer to your question," Joe said, trying to fill in an awkward pause, "I asked a girl once, but she turned me down."

"I know how that is," Kea said with a faint smile. "I wanted a man once, but he didn't want me."

211

Joe raised heavy brows. "You're kidding, aren't you?"

Kea made a wry face. "I swear it's the truth."

The music ended, and Kea didn't know which of them was more relieved. The dance had been awkward at best. Joe thanked her, then wandered over to a table laden with food. Before Kea could sit down, she was claimed by another partner. The band struck up another song and she found herself in the arms of a heavyset Mexican man who attempted to converse with her in rapid Spanish. He kept flattering her with pretty phrases, and before she knew it, she was laughing and joking with him, making light of his compliments and teasing offers of marriage. He was spinning her very fast to the music, and she was breathless in his arms. Once when he turned her, she caught sight of Rafe, but before she could focus on him, her partner had spun her again.

The song ended, and to Kea's amusement she was quickly claimed by another man, this one young and handsome, his eyes all too admiring as they lingered on her red hair and the creamy swell of her breasts above the bodice of her dress. She could think of no good excuse to refuse him the dance without seeming rude, so she smiled and let him take her in his arms. He was an accomplished dancer, and Kea found that she enjoyed the dance tremendously.

Sitting across the floor from the couple, Rafe told himself that the party was a timely lesson for him. Here was the woman who he had thought had once loved him, the woman who had easily left him for another man, in the arms of an attractive and attentive partner, and obviously loving every minute. Even with her scars, she was winning the hearts of all the men; and she was thriving on the attention. Rafe knew he was jealous, but he couldn't help himself.

Kea was glowing under all the praise she was receiving, smiling and laughing with the men who held her, and Rafe knew that he wished he were the one she was flirting with. A dark and forbidding flame blazed in his eyes, and he knew that Kea was in her element here at the party, with the luxury and the gaiety. This was the kind of world she belonged in. She would be content in no other.

The next time Kea looked for Rafe she didn't see him anywhere. Trena was also gone, and for a moment Kea didn't know what to do with herself. The dance had ended and the music momentarily ceased. Finally, she walked over to the bar and ordered a drink. She barely had time to take two sips before the band began another song and she was pulled into a man's arms. Determined to enjoy herself, she did her best to forget about Rafe and Trena, and she had almost succeeded when, a few dances later, she saw the two of them walking down the stairs from the upper rooms. She quickly devoted her attention to the man she was dancing with, pretending to have a splendid time, but the evening was suddenly in tatters for her.

When Rafe walked up behind her partner and tapped him on the shoulder, Kea sucked in her breath. The man nodded, grinned broadly, and moved away. Kea's heart was pounding as she went into Rafe's arms. Their bodies fit perfectly, as she had long ago discovered, and she recalled a hundred other times when she had been in his arms. She looked into his eyes, and unable to read the dark expression there, she offered him a hesitant smile. He didn't return her smile, but he let his fingers spread out over her back and he drew her nearer.

Closing her eyes, Kea let him embrace her more tightly, and she sighed with a mixture of regret and contentment. She didn't know what he was thinking, but she had always thought she belonged here in his arms. Even if she knew it wasn't true.

Rafe spun her agilely about the floor to the throbbing beat of the music, and she didn't dare open her eyes, for then she would have to come out of her memories and face reality. She would have to wonder where he had gone with Trena, and she didn't want to. After the song ended, Rafe still held her hand.

"Would you like a drink?" he asked, his penetrating gaze studying her face.

"I have one—over there at the bar," she replied, and Rafe led the way back there. He ordered a drink for himself and the two of them found a small table where they could sit down. Rafe didn't say anything, and Kea wondered what was on his mind. He was staring down into the liquid in his glass, and finally he lifted it to his lips.

"Would you like to see the rest of the house?" he asked. "It's very beautiful. Trena and I have already been given a guided tour by the host, and I'm sure he won't mind if I show you."

She felt an unreasonable wave of jealousy wash over her because Rafe had already seen the house with Trena, but she didn't refuse. "Yes, I'd like that," she said, forcing her smile.

She felt the warmth of his hand burn against hers as he led her up the stairs to a beautifully furnished library. The dark paneled walls held a number of book-laden shelves and many beautiful art objects, from pottery to sculpture. Kea recalled Rafe's great interest in art, and she was an eager pupil as he pointed out different pieces to her.

The party noises continued, drifting up to the couple through the open windows, but Kea sensed that Rafe had something more serious on his mind than showing her the house. Neither of them missed the party gaiety. The upstairs tour was hasty, although it included bedrooms, baths, and a lovely den. When Rafe had shown Kea the downstairs, he seemed to have made up his mind about whatever was bothering him, and he asked, "Would you like to see the rose garden? It's more beautiful than any spot in town. Once when I was here, I was invited to lunch there."

"It sounds lovely," Kea said. "How can I resist?" Her eyes held his, and the night was magic, the town enchanting, Rafe's company heady, as always. Kea was at the mercy of fate with this man, and no one knew it better than she.

She forgot all about Trena as they walked out into the courtyard, through the milling, laughing people to a small area near the back of the property. Tall rose bushes surrounded a little brick patio with several wrought-iron benches. The night was fragrant with the sweet smell of the roses, and the moon hung low in the sky.

"This is beautiful," Kea agreed, her heart pounding wildly in anticipation of the uncertainty before her. Surely Rafe hadn't separated her from the crowd without any more purpose than to show her the roses, had he?

He didn't release her hand until they had sat down on one of the benches. He rested his arm on the bench back, near Kea's shoulders, and she ached to slide over close to him and be enfolded in his embrace. Instead, she nervously waited for him to make the next move. She sensed the turmoil inside him, but she didn't know the cause.

Beside her Rafe wrestled with his thoughts. He was afraid Kea's experience at the hospital today had been a new turning point in their relationship, and he had to find some way to hold on to her awhile longer before she slipped away from him again. His bid to have her understand his way of life had failed, and though he knew it was too soon to get any kind of commitment from her, he had to know where he stood with her. He was faced with the same problem he had always had with her: She didn't fit into his world. But now he realized that he didn't want it without her. He would have to try and live life her way.

He could give up his jaunts to other parts of the world and stop bringing patients into his home. His practice in Beverly Hills would provide a handsome income for them if he restricted his work to that, and it would leave him plenty of time to spend with Kea. He would rather live in that world with her, he told himself, than live without her again—if she would have him.

He tipped her chin back with his forefinger, and as he looked into her eyes, he felt himself drowning in them. He was going to make a fool of himself, he was very much afraid, but to lose her without even trying would make him an even bigger fool.

She returned his gaze, her eyes bright and pensive, and when he saw that her mouth was parted, he was unable to resist claiming it in a possessive kiss. Kea moaned in surrender. She had longed for this so many times in recent days, and she had almost given up hope of finding herself in his arms again. His mouth moved against hers, stirring a passionate response.

Kea opened her eyes abruptly when she heard someone's sharp intake of breath, and she looked up in time to see Trena turn pale in the moonlight. Kea was sure she could hear the woman whisper Rafe's name in torment, but she quickly recovered.

After clearing her throat to attract Rafe's attention, she said in a relatively calm, although unusually thick voice, "Rafe, there's an emergency inside."

Rafe turned toward her in surprise, a frown on his face.

"One of the women tripped while coming down the stairs. She landed on the tile. The glass she was carrying shattered, and she's pretty badly hurt."

Rafe paused a moment to gaze at Kea with a strange expression in his eyes before he stood up. She rose too, and all three of them rushed into the house. The woman was still on the floor, but she had been placed on her back and she was bleedingly badly from her neck.

Kea gasped when she saw the shards of glass, and the blood. Feeling faint, she turned away to cling to the banister. Sick with shame over her weakness, she could see Rafe and Trena working quickly and efficiently to stop the

216

bleeding and soothe the patient, and she was filled with a sense of uselessness. Trena and Rafe had both been right; she didn't belong here with them. For the first time she admitted that they belonged together: they were a team. Trena knew all about Rafe's world and how to live in it and work in it side by side with him.

She stood all alone as Trena and Rafe worked on the woman, and she looked up in surprise when Rafe finally walked over to her. "The Mendozas will see you home," he said curtly. "We're going to take this woman to the hospital."

Kea didn't need to be told who the "we" was, and she wondered suddenly if Rafe was disgusted with her because of her weakness. She nodded, then watched as they removed the injured woman, but she did not wait for the Mendozas to escort her home. Although the party resumed with less gaiety, Kea stayed only long enough to make her excuses to the host, and then she fled out into the night.

Hours later, when she and the rest of the household were in bed, she heard Rafe's soft knock on the bedroom door. She lay in tense silence waiting for him to go away. She didn't wish to see him again tonight. The knock sounded again, only slightly louder, and Kea slowly made her way to the door to open it partially.

His dark eyes roamed over her face. "Are you all right?" he whispered.

She nodded. "Yes." She didn't want him to know how ashamed she was of her response, or how the memory of him and Trena working on the patient burned in her mind.

"I'm sorry I had to run out like that," he murmured.

Kea knew that he shouldn't be apologizing to her; his work was more important than leaving her stranded at a party. She had learned too late just how important his work was. "It didn't matter," she murmured. "How is the woman?"

Rafe smiled for the first time. "She's going to be fine."

He looked at her for a moment longer, then whispered, "Good night, Kea. Sleep well."

"Good night." She closed the door, then retreated to her bed. But it took her another two hours to get to sleep.

CHAPTER ELEVEN

Kea debated whether or not even to go to the hospital the next day. She had purposely lain in bed so that she wouldn't have to face Rafe at breakfast, but she couldn't linger any longer. When she had dressed and had a cup of coffee and a hot tortilla dripping with butter at Señora Mendoza's insistence, she forced herself to walk to the hospital.

Much to her chagrin, when she went into the courtyard, she found Trena there taking a morning break, and the woman wouldn't even look at her. "Good morning, Trena," she said hesitantly. "How are you today?"

Trena looked up briefly, and it pained Kea to see the misery in her troubled brown eyes and the dark shadows beneath. It was all too obvious that Trena was terribly unhappy, and Kea knew without asking that she was the cause of that unhappiness. Her sleep had been tormented by the look on Trena's face when she had discovered Kea with Rafe in the rose garden. She regretted it deeply; she genuinely cared for Trena, and she had no more wanted to hurt her than Ellen. She sighed at the memory of her long-time friend. Was it her destiny to spend her life unintentionally hurting those she cared about?

Trena glanced away, but not before Kea had seen the tears shimmering in her eyes. "I'm all right. How are you?"

Kea sighed tiredly; she had no choice but to pursue this,

even if it meant learning a truth she did not wish to hear. "I don't believe you are all right," she said softly. "Do you want to tell me what's wrong?"

Trena turned on her heel. "Nothing," she said over her shoulder as she hurried into the hospital, but her voice was filled with emotion.

Kea followed her inside to the room where Trena usually worked. "Can we talk about it?" she pressed, knowing deep within that she should not do so. Yet she needed to know if Rafe was still involved with this woman—she had to know.

Trena folded and refolded some white gowns lying on the table before her. Her full mouth trembled, and still she would not look at Kea. "Why do you torment me with these questions?" she murmured bitterly. "Do you take pleasure in breaking my heart, then asking me about it?"

Kea sucked in her breath, deeply wounded. "No, of course not," she returned. "Trena, let's talk about this, please."

Trena didn't reply, but when she turned around to put some instruments into a sterilizer, Kea saw how badly her hands trembled, and she was moved by the woman's distress.

Unable to resist, she walked up behind Trena and touched her shoulders. Trena whirled around to face her. "Please don't take him away from me a second time," Trena pleaded vehemently. Her dark eyes filled with tears again, and they spilled down her cheeks. "You can have any man you want. I've loved no other one but Rafe since he found me in my village nine years ago. There will never be anyone else for me." Her voice caught and she put her hands up to her mouth to stifle her sobs.

Kea's heart pounded wildly. Her own eyes filled with tears, and she knew a burning pain deep down inside her, a pain no medicine could heal. "Are you and Rafe lovers?"

she made herself ask. At the moment it seemed to be the most important question in the world.

Trena turned her back to Kea, and Kea ached deep inside when she saw how the woman's slender shoulders shook with sobs and misery. "Rafe and I became lovers the day I finished my nurse's training five years ago. I knew then that there would never be anyone else for me. Then you came into his life." Her voice cracked, and it was a moment before she could continue. "When you married, it was like a rebirth for me, for Rafe came back to me again." The last words were but a ragged whisper. "Now you're here again."

Unexpectedly, she turned back around, tears streaming down her face. "Please, I'm pleading with you. Don't take him away from me again. I have too much pride to take him back a third time when you've finished with him and have found someone else. Don't do this to me—or to him."

Kea was suddenly reminded of Ellen's words to her about using Rafe. But the tragic truth was that she, like Trena, had never wanted anyone else but him. Her throat was so thick with pain that she didn't know if she could say a coherent word. "It—it wasn't like that . . ." she began.

Trena's tears turned to anger. "It wasn't like what?" she demanded. "One week Rafe thought you were in love with him—and the next you had married another man. That's how it was! For weeks he was no good for work or anything else. You were never right for him. Ever since he met you, you've twisted him inside out—insisting that he be in town for your silly parties and vacations in the summer *season.*" She said the last word with such contempt that Kea winced. "The summer is the time when Rafe takes the patients no one else cares about and gives them a new life. Don't you care about that?"

Kea drew in a steadying voice. "Yes, of course, but—"

"Then go away and leave Rafe alone. You gave him up once, and when you've gone back to your social world with your television friends, you'll find someone who fits into your life better. You don't understand Rafe. You're no good for him. You turn him all around and make him question his priorities. You're not the kind of woman who can give wholly of herself. You're not the woman for Rafe. Go back to your show where you can get all the attention you need."

Trena's words hit Kea with a truth she couldn't deny. She closed her eyes, willing the tears not to come.

"Do you care for him at all?" Trena asked more gently, and Kea could see in her eyes that she was afraid of the question.

Kea's own reply was quiet and restrained. "Yes."

"Then let him go and leave him alone." Her gaze was steady for the first time when she met Kea's eyes, and she straightened her spine. "Not just for me, but for people like those out in the courtyard who need him. Don't pull him in two directions. I know him. I work with him. His life and mine are the same, and he *can* be happy with me, if you'll just go away."

Kea pressed her fingertips to her lips as if to hold back the cry rising from deep within. Trena was right; Rafe needed her. And she, herself, had made her decision long ago when she married Roxwell. It had been a cruel trick of the gods that she was here in Mexico with Rafe at all. She would take what she had learned from him and her memories and go home. It was only right: Trena was right. There wasn't room here for two women loving the same man.

For a long time she couldn't make her lips say the words her mind had agreed to, for her own heart was breaking. Yet she knew she couldn't refuse this woman's plea. Rafe certainly had never said he wanted her again, and if Trena could hold him, she had more right to him than Kea did.

She knew it was all true, and still she couldn't find the words to say so.

Biting down on her lip, she nodded to the other woman, then she ran out of the room. She didn't belong here in Mexico by Rafe's side. If it was anyone's place, it was Trena's. Trena had earned it; she belonged in Rafe's world. But the admission didn't ease the ache inside Kea. It was all too true that she had given up Rafe when she married Roxwell, and it was true that he hadn't really been hers even then. It was also true that she had suspected all along that Rafe and Trena were lovers, but the truth didn't set her free. In fact, the knowledge made her want to die inside.

She didn't want to cause anyone else, or herself, more misery. She would return to Beverly Hills where she belonged and begin her life again as she should. She understood Rafe better now, but that could not change their different goals. In many ways this trip to Mexico had been her salvation; in others, it had merely prolonged the eventual final separation from Rafe.

Feeling bereft, Kea left the enclosed patio and wandered toward the river, recalling how at peace she had been the times she had gone there with Rafe. Several children were playing in the water, and Kea worked her way past them, under the heavy, ancient branches of the trees to a secluded spot. There, with the lazy river winding past, whispering comfort to her, she tried to plot her uncertain future. She would miss the people and this town, but she didn't belong here. She was the outsider. She was Kea Montgomery, the Los Angeles talk-show hostess, trying to play nurse to a people in a foreign land.

She thought of Rafe and all the hours, the days, the nights she had shared with him here, and her heart begged her not to leave. But somehow she turned her back on its desperate plea. She had made up her mind: She was going home.

She laughed aloud at the thought, for she didn't even know if she had a home. She knew that the court battle over the will hadn't come up, for she had given her lawyer this address and he hadn't contacted her. Anyway, it was too soon. The courts were full these days, but it amazed her that she hadn't given it any thought.

Sighing wearily, she reminded herself of all she had to do once she got home and the idle days were over. She had to find an apartment and secure her personal belongings from Shane. Although she would give him the house, some of the furniture was hers, and she wanted that. She would settle into a nice apartment near the station.

The station. The battle at the television station would be long and painful too, she knew. Leaning over, she tried to see her reflection in the river water, but the wavering face mocking her did nothing to reassure her about her chances of getting her job back.

And there was the troubling matter of the contract; hers had nearly lapsed with the passing of the weeks. She realized, suddenly, that it had been over five weeks since the accident. The time had passed with incredible rapidity—perhaps because she had spent most of it with Rafe.

She wondered how she would tell him that it was time for her to return to Beverly Hills. They hadn't discussed how long she would stay here; she had imagined that Rafe expected her to stay the entire time. But he would be here two more weeks—with Trena—and Kea was going home, alone.

A young woman came to the edge of the river with her wash. She looked up in surprise when she saw Kea, then waved and smiled. Kea waved back, and the solitude of her santuary broken, she stood up and slowly wandered back toward the Mendoza home.

Carmen wasn't there, and she went in and helped the girl's mother prepare an afternoon meal, which would be taken to Rafe and the others at the hospital. When the time came for someone to carry it over, Kea pleaded a headache and retired to the room she shared with Carmen.

She didn't come out of the hot, stuffy room until it was time to help with the evening meal, and then she was shy and withdrawn around Rafe while all the time her mind was spinning, trying to discover a way to tell him she was leaving.

While she was helping with the dishes, Rafe walked up behind her. His tone was both serious and questioning. "Will you take a walk with me?"

Why did the blood pound so wildly at her temples at the question? She needed to talk with him and had hoped he would ask. "Yes," she murmured, but she couldn't turn around to face him.

Kea's heart ached at the thought of all the days and nights she would not spend with him, nights he would again seek comfort in Trena's embrace. She loved him more than ever, and she hadn't thought that was possible. She would have to get used to doing without him a second time, and it seemed a grossly cruel punishment to lose him again. Suddenly she wondered if, like Trena, she should be content to have whatever portion of Rafe she could get and ask no more. But that had never been her way. And perhaps someday Rafe would offer Trena marriage; she was more what he needed than Kea ever had been.

With trembling hands she set the last dish in the sink, then dried her hands on a muslin cloth. When she turned around, she saw Rafe leaning against the counter, staring at her speculatively. His beautiful eyes were dark with thought, and she wondered what he was thinking. Was she worrying for no reason? How much would he care when she told him her plans?

As he led the way out onto the street, Rafe sighed softly. He was seeing signs of the inevitable; Kea was restless. He had already lost her again. He had hoped for some miracle when he brought her here with him, but he should have known last night that it was over. She had allowed him to kiss her, it was true, but with Kea a kiss didn't mean a commitment.

Hadn't he also seen her with Jon? Was Jon the source of her discontent? Did the men last night make her long for her other lover? He had been both pleased and impressed with Kea while she had been in Mexico, but it had only made him dream foolish dreams. The newness was gone from the place now, and Kea wanted to go. He was sure of it. He had suspected it yesterday at the hospital and again last night at the party. And he had seen it in her eyes when she looked at him.

Kea saw that he was leading her toward the riverbank, and she had an urge to tell him to go anywhere but there. However, she didn't. She had shared so many marvelous times at the river that she would hate her final memory of it to be a painful one, as she knew it would have to be. They walked along in silence for a while, and then Rafe faced her, both of them caught in the moonlight spilling down on the trees huddled near the flowing water.

His hands closed down on her shoulders and he held her immobile before him. "What is it, Kea?" he asked. "Have you decided you've had enough?"

She gazed up at him in bewilderment. What exactly was he asking? "I don't know what you mean."

"I've seen the faraway look in your eyes. You're thinking of leaving, aren't you?"

For a moment she was so stunned that she could not speak. Somehow he had guessed, though she hadn't said a word. Perhaps he knew her better than she had thought. "Yes," she finally whispered. "It's time."

Rafe's fingers tightened brutally on her shoulders before he released her. For a long while there was no sound at all except Kea's breathless words hanging heavy in the air and the sound of the river going on endlessly. Finally, it carried her words away and Rafe sighed in resignation.

He wanted to argue with her, to use all the wit he had to convince her to stay, but he knew it was hopeless. He had been expecting this; he had known this time together could not last indefinitely. When he had recognized her tense withdrawal this evening, he had guessed that her decision had been made. Her new life was calling to her now. He couldn't hold her even if he tried.

With a strength of will he hadn't known he possessed, he spoke to her in a normal voice. "I'll make the arrangements at the end of the week. I can have someone drive you to the closest airport, about a half day's ride from here."

He had made it so easy for her, so incredibly easy, and unaccountably, that hurt even more. She looked up into his eyes, but the shadows kept his expression hidden from her. Was that concern she heard in his voice? For her? For him? For both of them? Or had she imagined it because she couldn't accept the fact that he would let her go so easily. Had he honestly brought her with him only to help her mental state? Her mind was running wild with her anxiety.

His willingness to send her on her way left her with an empty feeling deep inside. She didn't know what kind of response she had expected from him, but this ready acceptance was crushing. At the very least she suspected that she had thought he would ask why or urge her to stay until the end so that he could drive her back. The long, dark moment closed in around them, and Kea sadly told herself that there was nothing more to say. It was over for her and Rafe—whatever they had tried to revive in these past weeks—but then it had been over for them a long, long time ago.

Oh, yes, if she had her scars revised in a few months, she would have one more chance to be with him, but now she was sure she would get another doctor. She couldn't bear to go to Rafe's office now, to see Trena there again, and to know that the woman had the man Kea wanted for all her life.

"I think we should get back," Kea murmured. "It's late."

When Rafe didn't move, she started to turn away. Unexpectedly, he reached out and spun her around. For an interminable time he held her before him, his hands on her shoulders, then ever so slowly and gently, his mouth descended to hers and he kissed her as though he were starving and she were the food of life.

With a groan he drew her against him, molding her body to his with an urgency that alarmed her. That he wanted her, she had no doubt, but she couldn't give in to him now, under the circumstances, even though she wanted him with all her heart and soul. He wasn't hers and he never would be. Making more memories by this river deep in Mexico couldn't accomplish anything but more heartache.

But the night suddenly closed in on them, and Rafe's powerful seduction made Kea aware of nothing else. She tried to turn away from him, but her heart and body wouldn't permit it. She stopped questioning why he wanted her now, when he was letting her go for all time. Knowing that this would be the last time with him, wanting him too much to pull away, Kea let him ease her down on the sandy riverbank, and she closed her eyes as his mouth scattered kisses along her mouth and down her throat to her rapidly rising and falling breasts. She could hear her heart pounding in her ears against the background of water, which seemed to be rushing faster and faster with the pace of her heartbeats.

Rafe unbuttoned her blouse, and Kea moaned hungrily as he gently sucked on the rosy tips of her breasts, his mouth and tongue working their skillful magic, sending little rivers of fire washing through her veins. He cupped a breast, then licked it, his tongue creating smaller and smaller circles, until it probed the throbbing tip, driving Kea mad with desire. She had thought Rafe had taken her as high as he ever could in the many times they had made love, but here in this secluded spot, with the moonlight spilling down on them and the river whispering to them, she wanted him as never before. She longed to take him inside her and make him so much a part of her that when she went away from here, she could still believe that he had cared for her.

She arched her back in her eagerness to belong to him, but Rafe's loving was slow and unhurried, as though he were determined to savor every erotic moment, to taste every pleasure that was to be had. His fingers trailed slowly over her body, causing her breasts to tingle and her passion to rise. He sought her mouth again with his own and she submitted eagerly, her tongue meeting his to engage it in a timeless love battle.

When he drew back from her this time, it was to remove his shirt and pants, and Kea held her breath as she watched him silhouetted against the night by the moon. His body, too, had grown tanned and more beautiful here in Mexico, and his hips stood out, lighter in contrast to the rest of him, making his virility even more visible. Kea ached inside to know his power again. For some reason she was painfully reminded that he only made love to her in the darkness, but it didn't matter now.

She drew in her breath sharply when he bent down over her, resting on his knees in the sand to help her disrobe. He made a blanket for them from their garments, and Kea held her arms out to him when she had settled back down.

Rafe lowered his body to hers, burning along the length of her, but he did not yet claim her. She was so aware of him that she was trembling with need. There on the darkened riverbank Rafe scattered kisses along the length of her, hot, urgent kisses, telling her that his need was as desperate as her own. Refusing to think that this was their last time together, she reveled in the wonder of him, and when he gathered her up in his arms, she pressed against him, wanting to feel his magic.

Drawing her forward, Rafe rolled over on his back and brought her down on top of him, her legs on either side of him. Kea gasped as she felt him fill her with joy. The river rushed on past them, moving faster and still faster. Kea gazed at the moon high in the sky and she closed her eyes as she raced toward it with each tantalizing movement of Rafe's body. The night exploded into a thousand bright stars and Kea clung to him, wanting him for all eternity.

Long after their passion had cooled, Rafe lay cradling Kea's body to his, letting the night go quietly on its way, tiptoeing and whispering to the river as the water lulled the lovers into drowsiness. The night was warm and the moon shone down on the couple, holding its golden vigil as long as it could.

Finally, dawn began to push at the darkness, and Rafe stirred Kea from her half slumber. "We'd better get back before the entire town wakes up," he murmured thickly. He stood up and pulled her up by her hands. Both of them began to shake the sand free from their clothing and dress hastily. And soon they were walking away from their hideaway, leaving the river to talk to the trees and the moon to slide away behind forming clouds, leaving a part of themselves, and leaving each other.

Rafe glanced at the woman by his side as they worked their way back to the house. That he loved her, he had never doubted, but he knew he couldn't hold her. Somehow he found the strength to smile at her and tell her good night at her door.

She hadn't spoken to him on the way home and now as

she stood before him, she asked a single whispered question. "Rafe, have you ever made love to Trena?"

He was caught off guard. "Why?"

"Curiosity."

"Yes," he replied honestly in a very low voice, "but—"

She didn't give him time to finish. It hurt too much to know that she'd been sharing him with Trena, and yet she had had Roxwell. She shut the door and leaned against it weakly, willing Rafe to go away.

For a long moment he stood staring at the door, then he swore bitterly. It didn't matter anyway. She was going away. He had intruded in her life—she hadn't wanted him then; she didn't want him now. For just a moment he placed both hands on the door and pressed his forehead against it in utter despair, and then he turned back down the hall.

He couldn't see the tears in Kea's eyes as she leaned against the door on the other side, and he wouldn't have understood if he had. He thought that she was still grieving over her dead husband, and perhaps involved with Jon. He wouldn't have understood that she was crying over him. She would make her career her life, and she would get her show back, no matter how fierce the battle. But she would do so without Rafe. She had lost him.

The next two days dragged by in torturous slowness for Kea. The whole household was in an uproar at the news of her impending departure, and Carmen suddenly clung to her, staying by her side, wanting to talk, pleading with her not to leave. Kea was sad enough already, and it hurt to think of leaving this child she had come to love. She wondered how Rafe survived, leaving a little piece of himself here and there with the people he became involved with.

Kea had chosen not to visit at the hospital anymore, and the friends she had made came by the house in steady steams to bid her good-bye. She hadn't wanted to go back to the hospital because she hadn't wanted to see Trena again.

Feeling lost and alone, Kea kept away from her normal routine, busying herself with packing and saying farewell to her new friends—while Rafe gazed at her with dark, pensive eyes. Much to Kea's surprise, the night before she was to leave the Mendozas threw a big party for her. There was music and dancing, and gifts, and Kea couldn't keep from crying.

Carmen was the first to hand her a package. "So that you won't forget me," the girl said.

With quivering fingers, Kea opened it while all the guests looked on. It was Mickey! Carmen was giving Kea's friend back to her, and oh, how delighted she was to see the toy that had once meant so much to her. She needed him now more than Carmen did.

Drawing the girl forward, she kissed her on the forehead. "Thank you, Carmen," she whispered softly in Spanish. "I'm touched by your thoughtful gift."

The Mendozas gave her a beautiful clay flute. Joe, the anesthetist, gave her a shawl, and many of the others gave her small gifts of copper. Of course, Trena was there, and she approached Kea silently, holding out a lovely white lace mantilla to go with the dress Kea had bought for the first party. Trena gazed down at her hands awkwardly for a moment, then looked up, her eyes full of gratitude.

"Thank you," she whispered, "for what you are doing."

Kea thought her heart would break in that instant, but she managed a smile, and even through her own torment she saw that Trena was content at last. Her face shone with a peace she could not disguise. Kea touched the other woman's hand, and she knew, although the knowledge left her cold and empty, that she was doing the right thing.

Trena turned away and then, finally, Rafe, too, handed

her a package, but his instructions puzzled her. "Don't open this one until you get back to Beverly Hills," he said.

Kea gazed at him for a long moment, then returned her attention to the others at the party. But she couldn't forget the gift Rafe had handed her, for even though she didn't know what was in it, it meant more to her than all the rest.

The music started again, and Kea was drawn into the arms of first one man and then another and whirled gaily about on the little patio of the Mendoza home. The party was small in comparison to the one that had been given at the lavish home days before, but Kea wouldn't have traded it for a thousand fancy ones. The people were warm and loving, and they made her last day among them especially memorable.

Rafe was the last man to draw her into his embrace, and Kea didn't know if she could dance with him without weeping. She was truly afraid that this was the final time she would ever see him, and she was sure this was the last time she would ever be held in his arms. It was tormenting to be held so close once again, and she kept thinking of the hours they had spent on the riverbank, sharing each other as never before.

Their eyes met and held for a brief time, then Rafe murmured, "Take care of yourself in the big city, Kea. And I wish you all the luck in the world with the job."

"Thank you," she replied, but his words hurt, even though he had wished her well. It was very clear that he was through with her, that he was giving her back to the life she knew best.

His fingers tightened on hers ever so slightly and he thought of the gift he had given her. It was the closest he would ever come to letting her know how much she mattered to him. In his heart he was married to her—and even her leaving wouldn't alter that. He loved her even more than ever now, but he would have to shut her out

233

of his heart forever. She had made her choice and he must go on with his own life.

He drew her a little closer to him for the last time, and Kea rested her head on his shoulder. She didn't want anyone to see the heartache shimmering in her eyes, threatening to spill out and to make a fool of her here in front of all these people.

CHAPTER TWELVE

It was a subdued Kea who climbed into the old truck with one of the townspeople for the long ride to the airport. He, too, was going to catch a plane, and Kea was grateful for his company as she said good-bye to the crowd who had gathered around the vehicle.

Kea's eyes met Rafe's, darted to Trena, then back to him. She felt as if she were leaving her heart and soul in this country. She had grown closer to the Mendoza family in three weeks than to anyone else in a long, long time. And leaving Rafe was agony.

"Good-bye, Kea," he said stiffly.

"Good-bye, Rafe." Their words seemed so useless and foolish. She looked at him a last time, and she saw that his eyes were burning into hers accusingly, as if probing for a memory, and she realized that their *real* good-bye was said by the river that night. There would be no more touching, no more loving, and no more good-byes. Quickly, before she weakened, she nodded to the man at her side to drive off. And she did not look back again.

The ride to the airport and the plane ride back to Los Angeles gave her a lot of time to think. Slowly, thoughts of home came back to her, and she clung to them gratefully, wanting to concentrate on anything but Rafe. Her mind was a jumble of ideas as she tried to decide what to do about her future. One of the things she must do was confront Ellen and Jon, no matter what the outcome. She couldn't let the friendship slip away under the present circumstances, as though the three of them hadn't shared years together and hadn't cared so deeply for each other. She wanted the incident brought out in the open; she wanted either to restore the friendship or to sever it completely.

When the plane set down in L.A., Kea told herself she had come back to the real world; the idyllic interlude was in the past and it was time to get on with her life. It was an easy statement to make, but the memory of Rafe's accusing eyes wouldn't fade.

Running from the thought, she walked out of the plane and into the busy airport. By the time she had arranged for transportation to a hotel, she was feeling weary and more than a little uncertain about what to do next. She needed to talk with her lawyer and find out the status of the will before she hunted for an apartment, and she could not forget the upcoming battle with her producer over her job, but for the moment all she wanted was to settle in somewhere and rest. Her heart was aching, and no matter how she tried, she couldn't sweep the memory of Rafe from the corners of her mind.

She decided to stay at the prestigious and beautiful Beverly Wilshire Hotel right in the heart of Beverly Hills. She could take her meals in the coffee shop, and the location would be convenient for her other plans.

It was with tremendous relief that she settled in her room. Firmly shoving thoughts of Rafe as far aside as she could, she ran a tub of water and climbed in for a long, relaxing bath. More than anything, she wanted to discover her current situation at the television station, but she knew that would have to wait. She would have to plan carefully before she did anything. She juggled her problems in her mind, trying desperately to focus on something besides Rafe. How should she handle Jon and Ellen? Should she phone? Should she march right over to the house and take

236

the bull by the horns? Perhaps it would be best—less personal—if she went to the florist shop first; she was certain she couldn't be rebuffed as severely there as she would at the house.

She remembered the phone call and the note from Jon, and she pondered whether or not it would be best to try to talk with him first. That had been her original intention —how many weeks ago was it now? Thank God the incident had assumed less importance to her, and she felt that she could deal with it rationally, even understand Ellen's hostility better.

Her mind whirling, she reached for a towel and stepped out of the tub. After she had dried off, she wrapped the towel around her and walked over to her suitcase. She opened it and stood gazing into it for a moment. There on top of all her clothes was the gift Rafe had given her; she had deliberately put it out of her mind until now—in Beverly Hills. She removed it, then quickly took out a nightgown and slipped it over her head. The small gift in hand, she sank down on the comfortable bed. And then she could contain her anticipation no longer; ripping off the gaily colored paper, she exposed a tiny white box. Her fingers trembled as she lifted the lid, and there, nestled on a silver lining, was a ring. Kea's heart was beating rapidly as she lifted the ring up with quivering fingers. After all this time Rafe had finally given her a ring—and it was the very same ring she had admired in the jewelry factory, a simple, yet stunning band of gold, so close to a wedding ring that if she put it on her finger, she could almost believe it was.

For a long while she lay and admired the band, turning it around and around, letting it shine in the golden light. Then she eased it on the third finger of her left hand. The ring fit perfectly, but she was tempted to wear it only for a moment. She had vowed to put Rafe behind her, and she would not wear his gift so that every time she looked at

237

her hands, she would be reminded of him. Taking the ring off, she put it back in its box and dropped it back into her suitcase.

Sighing tiredly, she stretched out on the bed; it was the first time in weeks she had been afforded such luxury, and she was grateful for it. She closed her eyes and soon she fell into a deep, weary sleep.

And in her dreams she was still in Mexico with Rafe, making love that final wondrous time on the riverbank, hidden away in the dark under the sheltering trees that had formed a canopy over their love nest.

Kea smiled with contentment as she awakened, the sound of Rafe's name on her lips, the taste of him on her mouth, the clean smell of him in her nostrils. In her half sleep she stretched and smiled. And then she gazed around the plush room, seeing that she was not still in Mexico, and that she was not with Rafe. It had been only a dream, a magic and fulfilling dream that had vanished with the morning, leaving the air tinged with regret and disappointment.

Still disoriented after the quick return to California, Kea brushed back her short hair and struggled up in bed to study her posh surroundings. She had always loved this hotel; in fact, she and Roxwell had stayed here on occasion just to get a mini-vacation from the house and the insistent phone. She shook her head to wipe out Roxwell and the memory.

She would have to face the court battle soon enough too, but she had to take one task at a time. She wanted to wrap up the loose ends of her life so that she could move forward. Rafe had been the first—and the most painful. Jon and Ellen would be the second. The court battle would come when it came, but the job was the most critical of all. She already had an idea how she would approach McDonald; she wanted to take him completely by surprise so he would have no time to build false arguments to dissuade her. But that would take some special handling.

The first thing this morning she was going to the florist shop. She shuddered at the thought, but she had to do it. She went over to her suitcase and began to unpack her things, carefully putting the ring Rafe had given her in her purse. It was precious to her, but it had come much too late. It was a symbol of her parting from Rafe when she had always thought it would mark the beginning of their future together. She took out the copper clown she had purchased for Ellen and set it on a table; she would wait until she saw how she was received by her old friend before she attempted to give her the gift. When she took out her clothes, she discovered the things she had worn the night she and Rafe made love on the riverbank, the grains of sand still clinging to them. She quickly put them aside, for she could not bear to relive the bittersweet time.

She requested an iron and ironing board from housekeeping and pressed a few of her clothes, then selected a simple yellow dress and white sandals. When she had showered and washed and blown her hair dry, she stood before the mirror, assessing her image for the first time in a long while. She saw that her scars had lost some of their red, angry look, though they were still very noticeable. She hadn't expected any miracle, of course, but her attitude had changed, and she no longer saw the scars as a major obstacle to her future. She carefully put on her makeup, then once again marveled at how clever her hairdo was; she gave it a final stroke with the brush, then dressed in the clothes she had chosen.

She ate a relaxing breakfast in the coffee shop, then, fortified, she phoned for a cab. En route to the shop, she smiled faintly as she recalled how long she and Jon and Ellen had debated over the purchase of the business. The rent was exorbitant in that district, and though Jon had received an adequate inheritance and he and Ellen had both worked in florist shops at the time, they had been leery of putting all their eggs into this one particular basket. In the end they had leased the building and opened the shop, and though it required an enormous amount of time and energy, it had been a big success.

The driver parked in front of the building, and for a moment Kea sat still, unable to force herself into action. She gathered her courage around her like a cloak, not knowing what on earth she would do if she found both Jon and Ellen inside, and hostile. Kea paid the cabbie, then watched a little forlornly as he drove away, leaving her to her fate.

She pushed the front door open, listened for the familiar tingling bell that announced her presence, then walked across the room to the counter where an older woman stood figuring a bill for another customer. At least there was only one other person in the room right now, Kea told herself. If there was a scene, it wouldn't prove too humiliating.

Forcing a bright smile to her lips, she asked the woman, "Are the Wagners in?"

The woman peered at her uncertainly over bifocals, then removed them. "They aren't here any longer. I'm the new owner, Mrs. Phelps. May I help you?"

Kea was taken aback. Jon and Ellen had run the shop for almost ten years now. It was part of their lives. She felt a rush of guilt redden her neck and face. Surely she couldn't have been responsible for this too? She couldn't imagine them selling the business. They certainly hadn't mentioned it before the—the incident.

"When did they sell?" she asked in a tight little voice.

The woman smiled. "Almost two weeks ago."

"But why?" Kea blurted.

The woman frowned again and her eyes drifted momentarily to the man leaving with a bouquet of violets. "I beg your pardon?"

Kea licked her lips. "The Wagners—they're friends of mine. I've been out of the country," she hastened to add, "and I had no idea the business was up for sale."

The woman peered at her again, then lifted her glasses and perched them on her head. "You look like—yes, Kea Montgomery! You are! I've seen you on television—*Meeting New People!*" she said triumphantly. "I heard about your accident, and I never see you on the show these days. It's done by that pretty blonde."

Forcing a smile, Kea responded as calmly as she could. "Yes, I am Kea Montgomery. I haven't been on the show for several weeks. About the Wagners—can you tell me why they sold out? Did they open another shop?" She hoped that was the reason, but deep in her heart she was afraid it wasn't. She didn't understand what had happened here; she had been totally unprepared to find a new owner in the shop.

Mrs. Phelps shook her head. "I don't know." She smiled broadly. "But I got a very good deal, and I can offer you a discount on the flowers. There's a special on roses. Can I interest you in a dozen long-stemmed reds?"

Kea shook her head. "No, thank you. I've got to be going now. May I use your phone to call a cab?"

The woman looked irritated, but she motioned Kea behind the counter, then ignored her to go back to work. In moments the cab arrived and Kea was spinning up the road toward the Wagner house, forgetting all about anything but finding Jon and Ellen.

To her utter dismay an unfamiliar face responded to the ring of the doorbell. Surely Ellen and Jon hadn't given up the house, too, in such a short time. What did it mean? Had they moved out of the area? Separated?

She made herself calm down; she was overreacting because of the shop. For all she knew this was a household guest. "Hello," she said to the man standing before her. "I'm looking for the Wagners."

He smiled at her warmly, and she saw two small boys playing behind him. "They don't live here anymore," he told her, his words sending a shock through her. "They've rented the house to me and my family."

Kea looked at the little boys again, thinking how odd it was to see children living in Jon's and Ellen's house after all the years they had so desperately wanted a child of their own.

Seeing the shattered look on Kea's face, the man expressed concern. "Is there some problem?"

Kea nodded. There was a very real problem. "I don't know where they've gone. Do you?"

"Are you a friend of theirs?" he asked curiously.

"Yes, but I've been out of the country. I had no idea they were planning to move. This is all—so—so unexpected."

He nodded sympathetically. "Now that does seem odd. I wish I could say where they've gone, but frankly it was none of my business. I didn't know them. I deal with a realtor service. I didn't have any contact with the owners except to see them when I was shown the house."

A spark of hope stirred in Kea, but it was unfounded. It appeared that they were still together, but just because they had both shown him the house didn't necessarily mean that Jon and Ellen hadn't parted. "I see," she murmured. "Thank you for the information."

He smiled again. "No problem."

As he closed the door, Kea turned on her heel and slowly walked back down the sidewalk, feeling confused and worried. What had prompted Jon and Ellen to give up both the business and the house unless they were planning a divorce? Had they made that decision on such an unfortunate misunderstanding—that one kiss? Climbing back into the waiting cab, she gave the driver instructions to take her back to the Beverly Wilshire.

Shaken by what she had discovered, she rushed up to

her room and began to call any and everyone who might know something about Jon and Ellen's whereabouts, and at last she found someone who knew where she could reach Jon.

She phoned the number, but there was no answer. Guiltily, she wondered if Ellen had pleaded with everyone not to give Kea her number. No one seemed to know where she could reach Ellen, or the Wagners' status as a couple, but Kea conceded that most people she called were more interested in why they hadn't heard from her before, and how she was. Her friends knew the Wagners only casually, for the most part.

She replaced the phone for the last time, abandoning the effort to locate Ellen. It was all so mysterious, and she wondered how the world had changed so much in the three weeks she had been away. She was determined that she would reach Jon sooner or later and see what she could do about this situation.

Suddenly Rafe and Mexico surged into her mind, and she sat down wearily on the edge of the bed. She didn't know what she would have done without Rafe in the past month, and she knew she should be grateful for the time she had had with him, but oh, how she missed him! Memories of him riding beside her in the car, walking by the river with her, dancing with her, making love with her, working with his patients, flowed into her mind, and she was powerless to turn the tide.

Knowing she could escape only by keeping her mind occupied, she went downstairs and ate lunch. When she returned to her room, she called her lawyer. She wanted to ask his advice about her contract with the station, and to determine how best to proceed; her career was the most important part of her life now, and she had to convince McDonald that she could be as good as ever on the show.

The lawyer made some suggestions, then went into the

243

matter of Roxwell's estate. He informed her that Shane had been waging a paper war, sueing her for undue influence, but that he really didn't have a leg to stand on, and his lawyer knew it. The will was too clear-cut. The case would be coming up soon, the lawyer told her, and then she could get it over with.

"I still want to give Shane the house," she insisted.

There was a pause on the other end before the man told her it would all have to be done legally, and the matter of the will contesting should be resolved first so as not to confuse the issue or make her position look weak. She had intended to speak to him about getting her furniture and personal belongings back, but now she realized that they no longer mattered as much as she had once thought.

Hanging up the phone, she resolved to begin again, without memories and items from the past. She could get a new apartment and go all contemporary. She was a new woman with new hopes; she wanted to shed the past and its painful ties. But how it hurt to leave Rafe behind after having discovered such new pleasures with him.

She longed to discuss her problems with someone, but there was no one. She had to keep busy and forget. With a plan for approaching the producer in mind, she set about to get on with her life. She needed a car, and she went to buy one, going to a company she had dealt with before. She would not wait for the court battle over the will; anyway, she had never really liked the sporty little red car Roxwell had purchased for her. It had always been too extravagant. This time she would get something more practical, more economical, less expensive to run and to maintain.

Before evening had come, she had purchased an attractive beige Toyota, and had also looked at several apartments, one of which she found very appealing. For one thing it was near the studio. It would be close to her work.

244

And she was determined to work again. She had to. What else was there in her life?

It was dark when she returned to the hotel, and after a quick meal in the coffee shop she wearily bathed and went to bed. She felt that she was making some headway, and she was feeling better about her life in general. And then the dreams came—the tormenting dreams about Rafe and the days and hours she had shared with him.

The next morning Kea made an appointment with her hairdresser, then hunted through her clothes for just the right outfit. Today she would face McDonald for the first time since the hospital, and everything had to be perfect. To her chagrin she remembered that many of her clothes were still at Rafe's. It had been pointless to pack her nicest dresses for roughing it in Mexico. She didn't know how to reach Mrs. Fortune, but on the off chance that she was still going to Rafe's house for her housekeeping duties, Kea phoned there. She was in luck.

"Mrs. Fortune?"

The other woman was taken aback by the phone call. "Kea! Where are you?"

"Here in Beverly Hills."

"Where's Dr. Jordan?"

"He remained in Mexico for an additional two weeks. I had to come home—to see about my job and all." She hurried on. "That's why I phoned. I need to pick up my dresses. Will you be there at the house long enough for me to come over and get them?"

"Yes, today's my cleaning day. I keep the place dusted and mopped even when the doctor isn't here. The dirt comes anyway, you know," she said with a laugh.

It was good to hear her voice, and Kea was looking forward to seeing her friendly face. "I'll be right over."

She smiled a little after she had hung up. It was amazing how much she had come to care for the other woman in such a short time. She had missed talking with her.

In less than half an hour Kea arrived at Rafe's front door. Mrs. Fortune wanted to hear all about Mexico, and the two of them settled down in the front room with coffee while Kea gave a lively version of the trip. Talking about it brought it all back so vividly that her heart began to ache as she discussed Carmen's family and how Rafe had worked with the patients. Her voice was tender and warm as she talked about the people she had grown to love.

Mrs. Fortune's eyes glowed with a bright sparkle. "And how did you two get on?"

"Who?" Kea asked, deliberately misunderstanding the question.

"You know who," the woman teased. "I can hear it in your voice. You're fond of the doctor, aren't you?"

Kea shrugged in a careless manner, but she was terribly flustered. "Who wouldn't be? He's an impressive man, isn't he?"

"I sense that your interest is more than casual," Mrs. Fortune persisted. "Your voice changes when you talk about him."

Laughing lightly, Kea tried to brush off the woman's comment. "Now you stop trying to be a matchmaker." Her voice became more serious. "If Rafe is interested in anyone, I believe it's Trena. She's more his type." Kea's eyes met the other woman's, and she knew she was digging for information, but she couldn't help it. "I got the impression the two of them were more than just doctor and nurse."

Now it was Mrs. Fortune's turn to shrug offhandedly. "It won't be the first time a doctor and his nurse have been drawn to each other," she commented, "but I don't know anything about the two of them. I've never known him to bring her to the house, but then I don't know everything, do I?" She seemed a little thoughtful, and Kea was sorry she had prodded. "Trena worships him, but then he did

246

a lot for her. He paid for her schooling."

Remembering Trena's anguished face the day she had made her plea, Kea nodded, then changed the subject. She looked at her watch, amazed by how fast the time had flown. "I'd better run," she said. "I have a hair appointment. I'm going to talk to my producer today—but he doesn't know it yet." She said it casually, as if her whole future did not depend on this interview, but in her heart she knew how desperately important it was.

"Let me help you with your clothes," Mrs. Fortune said, and the two of them went down the hall to the room Kea had occupied.

There weren't many things there; most of her clothes were still at the house, but the two women hastily laid the items out on the bed. "That isn't mine," Kea said as Mrs. Fortune took the beautiful gown from the closet.

"Oh, yes," the other woman said. "That's the one the doctor keeps on hand for patients who have nothing to wear. Some are very poor, and he says there's nothing like a lovely gown to boost a sick woman's morale."

Kea smiled, remembering how she had thought the gown must have been Trena's. "That sounds like Rafe's logic," she said with a trace of fond reminiscence in her voice. Then she quickly packed her own gowns and odds and ends in the bag she had brought along. Mrs. Fortune carried the dresses out to the car.

When she had loaded the car, Kea smiled at the other woman. "Will you have lunch with me soon? I don't want to lose track of you."

Mrs. Fortune laughed. "I just have a feeling that you and I are going to be seeing a lot of each other, but, yes, I'd love to have lunch with you."

"I'll give you a call as soon as I get a place of my own," Kea said. "You take care."

"You, too, honey. And good luck with the job."

"Thanks." Kea climbed into the car and made her way back to the hotel. She was already growing weary of staying there, and she vowed to apartment hunt again when she had left the station today. She hung up her clothes in the hotel closet, then selected a sophisticated jade dress with Chinese lines for the confrontation with McDonald Hollister, the producer. She would take it with her to the beauty salon, and when her hair had been done, she could change and do her makeup there.

An hour later she braced herself for the meeting and walked into McDonald's office. His secretary looked up in surprise. "Kea! How are you?" she cried, rising.

Kea forced a smile to her lips. "I'm just fine. And you?"

"Real good."

"Is McDonald in?" Kea couldn't engage in pleasantries any longer; she was too nervous. "I'd really like to see him."

"Gosh, Kea, I'm sorry. He's taping in Philadelphia this week. He won't be back until Tuesday."

Kea was devastated. Not only could she not see him today, but his secretary would tell him she had been here. He would know what it was about, and she wouldn't be able to catch him off guard as she had planned. It was a rotten bit of luck, but there was nothing to be done about it now.

"Shall I make an appointment for you next week?"

Kea smiled a little. Just weeks before she had walked into McDonald's office unannounced at any time. Now she needed an appointment. "Yes, that would be fine."

"Tuesday—eleven o'clock."

"Yes."

"All right. See you then," the secretary said. "And, Kea, it's great to see you again."

"Thank you. It was nice to see you." She turned on her expensively shod heel and walked out into the sunshine, but the day had darkened considerably. She was disappointed, to say the least, and she was sure she had lost the advantage she had been counting on. Of course she would return on Tuesday, but she knew instinctively that McDonald would be armed with reasons why she couldn't have her old job back. And the thought distressed her deeply. It was so important that she succeed in putting her career back together. It was all she had to be proud of.

CHAPTER THIRTEEN

Kea busied herself with her apartment search, finally finding just what she wanted, in the neighborhood she wanted. The rent was a little higher than she had expected, but she had no doubts that she would soon be working again—at something—and she took it. She was grateful that the inheritance her father had left her, and her own wise investments, had given her a back-up source of money, for she certainly needed something to fall back on now.

She had not tried to call Jon again, and now she put it off until she could have her phone installed. It was wonderful to be so occupied that she didn't have much time to think. Nothing banished the ache she felt over losing Rafe, but the hours flew by as she shopped for everything for her apartment—from furniture and bedding to household utensils.

At night she went to bed so drained that she hardly had time to review the day's events, much less worry about her problems. Rafe remained in her mind, a raw wound, but she would not let herself dwell on him, or the fact that he would be home in another week. It meant nothing to her; it had nothing to do with her.

By the time Tuesday came, Kea had settled into her new place and was quite content with it. She had even gotten used to the solitude, which at first had bothered her after being with so many people for those weeks in Mexico. She rose early and tried to keep calm as she reviewed the arguments she would use when she finally met with McDonald. Over and over in her mind she tried to outthink him, imagining how she would answer his objections, but she wasn't feeling very secure when she finally dressed—again in the jade—and went to the office. She was early, and to her dismay McDonald kept her waiting.

The tactic made her even more determined, and her temper was flaming when the secretary finally admitted her to the office. McDonald Hollister, a sharp-faced, fast-talking man in his forties, stood up and held out his hand when Kea entered.

"Kea, sweetheart, how are you? This is an unexpected honor." His eyes raked over her face in swift appraisal, and she could tell that he was not pleased with what he saw.

She raised her brows. "How's that, Mac? I had an appointment. You knew that I was coming."

A bright stain slowly traveled up his neck. "Well, I don't mean today—I meant that you were coming at all. And you look just splendid," he said much too quickly. "Here. Sit down."

He pulled a narrow chair over in front of his desk for her, and Kea was reminded that he was one of those men who liked to feel powerful while he sat in his own plush chair, some distance behind a big desk. "So, what brings you here? I'm so glad to see you."

"Good," she murmured, gazing levelly at him. "I'm glad you think I look—what was your term?—just splendid. I'm here because I want my job back."

He pretended to look surprised, although he and Kea both knew that he had anticipated her saying just that. He leaned back in his chair, crossed his leg at the knee, and smiled patronizingly at her.

"Now, Kea, sweetheart, when I said you looked splendid, I meant . . . well, I meant considering what you've gone through. You're still a very attractive woman, but, now you and I are old friends—" He uncrossed his legs, pulled his chair closer to the desk, and said in a low voice, "Honey, you know how the board feels—television is for the beautiful people. It's that way with all the stations."

Kea was a little shocked by his bluntness, but she had no intention of letting him know that. Imitating him, she pulled her own chair closer to his desk, perched her arms on it, and spoke slowly and distinctly. "Let's cut the bull, Mac. Television is what the ratings say it is. I've always been very high in the ratings. I want my job back."

He leaned away from her again, sliding his hands down into his pants pockets, and succeeding in infuriating her. Kea had to remind herself that she would have to be very calm and collected to get anywhere with him. He had made up his mind long ago.

"Sweetheart, I don't want to hurt your feelings. You know that. I've always thought the world of you, but women in television are basically pretty faces. That's what got them there, and that's what keeps them there."

Kea sucked in her breath at his condescending remark, and she was grateful that Mrs. Fortune had once said something very close to his last comment. "Mac, that's the most incredibly chauvinistic crack I've ever heard from you, and I've heard some real shockers." Suddenly she stood up and walked around to the other side of his desk, effectively destroying the emotional and physical distance between them.

"I got where I was in television by a lot of hard work. I was innovative and bright, and the audience liked what I presented. A pretty face never won me an Emmy, and you know it!" She was breathing hard now, and she knew her face was red with anger.

Mac let her fume for a minute, then directed her back to her chair. "Sit down, Kea," he said in a more solemn tone.

252

For a moment she stood obstinately where she was. "Come on, sweetheart, sit down. Let's cut the malarkey and talk."

Kea hadn't realized how tightly her fists were clenched until she opened them. Drawing in several deep breaths, she sat down again. Then she stared at him, waiting to see what he had to say.

"The public won't want you, Kea." He shook his head before she could speak again. "Hear me out. You're scarred. People won't be expecting it; it's distracting. Now Janice is doing a commendable job, and the public has gotten used to her. I've no intentions of letting her go."

"That's discrimination!" she cried angrily, losing her temper in spite of all her talks to herself beforehand.

"It's *business!*" he shot back brutally. His tone softened. "Kea, no one was more sorry than I about your misfortune, but it rules you out in this business. I can't put you back on the air."

"You mean you *won't!*" she flung at him.

"Make it easy on yourself. I'm trying to do you a favor. Let's be honest about this. If I let you go back on, you might attract attention from the curiosity seekers—the 'let's see how bad she looks' people—and once they had seen, that would be it. Our ratings would drop, and you know it."

His sheer callousness amazed her. "You've got to be kidding," she practically yelled at him. "Do you think that badly of the public? Do you mean to sit there and tell me you think they only watched me because they found me physically attractive? My God, man, what have you been thinking? Where have you been? They might be curious, sure, and they might be a little surprised—but so what? I have scars I didn't have before, but I don't look hideous, for crying out loud."

"Come on, Kea, give it up. I'm sorry you're making this so hard on both of us."

"Mac, I'm still the same me. I still have a brain. I can still keep a lively show going—and, Mac, the show is for the guests, not the interviewer." She knew she was making an impassioned plea, and she hadn't wanted to humiliate herself this way. Her stomach was quivering and she felt sick. He was making this so degrading, but she couldn't give up. She *wouldn't*. She wanted her show back.

Her eyes met his. "Give me a chance. If the public doesn't go for it, I'll quit."

He stared brazenly at her, and she was taken aback when he asked bluntly, "Can't anything be done about those scars?"

"Yes," she said coldly. "In four months they can be revised, but there will still be some scarring."

"Tell you what," he said as if he were offering her the crown jewels. "Come back then, after the surgery. We'll talk."

"I want to go back to work *now*," she stated.

He shook his head. "I can't do it, Kea. I can't take that kind of chance. Besides, if I let you go on, people with all kinds of flaws will think they can do it too."

"Mac, don't make me fight all the way to the top with this," she pleaded, suddenly feeling very let down. "Give me a chance."

He was resolute. "Your contract is almost up. There's nothing to fight about."

"Oh, yes there is. The contract still has a few weeks to run. I'm going to get my job back, if I have to go all the way to the top. Now *you* make it easy on *yourself*."

He shrugged carelessly, and although she refused to show it, Kea was deeply discouraged. "Do what you have to," he told her offhandedly, "but you'd be wiser to try producing."

Kea couldn't keep back the retort that came to mind. "I'm too smart for a job you can do, Mac." Spinning on her heel, she left the room with as much dignity as she could muster, but she was sure her knees would buckle at any minute.

Damn the cold-hearted bastard! she told herself. She had always known he was difficult, but some of the statements he had made today were horrible! Women were basically pretty faces on television indeed! How she wished she had had a tape recorder. The newspapers would have a field day with that remark if she wanted to get nasty.

She forced herself to bid the secretary good-bye, and she kept herself together until she was out in the hall. Then she had to support herself against the wall for a few minutes before she could even flee into the ladies' room. Once inside she walked over to the mirror and stood before it as if she were mesmerized.

For a long time she stood there staring at her face, and from deep within her strength came to her rescue. He wouldn't treat her like that and get away with it. She would fight, even if she lost. The memory of that first night in Rafe's arms when she had known she had a future washed over her, and with it a warmth that lifted her soul. The thought gave her the courage to go on, the courage she needed so desperately now.

She didn't even remember the drive back to her apartment, but once she was inside, she called her lawyer and instructed him to start a discrimination suit against the station, including the producer, the chairmen of the board, the general manager, the program director, and the vice-president. If nothing else, she would have the satisfaction of airing her grievances. And she did still have a contract, at least for a few more weeks, that just might give her the leverage she needed. She was sure she would be all right it she could just get her foot back in the door.

Her lawyer was delighted. "We'll give them hell!" he promised her. But Kea took no comfort in his words. She didn't want to give them hell; she wanted her job back.

"By the way," he added, "I wanted to call you, but I

didn't even have a phone number for you. We go to court over the will week after next."

"Oh," she said, not at all thrilled by the news. At least she would be getting that matter settled. When he had told her the time, she replaced the receiver.

Feeling blue, missing Rafe as never before, she took a long, hot bath, then went to bed. Suddenly she wanted desperately to talk with Rafe, to share her problems and ask his advice. She had grown accustomed to those comforting evening walks. Sometimes they had just walked in companionable silence, sharing a relaxed intimacy that, she realized now, had been very precious to her. Other times they'd discussed whatever came to mind. Tonight, in the silence of her room, the absence of his voice was like the loss of music to a pianist who cared for nothing else. She had thought she would find a nap refreshing, but it proved elusive. Finally, she went to the kitchen and fixed a sandwich for dinner. It was eaten in haste, and she again retreated to the security of her bed. But sleep was a long time coming.

When Kea awakened the next morning, she felt as if she had been sleeping for weeks. It took her a long time to get herself motivated, but by the time she had finished her third cup of coffee, she had decided on a plan of action.

She went to the phone and dialed Jon's number.

"Hello."

"Jon, thank God," she breathed. "I've been trying to get you for almost two weeks. I've been frantic. I didn't know you had moved, and I went to the shop and found a new owner there."

"Kea!" he cried, his voice filled with excitement. "I've been trying to call you, but it seemed that I never received an answer at Rafe's, and I didn't know what to think."

"I've been out of the country with him—Mexico." she said.

256

"Why didn't you let me know?"

Kea paused for a moment. "Under the circumstances it didn't seem advisable. I tried talking to Ellen a couple of times, but she wasn't very receptive. How is she, Jon?"

"She's fine. Just fine. She's in Europe right now. Listen, Kea, I'm right in the middle of all kinds of unpacking and rearranging. I've been at my wit's end moving into this place and hunting for the right shop to open. How about dinner tonight?"

She hesitated, and Jon immediately reassured her. "Just to talk. I want to get this whole thing straightened out. Meet you at the Sunset at eight."

"Yes. Yes, that will be fine. See you then."

She hung up, not quite sure what to make of it all. So Jon was going to open another shop. Why was Ellen in Europe? Well, it wouldn't do any good to speculate. At least she had reached him, and at last she was going to get some answers. She found herself anxiously looking forward to eight o'clock, and the entire day stretched out before her, long and never-ending.

She kept hearing Mac's words play over and over in her head, and the more she thought of it, the more enraged she became. Finally, she dressed in shorts and a sweat shirt and began her exercise campaign. She had healed from her accident and there was no longer any reason to put it off.

Somehow she found ways to kill the rest of the day, and when eight o'clock came she was nervously awaiting Jon in the restaurant bar, sipping a Tom Collins. She stood up when she saw him coming toward the table, and with mixed emotions she allowed him to embrace her. He gave her a quick hug, then held out the chair so that she could sit back down.

"Kea," Jon said, "I've wanted to get this off my chest so many times. In fact, I tried calling Rafe's twice, but I couldn't make myself speak when you answered the phone. I left a message once. I was so embarrassed about

257

what had happened that I didn't know what to say to you." He stared down at the table. "I never meant it. You must know that."

Kea had no doubts about what "it" was. "I didn't think you did, Jon. I knew you were only trying to comfort me." She laughed nervously. "You went about it all wrong, and your timing was about the worst I've ever seen."

They both looked up when a waitress came over. Jon ordered a drink, then said, "I was so moved by your pain, and I knew you had lost so much. I only wanted to help. But I sure loused things up, didn't I?"

"How badly?" Kea asked, her voice full of anxiety.

Jon sighed. "At one point it looked real bad. I swear I honestly thought Ellen was going to divorce me, but it all worked out for the best. You know what they say about finding the good in the bad. Well, seeing us together unleashed a torrent of unhappiness and disappointment in Ellen."

He looked up as the waitress served his drink, then kept Kea waiting on pins and needles while he sipped it. "Ellen had been feeling chained to the shop. We were putting in more and more hours, and not enjoying the money. And she had begun to hate the house because she saw it as a reminder of our failure—all those bedrooms and she couldn't have children. When she finally began to shriek at me about you, all this other stuff came out."

He looked as if the discovery still amazed him. "She's always wanted to travel, but we would plan a trip and then cancel it because of the business. That's why she's in Europe now. A friend of hers was going, and when she threw it up to me, we decided she really needed to get away. It's worked out fine."

He reached over and patted Kea's hand. "I know we abandoned you at a very bad time, but we couldn't get ourselves together. Everything's fine now, and we want desperately for you to be our friend again."

Holding up his right hand, he said, "Scout's honor—nothing like that kiss will ever happen to you again. Ellen feels the same way I do about the entire mess. She knows she was rough on you, but you were only the tip of the iceberg. What was really bothering us both had nothing to do with you. That's why we rented out the house and leased a smaller place. We're also looking for a smaller shop. We plan to get a good manager—and close every day at five." He smiled. "Mrs. Phelps, the woman who took the business, had been after us for months to let her have it. She used the same arguments that Ellen had—we were too young to be tied to a busy shop like that, working day and night at it. She had nothing else in her life, and she had been badgering us for a long time. The last time she was at the right place at the right time, and we let her have it."

Kea smiled. "Well, you've sure made some changes, but it sounds like you're getting your life back in order." She shook her head. "I don't mind telling you how upset I've been. I thought both of you hated me."

Jon nodded, and all the mirth was gone from his face. "It's been hell," he agreed. "I thought I'd lost Ellen. I didn't realize how much you meant to me until the accident, and I didn't realize how much Ellen meant until she started telling me all the things that were wrong with us. We took a house down on the beach because Ellen's always wanted that. You're going to love it. I'm still trying to get settled in, but wait until you see it. It's wonderful."

"I will wait," she said evenly. "Until Ellen comes home."

Jon looked a little sheepish. "I wish there was something I could do to make it up to you, Kea, but I can only apologize. I swear I didn't know what I was doing."

Giving him a faint smile, she said, "I'm convinced."

Jon had made reservations and their name was called.

Feeling that old sense of camaraderie, they walked into the restaurant and settled down for a long and pleasant meal.

Kea slept late the next morning. She had dreamed about Rafe again, and he was on her mind when she awakened. She found herself wondering if he had returned, and for a single foolish moment she tried to think of some logical excuse for phoning his house. She quickly shoved the thought from her mind. That was just what she didn't need. She was getting her life back on solid footing, and that meant no Rafe. She had a new apartment, she had reconciled with Jon—and she was sure she could believe him when he said Ellen wanted to re-establish their relationship. Her life was definitely taking shape again.

She was startled from her thoughts when the telephone rang. It was her lawyer, telling her that the executives at the station wanted to meet with her this very afternoon to discuss her contract. He offered to go with her, but she told him she wanted to fight this one alone. Kea could feel her heart soaring, and it was all she could do not to shout with joy when she had hung up. She knew it was way too soon to think of victory, but the meeting was a step in the right direction.

The phone rang again, and she jumped in surprise. This time it was Mrs. Fortune. "Can we have lunch today?" the other woman asked.

"I'd love it," Kea exclaimed. "It will fit right in with my plans. I'm meeting with the bigwigs at the station this afternoon to talk about my contract."

They agreed on a place for lunch, and then Kea rambled about the apartment, trying to decide what to wear today. She was too excited to eat, and she decided that a cup of coffee would hold her until the appointed time. She was looking forward to seeing the other woman with the utmost relish, and then and there she promised herself that she wouldn't ask a word about Rafe.

The promise couldn't be kept. Rafe had come home in a brooding mood, and Mrs. Fortune was concerned about him. She spent most of the meal talking about him. As they sat across from each other in a little café, she frowned worriedly.

"He's in such an agitated state that I don't see how he'll work. I've never seen him like this in the seven months I've worked for him. He won't talk to me about it, but he's so irritable that I know he's really upset about something. He's not eating well, and he hardly sleeps at all. Why he got up at three this morning to go jogging. Now I don't need to tell you that in this city—any city nowadays—that's just plain dangerous. Sometimes I wonder if he just doesn't care about himself anymore."

Kea didn't know what to think. Had Rafe had a spat with Trena? Her heart began to pound. Or could he be upset over her? The idea seemed much too impossible. He hadn't seemed to care at all that she was leaving Mexico. He hadn't even suggested that she stay, she reminded herself firmly.

"I thought you might know what's wrong with him," Mrs. Fortune said, drawing Kea's gaze to her face.

"Why?" Kea asked. "I don't know what to tell you."

Mrs. Fortune shook her head. "I'm not sure. I can't put my finger on it, but somehow I sense that you're part of this. I'm not trying to pry," she added quickly, "but I thought you might be able to help."

Kea shook her head. "I'm sorry. I can't help." She raised her eyes and gazed around the room, uncertain if she should go into the painful past or leave it where it was. But then she realized that Mrs. Fortune deserved to know the truth. "Rafe and I dated for three years, but nothing came of it." She looked levelly at the other woman. "I married Roxwell."

She could see Mrs. Fortune's mind spinning feverishly,

261

but no light dawned in those compassionate brown eyes. "I see," she said at last.

Perhaps she did and perhaps she didn't. Kea changed the subject, smoothly gliding into her situation with the station, and then the court case week after next. "At last," she said, "I'm tying up the loose ends of my life. I feel like I'm really in control again."

Despite her cool words, she was disturbed about what Mrs. Fortune had said. Even though she wanted to forget him, she could not stop caring for Rafe. And whatever was bothering him, she wished she could go to him and make it better. She knew that was impossible, of course; he had made it clear that he didn't want her. Still . . .

Still, she could not get him out of her mind. And she realized that, no matter how far away he was, no matter how easily he had cut her out of his life, no matter how often she wished it were not so—he was the other half of her troubled soul. And he always would be.

"I'm glad, Kea. You deserve the very best."

Mrs. Fortune's reply drew Kea out of her reverie, and she remembered that she should leave for her appointment. She was actually shaking as she paid her bill and left for the station. It only took her a few minutes to get there.

Never before had she seen so much studio brass gathered in one place as in the room she was led into. She glanced down the length of the table, seeing everyone from Mac to the head of the station, and for a single moment she was intimidated; suddenly she wished she had brought her lawyer with her. Then she straightened her spine and took the chair one of the men had pulled out for her. This was her battle and she would see it through.

The next hour was grueling. First they mentioned subtle reasons why she should drop her suit, then they openly threatened that she would never work in television again if she pursued it. When that didn't work, they tried to persuade her, as Mac had, at least to wait to make a decision about the job until after her scars were revised. After she adamantly refused, they tried to reason with her, to plead the station's position, with considerably more tact than Mac, Kea noted.

Twice Kea felt herself weaken under the pressure, but she would not give in, and the men had to agree that she had the ratings and the prestige. Also they knew that if it actually came to a court battle, the public would sympathize with Kea. She began to take heart when she saw that they were stymied. Finally, amid much grumbling and exchanging of glances, they told her they would discuss it among themselves and get back to her.

A smiling Kea bid them a good day. They had been stern and negative, but she had held her own with them, and she sensed that at the very least she would be reconsidered for the job. She kept her poise until she was out on the street, and then she threw up her arms and laughed at the sun.

CHAPTER FOURTEEN

The next two weeks passed in a blur of confusion for Kea; her lawyer was constantly in touch with the station executives, and the battle was bitter, with much bickering back and forth. Kea knew that they were playing for time, and in exasperation, after one of her lawyer's lengthy reports on a counteroffer from the station, she insisted that he go ahead with the suit immediately. On the heels of that decision came the court battle over the will.

The verdict on that one was anticlimactic after all the tears, uncertainty, and pain. The judge ruled in Kea's favor, and a bitter, sullen Shane stalked away from the courthouse. Kea gazed after him, feeling sorry for him, but she had made her decision. She knew the blow of losing his father's fortune would be softened somewhat when she turned the house over to him, but first she wanted to remove a few of her personal belongings. She would arrange it all through her lawyer.

She left feeling less than triumphant. She saw the inheritance as more of a burden than anything else; however, an idea had been forming in her mind since she and Rafe had first discussed whether or not she should accept it. Once she had gone to Mexico and seen the dire need there for modern medical facilities, she had let the idea simmer more and more on the back burners of her mind, waiting only for the resolution of the case to decide what to do. She didn't want the money; Shane wouldn't put it to good use; but there in Mexico, and around the world, people were suffering intensely.

If she donated the money to charity, she could be of real help to people like Carmen. Suddenly she realized how ironic it was that she was burning with the same fever to do good that she had so resented in Rafe those many months ago. And she wondered what Rafe would think if he knew. Abruptly, she dismissed the idea; it had nothing to do with Rafe other than the fact that he had been the one to open her eyes to the need all around her. She thought of how much her own life had changed in the past few weeks; it had been incredible, a painful, soul-searching time of growth and learning, all caused by an accident that had altered everything. Now it was in her power to help other victims of accidents and misfortune.

Kea spent the balance of the day shopping, trying to unwind. When she returned home, she had a call from her lawyer, telling her to contact the station's program director first thing in the morning. "Can't you tell me what he has in mind?" she asked over the pounding of her heart.

"No, but I suspect it's good news. Let me know."

"I will," she assured him. Then she held the phone to her ear a moment longer, tempted to call the director now. What could one day matter? She sighed tiredly, knowing it was all part of the game with them. She would be kept in agony another night.

And a long night it was; so much hinged on what the director would say, and Kea found that she couldn't sleep a wink. She would lie in her bed, toss and turn, and finally get up in desperation. At last the dark night was over.

At nine o'clock sharp she phoned the station, too eager to care that they knew how eager she was. When he came on the line, the director was curt and impersonal.

"We've decided to put you on the afternoon show until your contract plays out—if you want to do it. When we see the response, we'll re-evaluate your position."

The blood was pounding at her temples, but Kea tried to match his aloof tone. "That will do for the meantime. When shall I start?"

He told her she would start on Monday, on the pretext of being guest hostess for Janice, who would presumably be taking a vacation. It wasn't a complete victory, but it was a victory—and Kea was ecstatic. She had full confidence that once she was on the air, she would be able to secure her job. And she was to begin on Monday—a live show!

The weekend passed in a blur as she fell back into the old routine amid rushes of ecstasy and excitement. She was sent the guest profiles by special courier, and her return to the station was being ballyhooed several times a day. With much indecision she finally settled on what she would wear: a lovely teal-blue dress with a high neck, long sleeves, and a full skirt that swirled softly and femininely about her legs. She would complement it with tall blue shoes that showed off her legs to advantage.

When Monday morning came, she was a nervous wreck. She spent the entire morning trying to calm down, but her knees were knocking when she settled down on the sofa on the plush set and tried out her camera smile. She gazed out into the audience, and her heart filled with love when she saw their support. Some had signs saying "Welcome Back, Kea!" Others said, "We've missed you!" or "We Love You!" and she was moved to tears.

When Mac gave her cue and the cameraman began to do a countdown with his hand signals, Kea suddenly settled in like the natural performer she was. Her makeup had been impeccably done, and her scars were discreetly camouflaged, though still evident.

She knew when the first guest was introduced that they both would do fine. The show went smoothly from beginning to end, with the guests going out of their way to make things easy and pleasant. Along the way Kea lost her nervousness, and the applause was enthusiastic and frequent. When a guest asked about her accident and what had helped her recovery most, she responded readily, "A doctor took me with him on a trip to Mexico, and I saw how fortunate I really was." She smiled. "I'll tell you something—I don't worry about wrinkles the way I used to."

The guest laughed. "No," he agreed. "I suppose you don't."

The applause that met the exchange was so loud that they had to wait until it stopped. At the end of the show the audience gave them a standing ovation.

Before she even left the stage, calls were coming into the station from well-wishers delighted to see her back. They might have tuned in, as Mac had predicted, to see how bad she looked, but they had apparently found her all too human, and they had loved her for it. She was already receiving flowers and gifts. And she was overwhelmed by the generosity and kindness of the audience.

The people who had attended the show waited in line to wish her success and to tell her how glad they were to have her back. "No one has your style, Kea," a little lady called out, and Kea had tears in her eyes when she thanked the woman. "You're beautiful, babe," a burly man told her, and she wouldn't have taken a thousand dollars for the compliment.

Mac stood on the sidelines, reserving judgment, perhaps thinking it couldn't last, but the next day and the day after was a repeat. She was back in, and she knew it. By the end of the week she was told that she would be given a new contract, and although it was only for the afternoon show, as Janice had been allowed to keep the evening show, Kea was well pleased. She had done something no one else had dared to do, and she had succeeded. Television wasn't just for pretty faces; she had proven that. And how she longed to tell Rafe so. But it was only wishful thinking.

Every day of the week Rafe had left the office early so that he could go home and watch Kea on TV. He had been compelled to, both to see how she fared—and to see her. He was proud of her accomplishment, even though it symbolized all that had kept them apart. By Sunday he could think of little else; before he could reconsider it, he picked up the phone and dialed the number Mrs. Fortune had conveniently left on the kitchen counter. He told himself that the least he could do was congratulate her; after all, they were not enemies.

When the phone rang, Kea was surprised by the deep male voice on the other end. "Congratulations. I caught your show on Friday, and it looks like you're back in."

The sound of Rafe's voice took her breath away; she honestly hadn't expected to hear from him again. For a moment she was at a loss for words. "Thank you," she murmured at last. "I'm very pleased about the show."

"I'm glad," he said. There was a pause, and Kea wondered if he had something more to say. Would he ask to see her? All her foolish hopes were quickly dashed.

"I'm glad things are going well for you," he said. And then the conversation was over. "Take care of yourself, Kea. Good-bye."

He hung up, and for a moment he stood staring at the phone, not sure why he had called her. What had he accomplished except hearing her voice again, and starting all the pain once more? He had seen the show, and he had phoned her. It had proven nothing.

Kea stood with the phone to her ear, aching for something more from him. Was that what it was then—good wishes? No desire to see her? To talk to her? She thought of calling him back, but she didn't have the nerve. His phone call hadn't really given her any opening.

She told herself that it didn't matter—that he didn't matter—but it was a lie. Hearing his voice again made her feel all weak inside, made her want him again. It brought

268

to mind Mrs. Fortune's words about him being upset, and she wondered if he had decided he didn't want Trena either. She didn't want to think about that pain again. She was sorry Rafe had phoned at all, for it was apparent he didn't want her either, so why didn't he just leave her alone?

His phone call put her recent accomplishments in cruel perspective: She had her job back; she had a new apartment; her scars hadn't appalled anyone; she had her friends back; but there was something frighteningly wrong in her life. Some key ingredient was missing—love. Love that only Rafe could give.

Pushing the haunting reality aside, she made herself count her blessings. She was deep in thought when a knock sounded on her door. At first, having thought so recently of him, Kea imagined that it was Rafe, but when she opened the door, she found Ellen and Jon on her doorstep.

For what seemed an eternity both women just stared at each other, then they rushed forward at the same time to embrace, tears streaming down their faces. "I'm sorry," Ellen murmured.

"It wasn't your fault," Kea assured her tearfully.

Jon stood in the background, looking sheepish, and Kea stepped away from Ellen to usher him in, her smile warm and welcoming.

"I'll put on some coffee," she said. "Make yourselves at home."

"I really like the place," Ellen said, her voice still thick as she looked around. "It's more like you, contemporary and all." She sniffled. "I never could see you with those antiques."

Kea handed her friend a tissue and took one for herself. She laughed lightly. "I guess I thought they meant permanence and stability, or something like that."

Both women smiled, their eyes still bright with tears.

Ellen joined Kea in the kitchen. "Jon said you were in Mexico. I want to hear all about it." It was clear that they would speak no more of the unfortunate incident. "I've just come back from Europe, you know."

Kea nodded. "Yes, and I'm sure that's more exciting than Mexico."

"Are you kidding—and you went there with Rafe? Tell me about it."

Ellen's green eyes shone with anticipation, but Kea's gray ones suddenly clouded over. She shrugged, finding the memories still too painful. "It was a a fascinating experience, and I learned a lot about how the other side lives. We truly don't know how lucky we are, Ellen."

"Oh, my God!" Ellen threw up her hands in mock exasperation. "Rafe's gone and turned you into a crusader." She laughed delightedly, but when she saw that Kea wasn't laughing, she became solemn. "You're serious about this, aren't you?"

Kea nodded. "I inherited Roxwell's money—in spite of Shane contesting the will—but I don't want it for myself. I thought maybe—" She stopped, deciding it would be best to keep her plans to herself.

"You thought what? If you don't want it for yourself . . ." Then it dawned on Ellen what Kea must want to do with the money. "Don't tell me you want to give it to Rafe for his causes?"

Kea shook her head. "Not to Rafe personally, but I do think I'll donate it to help people like those Rafe helps."

"Aren't you doing this to impress Rafe?" Ellen asked.

"No, of course not," Kea denied. But she wondered if perhaps there wasn't some tiny bit of truth in Ellen's question. She didn't expect Rafe to find out what she was going to do with the money, but if he ever did, she wanted to believe that he would be proud of her.

For a moment Ellen just stared at her friend. Then she

asked, "If you inherited, why are you in this apartment? Did Shane get the house?"

"He will. My conscience would barely let me take the money, despite Roxwell's explicit instructions. I can't take the house too."

Kea didn't comment, and Ellen changed the subject. "Tell me what happened with you and Rafe."

Kea busied herself with the coffee. "Not much, really."

"You don't expect me to believe that!" Ellen insisted. "*Something* must have happened—you and Rafe—in Mexico all those weeks."

"Me and Rafe—and Trena," Kea amended.

Ellen's green eyes grew wide. "Trena was there too. Oh, my God!"

"Of course she was there," Kea said as if she hadn't minded at all. "She's his nurse, after all."

"How could you stand it?" Ellen asked. She had known how humiliated Kea had been when she dated Rafe and Trena was always there in the background.

"I really got to like her, Ellen." She kept her eyes on the coffee pot, watching as the coffee dripped. "She and Rafe belong together."

"Says who?" Ellen demanded.

"Trena."

"And you took her word for it?" she asked incredulously.

Kea shrugged as if it were of no consequence, but just talking about it made her heart ache. "I realized that she was the one for Rafe. He needs her and he certainly doesn't want me. He's been seeing Trena all along."

"Are you sure?" Ellen asked.

Kea watched the coffee maker as the last bit of coffee dripped into the pot. "Yes."

Abruptly, Ellen turned Kea around so that she had to look at her. There were tears shimmering in those sad gray eyes. "You still care for him, don't you?" Ellen demanded.

271

"You've never gotten over him. I didn't think so when I heard that you went to Mexico with him. I knew then that there would be trouble."

Kea smiled sadly. "There was no trouble. Rafe took me on the trip for my therapy. He didn't bat an eyelash when I came home two weeks before he did."

"I don't understand," Ellen murmured.

A single tear slipped from Kea's eye. "There's nothing to understand. It was over for us before I married Roxwell, but I never wanted to admit it." She looked into Ellen's eyes. "Oh, Ellen, if you had seen him, the way the people love him and depend on him, you would know how incredibly selfish it was of me to want to chain him to Beverly Hills. He serves a real need. He's wonderful."

"You still *love* him," Ellen accused, correctly reading Kea's feeling for Rafe in her voice.

Kea turned back to the coffee, and she heard Ellen murmur sadly, "Oh, Kea, isn't there any hope for the two of you?"

Kea shook her head. "No. He belongs in another world. So does Trena," she added, the admission making her tremble. "Coffee's ready," she announced, pouring it in three cups. Ellen didn't see how badly her hands shook.

When they had again joined Jon in the living room, Kea skillfully changed the subject, but Ellen remained thoughtful. Finally, the talk turned to Ellen's trip and she began to entertain them with funny stories and purchases she had made. Remembering the copper clown, Kea excused herself to get it. Ellen fell in love with it, and vowed someday to visit the jewelry factory where it was made. The hours flew by on golden wings as the three friends caught up on the time apart, and finally Jon and Ellen had to leave.

"Have dinner with us at El Casa tomorrow night," Ellen urged. "Let's become the three musketeers again. What do you say? We've always had so much fun there."

Kea nodded. "That sounds great."

Before Jon could whisk Ellen out the door, she called over her shoulder, "Congratulations again on getting your job back. I've heard that you were better than ever."

Kea smiled. "Different, maybe, but I don't know about better."

"See you tomorrow night. Eight o'clock. Don't be late," Ellen said.

When Kea had bid them good-bye, she settled down with the book written by a guest who would be on her next show, but she couldn't concentrate. Ellen's disturbing questions had brought up fresh memories of Rafe. She kept asking herself why he had called. Then she reminded herself that he had always claimed to be concerned about her health—mental and physical—since the accident. Perhaps his call was just more of his professional interest. He had wanted to be sure that she really was doing all right with the show. There was no point in dwelling on it and making something out of it.

All day the next day she was excited about having dinner with Jon and Ellen. She saw this as the last bit of wrapping up her life—she was back on an even keel, perhaps she was better than ever, as Ellen had said. But she was different also; her priorities had changed. She found herself pondering the revision of her scars in the months to come.

She would have it done, she knew, for she wanted to look as attractive as she could, but she no longer felt that she couldn't leave the house unless her makeup was perfect, or every hair was in place. She had learned that from her accident—and from Mexico. How she treasured those hours in the Mexican town.

Before she could become lost to her memories again, she settled down on her couch with a cup of coffee and the book she had failed to read last night; this time she covered the high points so that she could discuss it intelli-

273

gently with her guest. Then she dressed and went to the studio.

When it came time to get ready for the dinner date with Jon and Ellen, she decided on the dress she had worn to the fancy party in Mexico. It was lovely, and she wouldn't be overdressed for the restaurant Ellen had selected. She wore a fresh flower in her hair, as she had done then, taking a red blossom from the hibiscus growing in the front yard.

She had chosen simple white sandals to complement her outfit, and impulsively she took the gold ring Rafe had given her from her purse where she still kept it and slipped it on her left hand. She loved the ring, and she thought she had finally reached the point where she could look at it without a constant heartache. Then she draped the mantilla Trena had given her around her shoulders like a shawl, and she was ready.

The ride to the restaurant was brief, and Kea was in fine spirits when she walked inside. She gave her name to the girl at the desk, and she was told her party had already arrived. She was led to her table, and to her total shock she walked right past a table where Rafe and Trena were seated.

CHAPTER FIFTEEN

Kea was deathly afraid that her legs would suddenly fail her; the only reason she could continue to her table was that she knew Rafe had already seen her. For a brief moment their gazes locked. Kea saw a burning question in his, but it was quickly masked. With a strength she hadn't known she possessed, she nodded to them both.

"Good evening." She didn't know where the words came from, but she said them. Then she took the final steps to her table, the blood coursing through her veins so furiously that the resulting roar in her head prevented her from hearing if Rafe and Trena had responded or not.

She knew she had a smile on her lips, but she found the shock of seeing them together so suddenly almost intolerable. It had been the last thing she had expected, and though it wasn't inconceivable that they would all choose the same restaurant on the same night, she had thought it highly unlikely. She had a burning sensation deep in her stomach as if she were being scalded, and she thought, if it were possible, it was more painful seeing him here, like this, than it had been when she had left him in Mexico with Trena.

It seemed to her that an eternity passed, but she finally reached the table where Jon and Ellen sat. They looked very uncomfortable, and Kea was sure they, too, must have seen Rafe and Trena. "Well," she murmured, pretending to be discussing something pleasant, "it looks like you've chosen a popular night for this restaurant."

Ellen laughed nervously, but she could hardly meet Kea's eyes as the redhead sat down. She looked at Jon, then back at Kea. "I'm sorry, Kea." Her voice was soft and low. "I'm afraid this is my fault."

"Nonsense," Kea replied. "You couldn't know that they would be here tonight."

Ellen agreed. "No, I couldn't know that both of them would be, but I asked one of them." She could see Kea turning pale across from her and she hurried on. "I called Rafe's office and left a message for him to join the three of us here for dinner. I purposely didn't speak with him because I wanted to see if he would come." Even in the dim surroundings Kea saw Ellen's rosy cheeks flaming with color. "I saw."

Kea waged a mighty battle to contain her fury, but she couldn't keep the disappointment from her voice. "Oh, Ellen, how could you have done such a thing?" she questioned bitterly.

"I'm sorry," the other woman repeated contritely. "I only meant to be helping. I was sure Rafe still cared for you." She reached across and grasped Kea's hand. "I've always thought that, Kea, and when he took you to Mexico, I was sure of it. When I saw that you were still in love with him, I thought . . . I thought . . ." She released Kea's hand and her green eyes were full of misery. "I guess I made a mistake."

"I guess you did," Kea said with a lightness she was far from feeling. Rafe had deliberately brought his nurse, knowing that Kea would be here, and that hurt more than she had thought possible. The ache swelled inside her, throbbing throughout her body.

"Do you want to go somewhere else?" Jon asked.

Kea shook her head. She wouldn't dream of walking out, and she didn't know if her legs would carry her at any rate. "No, I wouldn't dare leave now." Her somber gray eyes met his. "Besides, this is foolish. I can't keep running away. We all live in the same area, and this is bound to happen now and again. Perhaps I should just get used to the sight." The words were rational enough, and though she did wish Rafe and Trena happiness, it hurt way down deep inside to see the two of them together.

Involuntarily, she glanced across the room at Rafe, and when she saw that he seemed to be drinking in the sight of her in the Mexican dress, she couldn't decide if she was glad or sorry she had worn it. There was a dark flame glowing in his eyes, and she didn't know what to make of it. Before it could burn her again, she looked away.

Across the room from her Rafe was struggling with his own emotions. He was finally able to pull his gaze away from Kea, but it had taken incredible willpower. Just seeing her had started the pain all over again. He was hardly aware of the woman sitting by his side, and he felt guilty because he had agreed to bring her to dinner, then ignored her. But all his thoughts were on Kea; she looked more beautiful than ever, and he kept thinking of her as she had been in Mexico—as the two of them had been— when he was still dreaming. The loving and the anguish of those days had mingled in his mind, and he longed to touch Kea just once more.

He glanced at their table again, and he wondered if he had been wrong about Jon and her. When he had first entered the restaurant and had seen Jon and Ellen, he had spoken to them; however, their cool reception told him not to intrude. Then Kea had joined them, and he didn't know what to think. They all seemed compatible, laughing and talking, touching each other; he decided that he must have been rash in his assumption that Jon and Kea were having an affair. Her hasty and unforgivable marriage to Roxwell had colored his judgment. He sighed. What did it matter now? He was only tormenting himself with futile speculations.

Staring blindly down into his drink, he wondered how many more times he would run into Kea. He really was going to have to give serious consideration to moving away, and that would entail an upheaval in his life. He would have to begin his practice all over again. But Kea was such an obsession with him that he was sure it would be worth it. He couldn't go on all his life wishing things had been different. Perhaps in a new city with new faces . . .

He was startled when Trena laid her hand on his arm. He forced a smile for her; he had forgotten that she was here with him. When he saw her brown eyes darken with pain, he looked at her questioningly. "I'm sorry. I'm being a bad companion tonight."

Her gaze held his. "You were thinking of Kea, weren't you?"

He laughed bitterly, and he couldn't hide the misery in his voice. "Was it that obvious?"

She nodded, and her words were very somber. "It's written all over your face. You love her very much, don't you?"

He gave her a half smile. "Is that written all over my face too?"

"Yes," she said quietly, the admission making her tremble inside. "You'll never be happy without her, will you, Rafe?"

He shrugged off the question. He had no intention of going into it with Trena. "It doesn't matter. It's a moot question."

"I don't believe that's true," she said, dragging each word from her lips. "She loves you."

"Who gave you a crystal ball?" He tried to inject some levity into his words.

"I don't need a crystal ball," she told him. "I know it's true."

"You'd better forget fortune-telling and stick to nursing. You're way off base. The woman you're talking about walked out on me twice. Even I learn the second time. It was just my misfortune that you wanted Mexican food tonight."

Something in the tense way Trena was gripping her hands captured Rafe's attention, and he looked at her sharply. She seemed to be struggling with herself, hunting for the words she wanted to say to him. Finally, she whispered, "It isn't a coincidence that they're eating here tonight."

"What are you talking about?" he demanded.

She pressed her lips together for a moment, then forced herself to continue. "Ellen left a message at the desk today for you to join the three of them for dinner. Mary gave it to me to give to you."

Rafe's dark brows met in a frown as he looked at her. "And why didn't you?"

Trena's heart was in her eyes. "Don't you know, Rafe, after all this time?"

Their food arrived then, and the world stopped while the waitress cheerfully set down the plates and poured more water. Across the room Kea and her party were also being served. She glanced up once again, and her eyes locked with Rafe's. Then she said something bright, and Jon and Ellen laughed.

Rafe turned his attention back to Trena when the waitress left. He studied her closed face pensively for a moment, and then he briefly shut his eyes. When he opened them again, he spoke with a world of gentleness in his voice. "I thought you and I both agreed that was over a long time ago."

Trena smiled sadly. "It was over for you. I've never stopped loving you. All along I thought you would come back to me if only you could get Kea out of your heart. And you did come back to me—that one night."

She lowered her eyes, and Rafe covered her hand with his. "I was weak and I was wrong, Trena. I didn't mean to make love to you that night, but I was hurting so over Kea that I didn't have the good sense not to. I wish for all the world that it hadn't happened."

When her eyes met his again, they were filled with tears. "I'm not sorry it happened," she whispered, "but I know that you're *still* hurting over Kea. I know now that you'll never get her out of your heart."

"God knows it's not because I haven't tried," he said bleakly.

"She really loves you, Rafe," Trena said softly. "She didn't leave Mexico because she suddenly grew bored." She lowered her glistening eyes and she did not look at him again as she spoke. "I told her that she pulled you in two directions, that she would prevent you from doing your work, that she was no good for you." She looked up, but not at him. "I told her that you and I were lovers and that you could be happy with me if only she would leave you alone. She tried very hard to be what she thought you wanted. She left because she loves you enough to want your happiness."

Rafe was too stunned for a moment to know what to say, and then he asked her in a weary voice, "Why did you tell her those things?"

She glanced across the room, and her gaze briefly touched Kea's before they both looked away. "I really believed that I could make you happy and that she couldn't. I've seen the way she twists you inside out, and I honestly thought she was no good for you." Her voice was choked with emotion. "Maybe I was just desperate, but now I know there will never really be any other woman for you, Rafe. You love her and she loves you. Go to her. There must be a way for the two of you."

280

Rafe shook his head. "You don't know what you're talking about," he said, but he felt new hope stir inside him. He had let Kea escape twice without question, and if there was any chance for him—if she did love him—he wasn't going to risk a third time. If Trena were right about the reasons Kea left Mexico, and if there were love between them . . .

He looked at his nurse and saw the pain on her face. She smiled valiantly. "Don't worry about me, Doctor. I've been thinking for some time about leaving you to go to medical school. It's time I got on with my life. And you and Kea got on with yours."

Rafe gazed at her fondly for a moment, then murmured, "You'll be one hell of a good doctor."

She kept her smile intact. "You're not so bad yourself." Then she quickly picked up her purse and rushed from the room.

Kea had been watching the interaction between the two of them, and she had wanted to die when she saw Rafe cover Trena's hand with his. She hadn't looked up again until Trena left the room, and now she saw that Rafe was coming toward her. Her heart began to beat erratically. What did he want? Why didn't he just leave her alone?

When he stopped beside her chair, she tensed. "May I join you?" he asked, his eyes only on Kea.

"Aren't you already dining with someone?" she asked coolly, not wanting him to know how hurt she was.

He shook his head. "She's gone."

"I'm sure she'll be back."

He shook his head again. "No, she's never coming back."

Looking up at him with a puzzled expression, Kea was at a loss for words. What was he talking about?

"I really want to talk with you," he said.

"I think we've already said it all."

281

His fingers closed down on her shoulder. "We haven't even begun."

Suddenly Ellen stood up. "I've developed a severe headache," she said. "If you'll excuse us." Jon glanced at his wife strangely, and when she glared at him, he stood up and tossed some money down on the table. Kea watched as they made their way out of the restaurant.

When she reached up to brush Rafe's hand away, he captured hers. There was a burning intensity in his eyes now, and Kea couldn't make herself look away.

"I want to know why you left Mexico so abruptly," he said.

Kea was surprised; he hadn't asked her that before. "It doesn't matter why I left. We owed each other nothing— you and I."

Rafe drew her up to his side. "*You* have owed *me* a hell of a lot for a long, long time," he said solemnly. "I love you, Kea. And I think it's time we talked about it."

She opened her mouth in surprise. He loved her! Her heart began to sing. He had said he loved her!

"We'll talk at my place," he said, and Kea, stunned by his announcement, let him guide her out to his car. The ride to his house was completed in absolute silence, but the air crackled between them.

When they had parked, Rafe wasted no time or words. He led her up the walk, opened the door, then ushered her inside. He guided her to the nearest couch and sat down beside her. "Let's start back at the beginning—or the ending—whatever you want to call it," he said. "I want to know why you married Roxwell. I have to know."

Kea's gray eyes met his blazing dark ones. It had been less than a year, but it seemed aeons ago. She knew that he *did* have a right to know, but what could she tell him? The truth? After all this time would she admit why she had done it?

Yes, it was way past time. "I was angry with you," she said in a tiny voice unworthy of such a huge mistake. "I wanted marriage. You wanted your career and Trena."

"And marriage with any man would do?" His question stabbed her to the quick.

She shook her head, but before she could speak again, he silenced her. "I saw the signs of you wanting a husband, and I knew it couldn't be me. We were worlds apart." His eyes met hers. "But until you married Roxwell, I honestly didn't believe you would give up what we had. I loved you, Kea."

She had questions of her own. "If you loved me, Rafe, why didn't you ever tell me? And why was Trena in your life? I know that you were lovers."

"Trena was part of my life before you came into it. I only touched her once afterward—when I learned you had married Roxwell. It wasn't fair of me to turn to her because I'd lost you, and I haven't made love to her since."

Kea's heart began to hope. She was back in her world, with her work, and he was still in his; a million mistakes and a million dreams had passed between them, but they loved each other. There was still reason for more dreams.

"I never loved Roxwell," she whispered. "It was always you, Rafe. I knew that I'd made a mistake, but I didn't think you wanted me anyway, so I decided to try to live with it. I lived in my own hell, thinking that you didn't even care enough to contact me after my wedding. I thought you were happy in your world with Trena and your work. There were so many times when we were together that I realized there was no hope for us. Times when I pleaded with you to share your world with me, times when I wanted to meet your family, to know about your past. When I couldn't get beyond your armor to reassure myself that you cared."

"Kea, Kea," he murmured, "I was so afraid you would

hate my world. I couldn't hold you, and I couldn't let you go. Then you made the decision for me by marrying Roxwell. When you came into my life a second time, I was fool enough to hope again, for you had been injured yourself. I thought you could understand. And a second time you left me."

Kea traced his lips with her trembling fingers. "I left you in Mexico because I *did* understand. I realized how very selfish it had been for me to want you all to myself. So many people needed you, and I was so proud of you. I didn't want to have any part of taking you away from what you loved best. Besides, I didn't think you wanted me."

"God, how I wanted you," he groaned. "But I didn't want to take advantage of you, or break my heart. There was always your world, your career. I know how much it means to you."

"It means a lot," she agreed, "but it isn't everything."

Rafe's eyes darkened. "And didn't you come back in part because you couldn't give up the glamour, the glitter here? Mexico began to bore you."

"No," she cried. "I discovered something in the last few weeks. I don't need the glitter anymore."

"I saw the way you sparkled at that party in Mexico, Kea, dancing with all the men, being the center of attention. You need the adulation."

She shook her head. "I sparkled because you were there, Rafe. You're the only man I need in my life."

He wanted to believe her, but he had lived too long with his doubt. "You don't know how it used to torment me to leave you alone so much. I was always sure one day a Roxwell would come along and steal you away. Yet I was too afraid to take you with me. I couldn't hold up under that torment again."

"He only stole me because I didn't know you wanted

me. I was fighting the same demons with you being gone with Trena. Oh, Rafe, I've changed—you've changed . . ." She paused, hoping that he would make the commitment to her that she had wanted, but she had stopped dreaming of.

"And Jon?" he asked. "What kind of relationship have you had with him?"

Kea shook her head. "There was never anything more than deep friendship between us."

His gaze was darkly solemn. "I was very much afraid that you were having an affair with him. The night I took you to my house, there was every indication that there was something going on with you two, something which had upset Ellen terribly."

Her gaze held his. "It was all a misunderstanding," she said simply. "Jon just meant to comfort me that night. He loves Ellen—and you were always the only man I wanted."

He caught her hand as it moved gently across his mouth, and when he kissed her fingers, he saw the gold band he had given her. "I gave you this as a parting gift because I was already married to you in my heart. Kea, I want you to be my wife; with me or away from me, I need to know that you're mine. I love you and you love me. We can share our worlds. You understand my work, and I respect yours. We can compromise."

"Oh, yes, Rafe," she breathed, knowing it was possible. "I can arrange to take the summers off so that I can travel with you." She looked up at him in embarrassment. "I can't help, but I can play my flute."

He gently kissed her nose. "No one expected you to help, Kea. You're not a nurse. I took you because I wanted you with me. I'll always want you with me, when you can be there. When you can't, I'll take you in my heart."

His mouth traveled down to her lips, and with a fierceness born of suffering and longing, he drew her into his arms and claimed her mouth with an all-consuming passion. Easing her down on the couch, he molded his body to hers, wanting to make her his for all time. She met the fire in his kiss and the yearning in his muscled body. She was being given another chance with him, and she reveled in his touch. This time she had no intention of ever losing him again.

LOOK FOR THESE
CANDLELIGHT ECSTASY SUPREMES™ IN
DECEMBER:

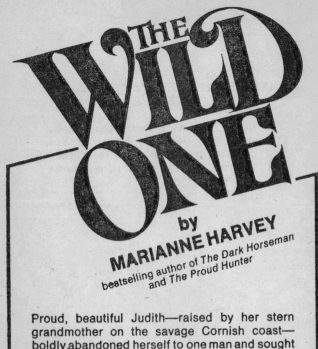

THE WILD ONE

by
MARIANNE HARVEY
bestselling author of *The Dark Horseman*
and *The Proud Hunter*

Proud, beautiful Judith—raised by her stern
grandmother on the savage Cornish coast—
boldly abandoned herself to one man and sought
solace in the arms of another. But only one man
could tame her, could match her fiery spirit,
could fulfill the passionate promise of rapturous,
timeless love.

A Dell Book $2.95   (19207-2)